Monstra Inter

The living, the dead, and the monsters in between.

- C. Britt -

CBRD Publishing

CBRD Publishing
Webb City, MO

ISBN (paperback): 979-8-9886143-1-9
ISBN (hardback): 979-8-9886143-2-6
ISBN (ebook): 979-8-9886143-0-2

Library of Congress Control Number: 2023911664

Cover art by Perky Visuals

https://www.cbrdpublishing.com

To my husband, who says this
is worthy of a movie deal.
And to whichever brilliant movie executive
who decides to prove my husband right.

CONTENTS

1

INTO CHAOS

- Southeastern Oklahoma -

-- Day 1 --

The quiet crunch of dry grass draws Abigail's attention toward the ground twenty feet below. She hardly dares to breathe. From her perch in the tree stand, she slowly leans forward as her hands rest on the camera in her lap. Her long hair shifts, sliding past her shoulders, momentarily blocking her view of the tall weeds that surround the base of the tree. She swipes the dark, curly locks behind her ears, then freezes with both hands still at the sides of her face. She gasps softly.

She'd been excited, expecting to see another deer. Instead, crouching below her amongst the tall weeds is a man she's never seen before. Abigail's enthusiasm quickly turns to fear. Her heart begins to hammer. She slowly lowers her hands to her lap and waits, silent and unmoving.

Minutes creep by.

The man carefully inches forward again. His eyes are locked on the doe roughly fifty yards in front of him. He stays downwind and moves cautiously; the doe's ears twitch, but the unsuspecting animal continues calmly chewing grass.

Abigail's curiosity is piqued. With one hand, she takes hold of the camera in her lap and lifts the viewfinder to her eye; the other hand slowly twists the lens until it's zoomed in enough for her to see the man a bit more closely. Then, she sits motionless once more, observing the strange scene unfolding below.

He isn't carrying a gun or bow. He isn't wearing the required hunter orange. In fact, he's dressed in what looks like workout attire. She can't help but wonder, *Why in the world would he be trying to sneak up on a deer like that?*

A chill runs up Abigail's spine. Both fascinated by this man's ability to move so stealthily and disturbed by such strange behavior, Abigail holds her breath and continues staring through the camera. She sits transfixed, trying to make sense of the sight.

Eventually, the man slowly and silently makes his way close to his target. He crouches low a few feet behind the oblivious deer. Only one narrow tree separates the two of them now. Waiting until the unsuspecting doe has its head down to get another bite of grass, the man lunges forward. In the blink of an eye, he grabs the deer and sinks his teeth into its flesh. The doe leaps forward, throwing the assailant to the ground. Blood drips in a thin trail from the man's mouth as he pushes himself back to his feet.

Abigail tenses, ready to flee, but forces herself to stay out of sight. The man takes a second to look around, and as she watches through the camera, Abigail catches a glimpse of his face. His mouth and shirt are drenched in blood, and small bits of the deer's hide hang from his teeth. But most chilling of all are his eyes. They're wide pools of inky black; they're soulless and inhuman. From this distance, they're so dark and bottomless, they look like gaping holes. Abigail shivers.

Turning his back on Abigail, the man casually wanders off, out of the field, into the woods, and disappears.

Abigail lowers the camera, presses one hand against her mouth, and wills her heartbeat to slow down. As she sits there armed with only a digital camera and a small can of mace, she's terrified to leave the relative safety of the tree stand.

After waiting for what feels like an eternity, Abigail sees the sun start to touch the horizon and knows she needs to get out of the woods before nightfall. With trembling, sweaty palms, she places her camera into its bag. She hurriedly descends the ladder. As soon as her feet touch the ground, she holds her breath and listens. Nothing disturbs the silence except for a gentle breeze through the budding treetops. She inhales deeply as she looks around. At last, gathering her nerve, she turns and sprints down the trail. A few minutes later, the terrified Abigail throws herself into her waiting SUV, locks the doors, and speeds off toward home.

Abigail slides the deadbolt into place and slumps against the door, and a subtle vibration in her jacket pocket catches her attention. She pulls out her phone to see her brother's name displayed on the screen. Quickly pulling her dark hair into a haphazard ponytail, she presses the green button and puts the device to her ear.

"Hey, Jake."

"Abby, where have you been? Are you okay?"

Abigail's brows knit together at the sudden question. Her mind races. *He couldn't know about what happened at the tree stand today. Surely I don't still sound that shaken up that he can tell with a two-word greeting either. What's so urgent that he couldn't even say hello first?*

"Abby?" Jake cuts into her thoughts. "Are you okay? I've been trying to call you all day!"

"Yeah, Jake, I'm fine." Abigail pulls one arm out of her jacket and shifts the phone to her other ear. She tugs at the other sleeve and hangs the jacket on the hook by the door. Kicking off her shoes, she continues, "Sorry I missed your calls. What's so urgent?"

"Why didn't you answer?!"

Abigail rolls her eyes. "What the hell has gotten into you? I don't answer for one freaking afterno—"

"Look, I'm sorry, Ab. I was... I just got scared, alright? I thought something had..." Jake's words trail away.

"Jake? Are *you* okay?" Abigail's tone softens at the sudden emotion in her brother's deep voice.

Jake inhales shakily, then exhales slowly. "I've just been worried for you, that's all. I guess this means you haven't seen the news yet today?"

"No. Why?"

"They're reporting that some crazy people are terrorizing the city. No one knows if they're junkies on some new kind of drug or if they're part of some crazy cult or what. Two people were arrested after biting people. At least—"

"What?" Abigail can't help but interrupt. The color drains from her face as she continues. "They were biting people?"

Thinking her outburst was due to incredulity rather than relatability, Jake goes on. "Yeah, biting. It's crazy, I know. They said on the news that at least a dozen people are in the hospital getting stitches, tetanus shots, and rabies vaccines. Sounds like those freaks even got ahold of a couple of pets too." Jake pauses a moment, then chuckles. "Of course, I guess that's why you bought that old house out in the boonies, huh? Surely those weirdos won't bother you out there in the woods, right?"

Abigail's knees threaten to give out from under her. She braces herself against the wall and slides down to sit on the cold floor. Her palms grow slick with sweat.

"Are you still there, Abby? Hello?"

"Y-yeah. I'm here." She swallows hard. "They're here too."

- Southeastern Oklahoma -
-- Day 2 --

"They're being called 'zombies' by many of the area locals. However, they're not zombies like those you've seen in movies: they aren't the resurrected dead, they can run, and they don't appear to be unintelligent. Preliminary reports indicate similar events in a few other cities as well. As events continue to unfold, we'll bring you more information about these so-called 'zombies.'" The news anchorwoman pauses momentarily to give the camera a somber look. "Now over to Nick, reporting to you live from the scene. Nick?"

The image switches to a man with a microphone. His usual on-camera smile is replaced by a more serious look today. "Thanks, Cheryl. We're coming to you live from the scene of the first known zombie attacks in the area." The reporter gestures to his left, and the camera pans over to reveal another person standing nearby. "With us today is Jeremiah Hamilton. He's been an area resident all his life, and he's here to tell us his thoughts on yesterday's events. Thanks for being here today, Jeremiah."

Abigail shakes her head in exasperation. *People are coming down with rabies-like symptoms for unknown reasons and running around biting each other. And the news is busy interviewing some random guy about how he feels!*

She stands up and walks away, scoffing. Leaving the TV on, she's only half listening as she begins sweeping the floors, washing dishes, and hoping to find enough busywork to keep herself from going crazy.

A few times throughout the morning, Abigail pauses to try to make phone calls to her parents and friends. The cell towers are overloaded, though, and the calls aren't going through. At one point, she stands there, tapping her foot against the linoleum, wishing she'd kept that old landline phone.

After running out of things to clean, Abigail plops back down in front of the TV and switches to a different channel.

"Preliminary reports now indicate that this zombie plague may not be as localized as previously thought. It appears to be happening in multiple cities throughout the country. In light of this, the governor has just declared a state of emergency for the region. All public transportation services are being suspended. This includes buses, passenger trains, taxis, and any other similar services. Flights will not be allowed to take off from or land in the affected areas. Residents are encouraged to stay in their homes until further notice.

"We'll bring you more inf—"

Abigail's heart sinks, and she turns the TV off. She's realized that since the airports are closed, Jake can't make it there tonight. Leaning back in her chair, she pinches the bridge of her nose. Suddenly, she slams her palms against the arms of the chair. "No!" No one is around to hear Abigail's complaint, but she can't help making it anyway.

Abigail stands up and paces through the kitchen, trying to figure out how to get in touch with Jake—or Mom, or *anyone*— when her phone chimes.

Of course email still works! Why didn't I think of that sooner?

She pulls the phone out of her hoodie pocket and unlocks the screen. "Hey Abby, flight just got canceled. I'm gonna start driving. See you tomorrow, stay safe. Love you. -- Jake"

Abigail taps reply. "Love you too. Be careful on the road. You heard from mom or dad?"

A few more taps as she hits send and then starts a new email to her mom. "Are you and dad safe? I can't make any outgoing calls. Call me if you can or write back. Please, I need to know if you two are okay. I'm alright, and Jake is on his way here now. I'll write again when he's made it. Love you both."

As soon as the second email is sent, Abigail leans her elbows on the countertop and rests her forehead against her palms. She barely slept a wink last night. And she's certain she can't handle another night alone, jumping at every little sound. She doesn't want to leave and miss Jake and wouldn't know where to go even if she did go. But even more than that, she doesn't want to run into one of those *things*—she can't quite bring herself to call them "zombies" yet—while she's out on the road, weaponless and alone.

She presses her thumbs to her temples and begins to massage as she mulls over her limited options.

A shower would be great right about now. Abigail knows she could use one after all the climbing into and out of the tree stand yesterday, then sprinting off through the woods. Besides, the soothing massage from the warm, falling water always helps her think. But she's terrified; what if while she's alone and vulnerable, shielded only by the thin, plastic shower curtain, one of those psychos finds their way inside? She quickly abandons the idea.

Standing abruptly, Abigail grabs the laundry basket and dumps the contents onto the floor. Then, she carries it around the house, gathering things: a flashlight, phone charger, pillow, a few blankets, an aluminum baseball bat, and the ingredients for PB&J sandwiches. She starts to head to the far end of the house but then stops in her tracks, grimacing as a thought occurs to her. Heading into the bathroom, she grabs the small trash can and a roll of toilet paper to add to her basket.

At last, she makes her way to the far end of the house. Setting the laundry basket down, Abigail yanks on the string hanging from the ceiling. With a loud squeaking groan of old springs and a light sprinkling of dust raining down, the overhead door drops open, and the attic stairs unfold in front of her. She picks up the basket and hurries up the steep steps.

Grabbing the old cot from the far corner, Abigail unfolds it and sets the laundry basket on top. Then she returns to the main floor and starts digging through the kitchen junk drawer. She finds a thick piece of cotton cord and takes it to the attic steps. She ties a knot around one of the wooden planks, returns to the attic, and gives the line a hard tug. The steps begrudgingly lift upward and refold into their closed position. Finally, she takes a couple chunks of plywood and jams them under each side of the ladder. Abigail presses lightly with her foot. The ladder doesn't budge, and she nods in satisfaction. Now, if anyone tries to open it from below, the plywood will catch against the attic floor, locking the ladder in place.

Relaxing ever-so-slightly now that Abigail feels somewhat secure, last night's sleeplessness begins to catch up to her.

- Southeastern Oklahoma -
-- Day 3 --

Abigail's phone chimes loudly and drags her from a fitful sleep. She pushes herself upright on the cot, blinking in the dim, early morning light. It takes some time for her to remember where she is, but her vision finally comes into focus.

Then, so do her memories of the previous day.

Running the heel of her palm across her closed eyelids, Abigail yawns. With the other hand, she forces her tangled mess of hair away from her face. Grabbing one of the blankets, she wraps it around her shoulders to ward off the slight springtime chill in the poorly insulated attic. She reaches for her phone but then pauses, listening intently for any sounds of movement downstairs. All is quiet.

Then just for good measure, Abigail stands up and creeps over to the small, round window. She peaks out, but the light is still too faint to see much on the ground other than vague shadows.

At last, reasonably confident that she's still alone and safe, she grabs her phone and brings up the email that had woken her up. "Have you talked to Mom & Dad? I can't reach them. I drove about 5 hours last night before I decided to check into a hotel. I'll leave in a few minutes. Be there this afternoon. -- Jake"

Abigail sends a quick reply to let him know she's safe and that she hasn't been able to reach their parents either. She swipes the email app off the screen and opens a browser window. A few taps later, a live news broadcast appears, and she sinks back onto the cot to watch.

"...that this sudden rabies-like behavior is more widespread than we had believed only just yesterday. Sightings have been confirmed in multiple cities throughout the western hemisphere. Authorities now also believe that the first presentations of these symptoms appeared in Central or South America sometime within the past week. The exact cause is not known at this time. Current theories include a new rabies variant, a previously unknown fungus, or possibly even some kind of biological weapon.

"The White House has declined to comment, other than to assure the public that scientists are working around the clock to find a cure for this illness. Additionally, they are requesting that the public remain in their homes as much as possible to prevent further spread.

"Now, over to Chuck as he brings us updates from the traffic watch helicopter."

The view on the screen changes abruptly from the anchor desk to a live, aerial view of a crowded downtown street.

"Thanks, May. As you can see, the city streets are quickly turning chaotic. Protestors have come out in droves, demanding answers about what exactly these 'zombies' are. Many of the protestors even carry signs hinting about conspiracies and bioweapons. In response, local police forces have been dispatched to keep things under control. There aren't enough officers to manage crowd control though, which means rioting and looting has alre—"

Abigail closes the browser and tosses the phone onto the cot. Standing up, she starts to pace. Worries and what-ifs have already begun tugging at the corners of her thoughts. Jake won't be here for several more hours. She knows she needs some kind of distraction before the negative thoughts completely take hold. She takes a seat on the dusty plywood floor, pulls her knees up to her chest, and drums her fingertips against her shins.

The trail cams! She leaps up as the idea forms in her mind. *I know it's risky to go out alone, but I can move the trail cams so they're pointed toward the house and turn it into my own makeshift security system!*

Letting the blanket fall from her shoulders, Abigail heads to the top of the steps. With her toe, she pushes away the plywood chunks that trap the ladder in its closed position, then presses on the steps until they start to extend down into the lower floor. They creak and groan but eventually unfurl completely. She waits, listening. Nothing but silence. She makes her way down slowly, stopping to listen after each nerve-wracking step.

At last on the main floor, Abigail hurries to the kitchen and grabs her car keys and some fresh batteries for the trail cams. She goes to the front door, puts her hand on the doorknob, then stops.

Setting down her stuff next to the door, Abigail goes to the bedroom. She strips out of her pajamas and throws on a pair of jeans, a turtleneck, a denim vest, and snow boots. She returns to the kitchen and finds an unused roll of duct tape. Meticulously, she winds the sticky, gray material around her pantlegs, sleeves, and collar. Going to a small closet, she finds a pair of rose-pruning gloves and slips them onto her hands. One more round of duct tape to wrap around the wrists of the gloves, and she returns to the door to regather her supplies.

Three of the six trail cams have had their batteries replaced and have been moved into better positions to face the house. The two cameras closest to the pond are difficult to get to quickly, so Abigail decides to leave them alone. Only one more to go before her task is done for the day.

As Abigail puts the last camera into place, the hairs on the back of her neck rise. She knows beyond a shadow of a doubt that she's being watched. Her pulse quickens. Holding her breath, she starts to slowly turn around. Before she completes her turn, she hears the pounding of footsteps from her right. She pivots toward the noise. The attacker is nearly within reach. Empty-handed, Abigail throws both duct-tape-armored arms up in front of her face. The assailant—a small, middle-aged woman—slams into Abigail and wraps her jaws around Abigail's arm, tight enough to prevent her from pulling away.

With her arm caught in the vice of teeth, Abigail's eyes widen. Her breath comes in shaky gasps as she quickly glances over her attacker's shoulder. She's blocking the path to the car. Fighting against the growing panic, Abigail slides one foot backward, twists, and slams the side of the assailant's head with a left hook. The woman's grip loosens, and Abigail stumbles back. Before the attacker can recover, Abigail shoves her away. The woman falls, and Abigail sprints past and to the waiting vehicle.

Throwing herself haphazardly into the SUV, Abigail slams and locks the door behind her. The attacker reaches it only a fraction of a second later and slams hard into the blue door. Abigail stares openmouthed, trying to catch her breath and watching as the assailant glowers back at her. The violent woman's eyes look strange. The pale, blue iris has nearly vanished behind the dilated pupil, much like a cat on the hunt. The whites of her eyes are now streaked with dozens of jagged black lines.

As Abigail gawks, the attacker suddenly screams. Abigail jumps. The scream isn't a normal sound, though. It's something animalistic, something between a shriek and a roar. At the same time, the attacker raises both fists and bashes them against the window. The zombie roars again as she slams her knuckles into the glass so hard that she draws blood. It leaves red trails down the window that start to drip down the side of the car.

All the color drains from Abigail's face. She shoves the keys toward the ignition, but her gloved fingers slip, and the keys fall to the floor between her knees. She lets out a frightened squeak and yanks at one of the gloves, but the duct tape holds it fast.

Crack! A vertical line appears down the center of the glass.

Still gloved, Abigail doubles over and swipes her hand across the floor until she finds the keys. At last, she snatches them up and jams them into the ignition, twists, and the engine revs to life. She throws the vehicle into drive and slams her foot against the gas. The unpaved ground doesn't immediately give much grip to the tires, and the SUV barely lurches forward. The attacker yanks on the door handles as the tires finally find purchase. The vehicle rushes forward.

Before long, Abigail looks in the rearview mirror at the attacker. She's sprinting after the car. The woman opens her mouth and lets out another blood-curdling roar. Abigail's breath catches in her chest. Suddenly, she brings the vehicle to a halt and switches into reverse. Backing up at reckless speed, Abigail slams into the assailant. Bile rises in Abigail's throat at the sickening crunch of the attacker woman's bones underneath the tires.

Abigail stops again and swallows hard, staring at the gory sight before her. The attacker's chest is completely flattened. Blood coats the ground and continues oozing from the woman's shattered torso and pooling on the dry ground around her. She appears entirely unfazed, still leering and chomping in Abigail's direction. A chill runs down Abigail's spine. She takes a deep breath, switches back into drive, and presses the accelerator again. Another sickening crunch. Another stifled retch.

Abigail turns toward home, ready to empty the contents of her stomach behind the safety of a locked deadbolt. From somewhere far off in the distance, Abigail swears she can hear the echoes of another shrieking roar.

2

DISBELIEF

- Southwestern Kansas -
-- Day 1 --

Grumbling under her breath, Charlie tosses the unopened mail on the table. On top of the bright flyers and restaurant coupons, the white envelope is unremarkable. The sender is some company she's never heard of from some city she's never been to, but with one brief glance, she's sure of what's inside. After all, the only people who ever addressed her by "Charlotte" were her husband, her mother, and the infernal bill collectors. And well, given that her husband and mother are both buried behind the old church down the road, there isn't room for doubt.

She glances at the newest bill and the stack of older ones next to it, debating whether to toss the whole stack in the burn pile. She grumbles again and shrugs off the thought. Then, she turns and walks to the front door.

Grabbing her keys and baseball cap off the hooks by the door, Charlie steps outside, pulling the wooden door closed behind herself. A chilled breeze whips across the porch and tousles her short, white hair. She pushes the hair back, away from her wrinkled forehead, and quickly slips the dark green and white cap on before the wind can restyle it again.

Charlie steps off the porch. The breeze goes past once more and sends a flurry of goosebumps across her skin. She pulls the sides of her denim jacket forward and covers up the dark blue bib of her overalls. The gnarled joints of her fingers crackle as she grasps the jacket's buttons and slides each one into place, blocking out the worst of the day's chill. Charlie climbs into the old, red pickup and pulls the cap's bill down low to block the glare from the mid-morning sun.

With a twist of the key, the pickup's engine roars to life.

"...from multiple cities, claiming that they are experiencing outbreaks of some new, fast-acting, and deadly illness. At this time, no one can definitively say what we're dealing with, but health officials indicate this could be a new variant of the rabies virus. This illness, however—"

Spinning the volume knob counterclockwise, the radio broadcast goes silent.

Charlie twists to the side, throws her arm across the seat back, and reverses down the gravel driveway. Then turning around in a little patch of grass, she switches into first gear and drives slowly up to the old, gray barn. She stops in front of the wooden structure. As the engine continues rumbling, she sets the emergency brake and climbs out.

Charlie walks over, unhooks the latch on the wide barn doors, and swings one side open. Without looking down, she takes a wide step across the threshold, habitually stepping over the sleeping, gray cat that calls the barn his home. The cat meows at her without bothering to open his eyes. Charlie picks up an unopened bag of chicken feed, carries it back outside, and sets it in the passenger's seat of the pickup.

She goes back into the barn and walks to the far back corner. On each of the next several passes, she grabs a square hay bale, hauls it outside, and hefts it into the truck bed. Finally, with the bales and the feed loaded up, she makes one last trip into the barn.

"You still catching mice for me, Tom?" Her voice comes out deep and hoarse, possibly even intimidating to those who don't know her well. But the old, gray cat doesn't mind. He blinks up at her and meows softly.

Leaning down, Charlie gives the cat a good scratch behind his ears. He purrs loudly. He's not the only cat helping her keep the rodent population under control, but he's the only one who's tame enough to let her approach without an offering of kitchen scraps. After giving Tom a few more pats and a bit more one-sided conversation, she heads back outside.

Charlie recloses and latches the barn door and climbs back into the truck. Reaching into her pocket, she fishes out a cigarette. She places the thin, white and yellow cylinder between her lips and pulls out a lighter. After a couple flicks, a flame springs to life, and she touches it to the end of the cigarette. Returning the dark green lighter to her pocket, she releases the emergency brake and drives the pickup into the pasture behind the house.

Keeping the pickup in first gear, she drives slowly through the rough, rocky pasture. Before long, she stops in the middle of a small, flat patch of grass. She takes one last puff of her cigarette before smashing it in the ashtray.

She steps out. Climbing onto the tailgate, she starts tossing each of the eight hay bales out of the pickup bed. Once they all lie haphazardly on the ground, she steps down and uses her pocketknife to cut the twine off them. Stopping momentarily, she straightens up and slips the ball cap off to swipe her jacket sleeve across her damp forehead.

Resettling the cap back into place, she heads over to the water trough and lifts the handle on the pump to start the water.

Her thoughts wander as she waits. She glances toward the beehive boxes by the fence. The bees are still staying sheltered from the cool air, but before long, they'll be producing honey again.

She'll be able to start gathering the sweet, sticky substance and selling bottles of it in town. Soon, she'll have enough eggs to start selling again as well. After a few months, she can sell off a couple calves. Eventually, she'll begin baling and selling the excess hay. Then maybe—*maybe*—she'll be able to put a dent in that ever-growing pile of bills.

Once the trough is full and the water is shut off, she heads back to the waiting vehicle.

As Charlie climbs back into the pickup, she sees the black and white, blurry shapes hurrying toward her from the shade of the distant trees. After doing a quick count—four Holstein cows and one young calf—she takes off again.

She drives toward the far end of the pasture and stops the pickup next to a pale blue, wooden building. Grabbing the bag of chicken feed, Charlie climbs out of the pickup and freezes in her tracks. The chickens always come running, clucking like mad, when food arrives. But this time, it's quiet. There isn't a bird in sight.

Setting down the feed bag, Charlie takes a peek through the small, screened window of the coop. Counting—and then recounting to make sure—she sees that while most of the birds are safe inside, four are missing. Stepping back, she looks at the ground. Near the corner of the building is a paw print in the mud.

"Damn!"

From inside the coop, several of the chickens squawk in response to the sudden, loud exclamation.

Continuing her search, Charlie goes around the side of the building. Hundreds of white feathers litter the ground, accentuated with reddish-brown droplets of dried blood. Just beyond the building lie two roosters and a hen, each drenched in a thick layer of half-congealed blood.

The other hen is nowhere to be seen.

Charlie crouches down and takes a closer look at the bird corpses. Each one seems to have received only a single, deep bite.

She stares for a moment, wondering why a coyote or dog would bite and then abandon the dead birds. With a loud sigh, she decides that's something to ponder later.

She picks up the hen and one of the roosters, carries them to the pickup, and lays the corpses in the bed. She'll bury the birds up by the house. No sense leaving an easy meal for the predators out here; it'll only encourage them to come back time and time again. She goes back over to the building, tosses some feed inside, and latches all the doors and openings of the coop. It's not ideal, but the birds will have to stay inside for a few days until she's put an end to the blood-thirsty coyote.

Making one more trip to the back of the coop, Charlie picks up the second rooster and brings it up for a closer look. Still hooked in its talons is a thick tuft of gray-brown fur with a long strip of bloody skin still attached.

- Southwestern Kansas -

-- Day 2 --

"Mornin', Charlie." Melvin scratches the dark mole on the side of his chin as he looks up from his magazine. "How's things in your neck of the woods?"

Charlie nods at the tall, thin shopkeeper as she places the foothold traps and the chicken feed on the counter before him. Scowling, she grumbles back, "Could be worse, I s'pose."

"Ah." Melvin slides the traps closer. He flips one of the traps over in search of the little paper price tag. Finding it, he types the number into the register as he looks at Charlie. "Coyotes giving you troubles again?"

"Yep. Got four of my birds yesterday."

"Oof." Melvin makes a pained face. "What about your cows? You got a couple of calves now, don't you?"

"One. Second one'll be here before too much longer." Slipping the ball cap off her head, Charlie scratches her forehead, pushes back her short hair, then settles the hat back into place. "I reckon the calf'll be fine. Coyote ain't gonna mess with an angry mama cow. More worried about it getting the rest of my birds."

"I don't know." He presses a few more buttons on the cash register, rings up the chicken feed, and then brings up the total. He turns his attention back toward Charlie. "Normally, I'd agree. But... Well, I don't reckon you watched the news last night, did ya?"

"Nah." Charlie shakes her head. She pulls a cigarette from her pocket and places it, unlit, between her lips. "Nothin' on the news anymore but bullshit and hot air."

Melvin chuckles at Charlie's gruff bluntness. "Well, according to the news last night, there's been several rabies outbreaks in the area. Rabid coyotes won't be too scared of an angry cow."

"Hmm. Hadn't heard about that. Guess I'll have to put the cows in the barn. For a few days at least, until I can try to deal with the one that got my chickens."

Melvin nods. He looks back at the register for the total as he tosses the traps into a paper bag. "That'll be eighty-six, forty-two."

"Add it to my tab."

"Charlie..." Melvin sighs. He shoves his hands into his jeans pockets as he looks at her. "I've already extended that tab more than I should've."

"Melvin, you know I'm still payin' off Isaiah's medical debts."

"I know. Rest his soul. And I hate doing this, but..."

"Look, Melvin." Charlie crosses her arms and leans on the counter. "I ain't gonna be able to pay you back or anybody else if all my livestock gets killed. Besides, me and Isaiah helped your folks out a few years back when they was struggling. Remember?"

Melvin presses his lips together and stares at Charlie. She stares right back, undaunted.

"Fine." He shakes his finger at her before pulling a black notebook from underneath the register. "Last time, though, Charlie."

Nodding, Charlie tucks the chicken feed bag into her left elbow and lifts the paper bag with her left hand. As she presses her hip into the glass door and the little bell jingles overhead, she grabs the lighter in her right hand, flicks it, and lifts the little flame to the tip of her cigarette.

After setting the last trap, Charlie reaches up and ties a thin strip of orange cloth around the tree branch overhead. Then she turns and walks back up the narrow game trail until she reaches the barbed wire fence. Bending down, she steps between the wires and returns across the pasture.

As she approaches the chicken coop, she sees fresh, deep gouges in the wooden door at the top of the ramp. Slivers of broken wood litter the ground. Charlie bends down to take a closer look at the damaged building. The door would need to be replaced, but it has done its job.

Grabbing the bag of chicken feed and stepping inside the small, smelly building, she refills the feeders. She sets the bag outside. She picks up the water dispensers, carries them outside, replenishes them, and returns them to the coop. Finally, she scoops up all the eggs she can find and gently places them into a small bucket.

She steps out of the building and relatches the door. With the bucket and the feed bag in hand, she returns to her pickup.

Charlie starts driving slowly across the broad pasture. She can see some blurry, black and white shapes next to a small cluster of trees in the distance. All of a sudden, the yipping bark of a coyote cuts through the air, followed by the loud bellow of an angry cow. Most of the blurry shapes take off across the pasture. But not all of them. At least one of the cows is still next to the trees. The figure is moving frantically.

Shifting into second gear, Charlie presses the accelerator harder. The truck obediently picks up its pace, bouncing hard against each hole and rock in the rough pasture. The eggs crack on the sides of the bucket, but she can't worry about that right now.

The sight before Charlie finally comes into focus. One of the mother cows is next to the trees, her head down low, and her calf is close behind her. A coyote stands in front of her, its head down and teeth bared. The coyote lunges toward the calf. The cow swings her head hard at the attacker, catching it in the ribs with her horn and sending it tumbling across the pasture. The coyote skids to a stop and climbs to its feet.

The cow charges. Waiting until the last second, the coyote dashes off to one side, toward the frightened calf. The calf bolts across the pasture.

Bellowing again, the cow turns and kicks both of her back feet as the coyote tries to run behind. The blow connects with the coyote's head, and the creature spends a second airborne before tumbling across the ground again. This time, it doesn't get up.

For good measure, the cow turns around and tramples across the coyote's unmoving body.

Charlie pulls up just as the cow runs off to find her calf. The woman grabs her shotgun from the back window of the pickup, loads it, and climbs out.

Walking over, Charlie looks down at the bloody mess that was the coyote. It's far too mangled to see if anything was visibly wrong with it, but Charlie's sure it was affected by that rabies outbreak. She decides to go ahead with her traps and quarantines to ensure there aren't any others.

After the better part of an hour, Charlie finally manages to get the last of the frightened cattle into their stalls in the barn. She piles fresh hay into each of the long compartments, then fills each water trough. The first three cows—those who had made it away from the rabid animal unharmed—calm down quickly enough when their food is placed before them.

Charlie stands in front of the back stall now. The calf is in the far corner, still shielded by its agitated mother. Charlie moves closer. Lowering her voice, she speaks softly to the cow. "Easy now, Mama."

The cow snorts and huffs in response. The coyote blood on the cow's horns and nostrils and hooves has long since dried and is already beginning to flake away. But the large, white spot of fur on her face has become stained with patches of pinkish brown as the blood gradually soaked in.

Charlie wants to check the pair for injuries and clean them up, but Mama isn't having it. So, the gruff, old widow steps back and gives the pair their space.

Moving away and leaning against the opposite wall, Charlie looks into the cow's dark eyes and feels a sudden chill run down her spine.

3

RETREAT

- Eastern Missouri -

-- Day 6 --

"Aaron," Nathaniel hisses the name across the darkness as he searches for his roommate. "Aaron! Come here!"

"Sh!"

Nathaniel spins toward the sound and finds Aaron's silhouette crouching a few feet away. Aaron's arms are outstretched as he tries to make his way in the dark.

Seeing across the unlit crawlspace is difficult, but at least by now, their eyes have adjusted enough to see each other's general shape if they're nearby. And they can see the large wooden joists that run the length of the house, so the bumping of heads has been reduced significantly. The cobwebs, though, are still invisible in the darkness. So, stretching out his own arms and swinging them side to side in front of his face, Nathaniel crouch-walks his way over to Aaron's side.

"So, I have an idea." Nathaniel plops down into the dirt and straightens his legs. Then he leans back on his elbows to give his back and thighs a break from the constant crouching. He lets out a low groan as the burning in his spine subsides. "After dark tonight, we'll go outside and head down the block—"

"What?! Have you lost your mind?" The whites of Aaron's eyes are just barely visible in the darkness. Aaron shakes his head. "No, we are not going outside! There are way too many of them. It'd be suicide."

"I know it's a little risky, but—"

"A *little*?"

"Okay, a lot risky. But just hear me out." Nathaniel sighs, then turns around to get on his knees. He grabs Aaron's wrist and pulls him along as he moves toward the small vent in the foundation wall. When they finally reach the wall, they squat down with one of the roommates on each side of the small opening.

"So, take a look," Nathaniel points to the right, up the street, "up that way. At the end of the block, we can turn left, and there's the fire station."

Aaron obligingly looks through the opening. As he leans into the small, lit square of space, Nathaniel can see the cobwebs stuck in Aaron's hair and the dirt that clings to his face and clothes. The mud is now so thick on Aaron that his pale blond hair looks like it's been dyed. "Yeah, I see it."

Pausing for a moment, Aaron looks around a bit more. He continues in a hushed, mocking tone. "Then what do you expect to happen once we're there? You think we're gonna steal a whole-ass firetruck? Just plow through the zombies, spray them in the head with the firehose while we drive around with the sirens blaring?"

"No. Although, now that you mention it..." Nathaniel smirks.

Aaron rolls his eyes and then leans back against the wall, hiding his face in shadow.

"Alright, so we wait until nightfall. Then, see that line of hedges over there? We can sneak along behind those until we get down to that third house. After that will be a little trickier, but I think we can manage if we're careful. Did you see how those trees along the edge of the street are spaced out?"

"Yeah."

"So there's one at the center of each house. We'll run from one tree to the next. We'll stop by each one and wait, look around, listen for any followers. When it's clear, move on to the next."

"Hmm." Aaron folds his arms across his chest.

"After we make it to the end of the block, we'll just have to make a run for it. But by that point, it's not too far."

Aaron waits, raising his eyebrows at Nathaniel. "And then?"

"Right. So once we get there, I'm sure we'll be able to find axes. Maybe crowbars and things like that too. I mean, we don't really have any weapons now, so those would be good to have."

Aaron starts to open his mouth in protest, but Nathaniel keeps going. "*And,* I imagine we can find a couple of those firefighter coat thingies to wear. They're made out of, like, Kevlar or something. Nobody's gonna be biting through that!"

"So—"

"*And, and* I bet there'll probably be one of those CB radios there. Right? We can try calling for help. Or even if they don't have that, they'll probably have, like, a police scanner. We can listen in and see if there's any more information coming over that."

Aaron draws a breath to try to speak up again.

Nathaniel carries on, growing louder the longer he talks. "*Plus,* I'm thinking we take it over, make it our new home. They have beds and blankets there, and there will be food, I'm sure. Basic medical supplies too.

"Oh, and hot showers and working toilets. Remember indoor plumbing?" Nathaniel lets out a long sigh. "Ah, indoor plumbing. How I miss getting to make use of it."

Nathaniel tilts his head as he thinks about relaxing in a long, hot shower. Aaron clears his throat and draws Nathaniel's attention back to the present.

"On top of all that, it's a lot sturdier of a building. It's definitely a lot newer than this house, and I think it'll be easier to defend than this place."

The pair sits in silence, staring at each other. Finally, Nathaniel blurts out, "Well?"

"Oh, is it my turn to speak now?"

"Yeah." Nathaniel feels his face get warm. He's grateful for the shadows now, knowing that Aaron can't see the bright color of his cheeks.

"Come on, Nate. It's a *big* risk. A truly, insanely big risk, and you know it. We've been safe here so far. Why should we leave?"

"Look. We're not going to have enough food to last forever. We've probably only got enough for a couple more days as it is. And what if one of those things does find us here? We'd literally be backed into a corner. There's only one way in or out of here."

"True."

"And honestly," Nathaniel slumps back against the wall and slides down until he's sitting in the dirt once again. "I can't stand that I can't... Well, *stand*. My back is killing me, man. I'm sick of the dark. I'm sick of crawling through this cramped space. I'm sick of the cobwebs and the cockroaches. I'm sick of only speaking in hushed whispers. I want to stretch. I want to be able to move around, to sleep in a real bed again."

Aaron twists sideways to look out the small opening again. Leaning back once more, he sighs.

"Really, man, what's the point of living if *this*," Nathaniel pauses as he gestures around the dark, filthy crawlspace, "is how we have to live?"

"Fine." Aaron closes his eyes and pinches the bridge of his nose. "But not tonight."

"What? Why?"

"Give me tonight to think. I want time to see if I can come up with anything better first. If I can't, then we'll try your plan tomorrow."

Nathaniel nods. "De—"

A roar rips through the air outside. Both men press their backs to the wall and inch away into the darkness on each side of the small vent opening. Their hearts hammer inside their chests. The zombie's feet pound against the sidewalk as it sprints past the crawl space vent. Someone far off in the distance screams.

Nathaniel's eyes slowly readjust to the darkness, and he searches for Aaron's silhouette. So hushed now that he can barely hear his own word, he whispers, "Deal."

- Eastern Missouri -
-- Day 7 --

"So," Nathaniel turns away from the vent just as the sun drops below the horizon. His eyes slowly adjust, and he locates Aaron. "We leaving as soon as it's fully dark? Or have you had some brilliant idea since yesterday?"

"No."

"No to which?" Nathaniel narrows his eyes as he looks in Aaron's general direction.

"Both. Sort of."

"Aaron, dude." Nathaniel drags the word out as he rolls his dark brown eyes.

"Sorry." Aaron shakes his head rapidly and sends dust flying loose from his shaggy hair. He moves a few steps closer and takes a peek outside. "Not trying to be evasive. Just kinda got lost in my thoughts. I've still been trying to think of something better. I just..."

Aaron stares down the street at the fire station in the distance as he drums his fingers on his shins. Finally, Aaron steps back into the shadows and turns toward Nathaniel again. "Anyway, what I mean is, no. I haven't exactly thought of a 'better' plan. But I also don't want to leave immediately after dark because I have a slight modification to your plan."

"I'm listening."

"It'll be easier to just show you, though. We got any duct tape in the house?"

"Um, no. Not that I know of, anyway. Pretty sure I've got some packing tape, though. Will that work?"

"Yeah." Aaron takes another look through the opening. By now, the sun is half-disappeared. "Let's go up into the house."

Aaron turns around and crouch-walks to the small opening that leads into the one-car garage. He waits, listening intently for sounds of movement up above as Nathaniel catches up.

At last, Aaron lifts the board and moves it out of the way. He climbs through and straightens up. As much as he can anyway after stooping and crouching for so long.

Aaron steps away from the opening to make room. The tiny nightlight in the wall socket almost feels like a floodlight after spending so long in the dark. Feeling suddenly exposed, he shivers. Nathaniel comes through, stands up, and gestures for Aaron to lead the way.

The pair walk to the door. Aaron twists the knob, and he winces as the door opens with a loud *squeak*. However, there are no roars or trampling feet, so they step inside.

Sending Nathaniel in search of the packing tape, Aaron heads to the hall closet. Pulling out four folding, metal chairs, he leans them against the wall.

"Here." Nathaniel hurries back in and tosses the tape to Aaron. He spots the chairs and frowns. "Uh, what—"

"Okay, dude. I know you're going to think I'm crazy. But just turn around."

"Okay..."

Aaron picks up one of the folded chairs and presses it against Nathaniel's back. "Hold that there."

Nathaniel looks sideways at Aaron but does as he's instructed, reaching backward and grabbing hold of the sides of the chair.

Pulling the end of the clear tape from the roll, it lets out a loud *sqriiick*! Both men wince and look around. Again, though, there are no signs that anyone—or any*thing*—was alerted by it.

Aaron exhales heavily. Pressing the end of the tape against the back of the chair, he drags it up over Nathaniel's right shoulder, down diagonally across his torso, horizontally around his back, and then diagonally again to go over his left shoulder. A few more passes and the chair is well-secured to his back. Turning around, Aaron tells Nathaniel to take another chair and tape it to his back as well.

"There. Back armor."

"Huh. Yeah, you're definitely insane. But I like it." Nathaniel jerks a chin toward the other two chairs. "What are those for?"

"Hold your arm out like this." He holds a bent arm out in front of himself. "Like you were holding up a shield."

"Ah," Nathaniel grins. "I see where you're going."

"I mean, I literally said 'holding up a shield,' so... Yeah."

"Oh, no. I meant an '*armchair*.' Get it?"

Aaron groans.

Within a few minutes, the chair is taped onto Nathaniel's forearm. Then, Nathaniel grabs the final chair from its position along the wall and attaches it to Aaron's arm. "Anything else?"

"Yeah, hold on."

Aaron goes into the kitchen, carefully maneuvering his makeshift shields so they don't slam into anything. A moment later, he returns with two large knives in his hand. He passes one to Nathaniel. "Let's go."

Nathaniel nods. Turning around, he opens the front door, steps outside, and quickly moves behind the row of hedges. Aaron is close behind.

They move slowly, listening to their surroundings and trying not to clang the metal against anything. After what feels like an hour, they make it to the end of the hedgerow. They dart out across the sidewalk. Their metal chairs rattle with the hurried pace, but they make it to the first tree unnoticed.

They rush to the next tree, and the next, and the next, until they finally make it to the last one. The pair stops to catch their breath.

"So far, so good." Nathaniel glances at Aaron. "Ready?"

"Whenever you are."

Nathaniel takes off, sprinting across the abandoned road toward the fire station. He can hear Aaron close behind.

Yanking the door open, Nathaniel hurries inside and then twists to hold the door for Aaron. Once he's through, he pulls it closed. There's no lock, but they'll figure that out later. The room is already well-lit, and they stand there momentarily, blinking as their eyes adjust to the sudden brightness.

Ready to celebrate, Nathaniel starts to turn toward Aaron. Suddenly, a roar reverberates off the walls and seems to shake the air around them. Nathaniel jumps, yelping.

Aaron wastes no time, charging at the zombie with his arm shield in front of his chest. Aaron slams into him, and the zombie falls, tumbling across the floor.

Nathaniel rushes up as the zombie leaps to his feet. The zombie roars again, then charges. Nathaniel plants his feet and bends his knees.

Aaron stands off to the side, watching now, unsure how to help without getting in the way.

The zombie crashes into Nathaniel's metal chair and stumbles to the side. Swinging his unshielded arm up and back down, Nathaniel jams the knife's blade into the zombie's chest, sending a spray of blood across the floor. Before he realizes what's happening, Nathaniel's hand slips off the grip and down the blade, leaving a deep gouge across his palm. Nathaniel jerks his hand away and stumbles backward.

The zombie lunges toward Nathaniel. Aaron rushes behind the zombie and slams into his back. The zombie stumbles forward, slipping in its own spilled blood, and lands face-first on the concrete floor. Aaron leaps onto the creature's back. He brings the knife down into the back of the zombie's skull. Blood squirts out, coating Aaron's shirt and hair. The zombie goes limp.

As Aaron kneels there, struggling for breath, some blood drips onto his lip, tickling the sensitive skin. Without thinking, he runs his tongue over the spot. As the taste makes itself known, he realizes what happened. The color drains from his face. Turning, he gags, then noisily empties the contents of his stomach onto the floor.

When his nausea finally passes, Aaron pushes himself to his feet and turns around. Nathaniel is leaning on the wall by the bottom of the stairs, pale and clutching his palm to his chest. Aaron yanks the chair off his own arm and jogs over to Nathaniel's side.

Aaron looks Nathaniel over. As far as Aaron can tell, the only blood on Nathaniel is from that horrendous cut on his hand. There's none on the chair shield, none on his face.

"Nate? Don't pass out on me." Aaron quickly removes the chairs from Nathaniel's arm and back. Then, he guides Nathaniel over to sit on the stairs. "Hang in there while I find a first aid kit or something."

Nathaniel nods, but his eyelids droop, and he leans precariously to one side as Aaron hurries away.

4

LEARN AND ADAPT

- Southeastern Oklahoma -

-- Day 4 --

After Abigail had gotten home the previous day and let her stomach settle, it had been time to slither out of the homemade duct tape armor. It had taken several minutes, but once she'd gotten free, she'd been relieved to find that it had done its job rather well. There was a gigantic, circular, purple bruise on her forearm, along with two lighter bruised streaks showing where the attacker's teeth had dragged across Abigail's arm when she'd landed that left hook. The skin was unbroken, though, and she hoped that was good enough. The knuckles along her left hand were also swollen and badly bruised. Thankfully, none of the bones seemed broken.

On top of the close call and the wounds, she'd arrived home to find another email from Jake: "Hey, Ab, flat tire. It's gonna take a bit to get it replaced and get back on the road. Be there by morning. -- Jake."

So, she'd spent another long night alone in the attic.

Now, sitting in the attic in the early morning light, Abigail stares at her darkened phone screen, willing it to chime with a message from her brother.

Where is he? Has something happened since last night?

Just as the dark thoughts threaten to overwhelm her, she hears the crunch of tires on the gravel driveway. She jumps up and rushes over to the small attic window to check. Abigail breathes a sigh of relief as a man steps out of the car, and she catches sight of the familiar wavy, brown hair. She moves toward the ladder, grinning.

Abigail begins to pry loose the boards that are securing the ladder in place but freezes at the sounds of shouting outside. The boards slip out of her hands. She rushes back to the window.

Jake is struggling with someone. A zombie. Realizing the attacker has his teeth buried deep in the flesh of Jake's hand, Abigail screams. Jake rears back, then headbutts the zombie straight in the eye.

The zombie's teeth loosen their hold on Jake's flesh, and Jake loses his balance, stumbling backward into the side of his car. The zombie staggers back, away from Jake, then sprints toward the trees. As soon as the zombie is a few steps away from the cover of the woods, he stops, turns, and looks back. The area around his eye is already swelling and turning purple from the hit, but his face is entirely devoid of emotion. He turns away once more and casually wanders off into the dense foliage.

Rushing back to the ladder, Abigail forces the boards away and flies down the still-unfolding ladder as she hurries outside to meet Jake. He's standing in the driveway, stunned and unmoving. His mangled hand is clutched tight against his chest, and blood quickly changes his yellow t-shirt into a deep orange hue.

Ignoring the gore, Abigail throws her arms around her brother's neck. Jake doesn't react. She lets go and quickly looks around, but as far as she can tell, they are now entirely alone. Gently lifting his uninjured arm, she places it across her shoulders. Then, sliding her arm around her brother's lower back, Abigail slowly maneuvers him into the house.

After making it in and securing the door behind them, Abigail leads Jake to the dining table. She forces herself to push back the adrenaline and focus on the most immediate concern: calm him down and stop the bleeding.

"Jake?" She waves a hand in front of his vacant eyes. "Jake, I need you to sit down."

No response.

"Jake?" She snaps her fingers next to his ear.

Nothing. Abigail moves him in front of a chair and pushes down on his shoulders until he finally bends his knees and sinks into the wooden seat. Stepping out of the room for a minute, Abigail double-checks the door locks, then retrieves the first aid kit. When she returns to the table, Jake is sitting there, still lost in his thousand-yard stare, mumbling something incoherent.

"Jake, you're gonna have to speak up." Abigail kneels down in front of him and tries to meet his gaze. "What are you saying?"

For a long while, his eyes continue to look straight through her. Abigail takes his face in her hands and brings her face close to his so they're nearly touching noses. Doing her best impersonation of their mother, she loudly says, "Jake Andrew!"

At last, he blinks. His eyes focus on his sister. In a shaking voice, he asks, "Why did it run away?"

Opening up the small, metal box, Abigail pulls out the bottle of rubbing alcohol. Abigail leans back and looks at him with her brow knitting together. "What was that?"

"Why did it run?"

His words finally sink in this time. He has a good point. Why did it run after biting him? She lifts her shoulder in a shrug and turns her attention back to his hand. She pours the alcohol over the wound, and the pinkish liquid runs down, soaking both his jeans and the floor.

Jake doesn't even acknowledge the burning his hand should be feeling. He continues in a somewhat more normal tone, "I'm sure it heard

you scream. I thought it would go after you because of that. It only bit me once... Shouldn't they, I don't know... Want to feed or something?"

Abigail blinks at him, utterly at a loss for words. Picking up a towel, she dabs away as much of the alcohol and blood as she can from her brother's hand and, for the first time, can really see the extent of the injury. There's a semi-circular pattern of teeth marks deep into both the palm and back of his hand. But there's no significant chunk of flesh missing.

Abigail reaches for the first aid kit again. "Let me bandage this and hopefully get the bleeding stopped. We'll talk about it later."

He meets his sister's gaze with his wide eyes showing a sudden earnestness. "Should we cut it off?"

"Jake... Honey, we..." Abigail's dealing-with-the-emergency demeanor abruptly falls away, and a tear rolls down her face. Reaching up, she cups his stubbled cheek in her hand. She swallows hard, fighting to hold the tears at bay for now. "We don't even know what will happen. And besides, I'm sure it doesn't work like that. It's already in your bloodstream. If we cut your hand off, you'll still have whatever germs are in their saliva, but you'd be without a hand and losing a ton of blood."

Jake simply nods and lets her wrap the bandage around his still-bleeding hand.

After bandaging him up, Jake says he wants to be alone for a while and goes to the attic to lie down.

Abigail sits alone at the kitchen table and mulls over his questions. The more she thinks about what she's seen (both in person and on the news), the more she believes these zombies don't actually want to *eat* people. They only want to infect them. All they do is bite and move on.

But why didn't it respond to my scream?

- Southeastern Oklahoma -

-- Day 5 --

Jake is lying on the cot in the attic. He stares, unseeing and unmoving, at the rafters overhead. If it weren't for the steady rise and fall of his chest, an observer might think him to be dead. Inside his head, though, his thoughts race. His lip twitches ever-so-slightly as a dark thought pops into his mind: *I guess I'll get to find out firsthand how accurate all those zombie movies are.*

Abigail had spent last night cleaning, pacing, and organizing. Basically anything she could think of to keep herself from worrying about her brother. She had tried to watch the news as well, but most channels are only broadcasting sporadically now, if at all.

Now, she sits at the kitchen table with her head resting atop her folded arms. Utter exhaustion finally puts an end to her physical movements, but her mind still races. Still fighting the urge to dwell on Jake's fate, she tries to understand these zombies instead.

So, these zombies obviously bite people. But other than that, they're so incredibly different than the fictional versions.

First of all, they only bite. They don't seem to consume, and they certainly don't want brains. From what they showed on the news and from what Jake and I saw, they bite until they draw blood. They spread this infection, then move on.

They're sure not slow and unsteady. They all seem to be able to run. That one that was out by the trail cams, in particular.

I saw that one attack the deer. Apparently, they can form plans. They can stalk and sneak up on their prey.

I'm pretty sure they hunt primarily by sight. I don't know if that's their only hunting sense, though. The one that attacked Jake...

Tears start to well up in her eyes. Abigail takes a deep breath, reminding herself to look at this from a purely analytical perspective. Now is not the time for becoming emotional. She inhales deeply, then slowly exhales as she returns to her thoughts.

That one didn't seem drawn to my voice, even after he was done infecting my brother. Was that a fluke?

Scent might be a factor. I doubt it, though, since humans don't have a particularly strong sense of smell to begin with. But I guess I can't really be certain about that.

So, they're fast and smart and don't eat brains. Not exactly the definition of a zombie. But honestly, it's as good a name as any for these monsters.

Abigail sits up as her thoughts turn again toward her brother's fate. Searching for a distraction, she grabs her cellphone and lights up the screen. The trail cam app has notifications of new activity. She taps the app icon, props the phone up on the table, and selects the first video.

This one is from one of the cameras mounted close to the pond. Two men are running: one as predator and one as prey. A short, thin man is being pursued by a tall, burly one. The thin man is headed straight toward the water, repeatedly looking back over his shoulder. Finally, the thin man stops, spins around, and fires a pistol at the pursuer. The pursuer barely flinches as the bullet tears through his shoulder, and a spray of blood flies out, painting his clothing and face. Another shot blows a hole through the pursuer's skull, just above his left eye. He stumbles but quickly rights himself. He begins running again. The thin man spins back toward the water, lets the gun slip from his hand, and sprints once more.

Abigail's heart hammers against her ribs as she sees the larger man gaining on his victim. The thin man redoubles his efforts as he tries to outpace his much larger pursuer. Abigail watches helplessly as the larger man speeds up as well. The small man reaches the edge of the pond and leaps in. He disappears beneath the murky water. A moment later, he bobs back up to the surface and begins paddling madly, swimming with all his might. The larger man runs straight into the water and immediately sinks to the bottom. Abigail lets out the breath that she didn't realize she was holding. Just as the tightness in her shoulders fades away, she sees a small splash. The thin man disappears from view. She gapes at the screen until realization dawns on her: he was pulled underwater by his attacker. After a few seconds with no visible movement, the camera's recording ends.

A chill runs down Abigail's spine. She had opened the video expecting to see a fox or a bird had triggered the motion sensors. So even though she'd known an attack like that *might* have been caught on film, she really hadn't been prepared for the sight.

She quickly swipes away the video and returns to the app's main screen. Another video is waiting. The timestamp is three minutes after the previous one, and it's from the same camera. Her shaking hand hovers over the screen as she hesitates. Finally, she taps the screen, and the video starts up. The burly man casually walks out of the pond. He stops at the water's edge and looks around. He glances at the camera for the briefest of moments. With the distance and the poor resolution, his eyes seem to be a solid pool of pitch black. Abigail recoils at the sight. Drenched and dripping, the large man slowly wanders away into the woods. Abigail looks at the water, wondering where the thin man went until she finally realizes the floating, motionless shape in the water isn't a log.

The video ends. Abigail swipes the app away and locks her phone, not caring if there are more videos.

"Abby?"

Abigail jumps. She spins around in her seat with her hand clutched against her chest.

Standing in the doorway is Jake. His eyes are red-rimmed and puffy. He sniffles. Abigail stands up and rushes over, wrapping her arms around him. He returns the tight embrace and buries his face against his sister's shoulder. For a long time, they simply hold one another.

Jake says something, but the words are too muffled for her to understand. Abigail takes half a step back and asks him to repeat himself.

"I won't survive this."

Abigail opens her mouth, ready to protest, but Jake cuts in again before she can find the words.

"Abby. Listen to me. I *won't* survive this. I can already feel it gnawing away at me. It's..." His eyes search the room as if the right words are hiding somewhere nearby. "I don't know how to explain it, but I can feel it. It's... It's changing me from the inside."

As her eyes fill with tears, Abigail momentarily meets her brother's gaze before casting a glance around the room. She draws a breath and tries to find the words to lessen his fears. He shakes his head, stopping her again before she can speak.

"No, Ab. It is *not* your fault." Jake pauses. He tilts her chin up so he can look her in the eye. "Do you hear me, Abigail Jane? You are *not* to blame."

Abigail bites her lower lip as the tears start falling freely down her cheeks. She squeezes her eyes shut. "Yes, it is my—"

"No!"

Shocked at the sudden forcefulness in his voice, Abigail blinks at him. "But I—"

"Don't you dare think like that. I *chose* to come here because I love you." Pulling his sister in close, he tightens his arms around her again. "I wouldn't change that decision for the world."

Abigail's mouth moves, but her voice is trapped behind the lump in her throat. She returns the gesture, squeezing tightly and hoping that he can feel just how much she loves him too.

"Hey, Ab?"

She pulls away just far enough to look up at his face.

"I do love you, but..."

Abigail takes a step back. "But what?"

Biting his lip, he looks away, across the room. "Well..."

Grabbing his chin, Abigail forces him to look at her again. "But *what,* Jake? Just spit it out!"

"If you don't go take a shower right now, I might actually start to regret coming here."

Bursting into laughter, she slaps Jake's arm. He grins. Abigail steps up close to him and wraps her arms around his chest again. He leans his cheek against the top of her head. The pair of them stay there for a long time, laughing together even as the tears continue to fall.

5

MAMA

- Southwestern Kansas -

-- Day 5 --

Charlie walks quickly into the barn. Tom is absent from his usual sleeping spot, but habit has her stepping wide as she crosses the threshold anyway. Her thoughts are already elsewhere. She heard some commotion up near the chicken coop a few minutes ago, and she needs to get up there.

She hurriedly tosses more hay into each of the cows' stalls. The first three stalls were low on hay, as expected. In her rush, Charlie doesn't notice that Mama hasn't drunk or eaten a thing since she's been in the barn.

Charlie steps wide again as she exits. She closes the door and returns to the truck, taking off across the pasture.

As she nears the building, Charlie hears the high-pitched yelping bark of a coyote. It's close. She stops the pickup a ways back from the chicken coop and shuts off the engine. She grabs the shotgun from the window rack and checks that it's loaded. Twisting the crank handle on the door, she forces the stubborn window down and listens. There's noise coming from the far end of the coop: claws scratching, teeth scraping against wood, a low growl.

Slowly opening up the pickup door, she quietly steps out and into the tall grass. She disengages the shotgun's safety. Her eyes never leave the chicken coop. Charlie walks forward, then moves in a wide arc around the enclosure. She lifts the gun up and places the butt against her shoulder. Raising the muzzle slightly with her left hand as she moves closer, she puts her right hand on the grip and rests her finger against the trigger guard.

Charlie slowly makes her way around to the far side of the coop and stops. There it is. But the murderous beast doesn't acknowledge her. It continues tearing away at the wall of the enclosure. She studies the coyote over the top of the gun. A thick, white foam drips from its mouth. Its gray-brown fur is thick, except for a few bald patches on its neck. And those same hairless spots are accented with scabbed-over gouges down its side. There's no doubt this is the one her roosters fought. It's the one that killed her birds. She takes aim and slides her finger toward the trigger.

Exhaling slowly, she's just about to fire the gun when she notices something. Charlie lifts her face and looks at the coyote's front left paw. Or rather, its lack thereof. The beast's left leg ends abruptly in a bloody stump.

Looking down the sight again, she exhales, then squeezes the trigger. The coyote is knocked off its feet and falls into a pool of blood. Her ears ring after the sudden blast, but she doesn't flinch.

Charlie lowers the weapon and starts to move closer. The coyote twitches, and Charlie stops in her tracks. The creature slowly climbs to its feet as though it didn't just have a hole blown through its side. Charlie raises an eyebrow at it.

The coyote turns toward the woman and snarls. She raises the gun once again. Just as the coyote starts to charge, she fires another time. Blood, fur, and brain matter go flying, coating the ground and the walls of the coop. The coyote twitches again, but this time it doesn't get up.

Lowering the gun, Charlie reengages the safety. She moves close and looks down at the creature. She leans over. She squints at the blood-encrusted front stump. It looks gnawed off, and recently too.

Straightening up, Charlie walks swiftly over to the edge of the pasture. She climbs through the fence, moves to the narrow trail, and makes her way to the nearest trap. Her hunch is correct. Sure enough, the paw is still lodged in the trap.

Charlie shakes her head. "Poor, rabid bastard."

After sliding her hands into a pair of thick rubber gloves, Charlie uses an old raincoat to scoop up the coyote carcass. Tossing the blood-soaked trap and severed foot on top of the corpse, she folds the coat around it all and ties it closed with a bit of rope. Soon, she'll bury it all at the far end of the property. But for now, she lays it in the truck bed. Sweat beads on her upper lip, but she doesn't dare wipe it away and risk getting the coyote's contaminated blood on her face.

She turns back toward the chicken coop. The ground is stained with the carnage. Scowling at the sight, she taps her foot and tries to think. Ideally, the whole area could be sanitized so that no other creatures come in contact with it. But she can't disinfect the dirt, and she couldn't find every last drop of spilled blood if she wanted to. Finally, she decides she'll cover what she can with a layer of soil from elsewhere in the pasture, let the chickens back out, and hope for the best.

- Southwestern Kansas -
-- Day 6 --

Charlie pulls the pickup beside the barn and sets the brake, then climbs out and stretches. The sun is beating down intensely this morning, and she can hardly believe it isn't summer yet. Sliding the ball cap off her head, she closes her eyes and takes a moment to relish the end of the freezing weather for the year. At last, Charlie settles the cap back on her head.

Opening the barn door, Charlie stops and blinks at the gray streak that bolts past her feet, through the door, and down the long driveway.

"Tom? What're you all riled up about?"

The cat disappears as he turns and runs past the end of the house.

With a shrug, the woman chuckles softly, steps into the barn, and closes the door behind her. She flips the light switch, and the fluorescent lights slowly buzz to life. Her eyes take a few moments to adjust after the brightness of the morning sun.

Inside the first three stalls along the left wall at the back of the barn, the cows are softly mooing and shuffling restlessly. Each one has pressed itself into the corner of its own wooden stall, as far toward the front of the barn as possible. Charlie stands there for a moment, staring, puzzled at the strange behavior. At last, shaking her head, she moves on.

At the far end, Mama is snorting and huffing. Charlie slowly moves past the first three stalls until the last one comes into view. Baby is curled up in the corner, barely visible behind Mama's shuffling hooves. Mama's gaze meets Charlie's. The cow snorts loudly and stomps her feet, then shakes her head as she starts to bellow again. Thick, white drool drips from her open mouth.

Charlie hurries away. She throws the barn's back door open, then rushes back to open the first three stalls. The frightened cattle move hesitantly at first, but then giving that farthest stall a wide berth, they dart past and out across the open field.

Reclosing the back door, Charlie turns again toward the angry cow. Mama glares. The former white patch on the cow's face is now stained brown by the long-dried coyote blood. Mama paws at the hay-covered, concrete floor.

Charlie's heart begins to race. As she stretches a hand toward the cow, she takes a tentative step forward and speaks softly. "Hey, now. It's alright, Mama. Ju—"

Mama rears up and kicks the wall behind her. She swings her head to the side, slamming one of her short horns through the thin wall beside her, and dust rains down from the wooden rafters. For a moment, the wall holds her trapped. She bellows. She steps to the side, twisting and jerking her head. Her eyes roll as she tries to free herself.

Charlie stares as she takes a step backward.

The cow jerks her head again as she steps backs up. Suddenly she's free. She bolts forward and slams headfirst into the wooden gate in front of her. It snaps down the middle in a shower of splinters. Charlie barely manages to pivot out of the way as the cow bashes into the opposite wall, horns first. Dust and bits of hay go flying through the air.

The cow snorts again but stumbles, stunned by the impact. Charlie bolts out the front door and latches it behind her before Mama can try again. She stands there by the pickup, catching her breath and listening. The noise starts up again inside the barn. Huffing, slamming, stomping, pausing, and then starting all over again.

Sighing heavily, Charlie walks over to the lean-to at the side of the barn and grabs a ladder. She carries it over to the wall below the opening for the hayloft and sets it in place, leaning against the wall. Then, grabbing her shotgun from the pickup and slinging it across her torso, she carefully climbs up into the upper part of the barn.

Charlie kneels and looks down over the edge at the rampaging cow below. She sets the shotgun against her shoulder. She takes aim and waits.

Mama charges again, slamming into the wall. The boards crack loudly as they begin to give way to the incessant attacks. The cow steps back, dazed and regaining her balance. Charlie holds her breath and squeezes the trigger. The projectile finds its mark, and the walls and floor are soon coated in a thick spray of blood and brain. The cow's knees buckle beneath her, and she collapses. What's left of her head flops limply to the side.

Waiting a moment, Charlie lowers the gun and looks toward the back stall. Baby still lies there, silent and unmoving. Charlie slaps her hand against the wooden boards of the loft, angry at herself for not putting the cow down sooner.

Shaking her head, Charlie stands up, walks to the edge of the loft, turns around, and climbs down the attached, interior ladder. She goes over to Mama and looks her over, studying her for any sign of a bite mark. She's careful to move slowly, avoiding the fresh blood and checking every inch of the body that she can see. Nothing. But she can't see the underside of the cow's round belly. She'll have to bring in the tractor to move the large carcass.

Charlie walks across the barn, internally cursing at herself for not getting rid of Mama sooner, before she could hurt Baby. Grabbing a tarp, she walks into the stall and carefully looks over the dead calf. Its chest is sunken in, the ribs likely crushed by Mama's hooves. No signs of bites, though. After a few minutes, Charlie uses the tarp to roll the stiff corpse to its other side and examines it again. Still, not a single bite mark.

Still crouching next to Baby, Charlie turns and looks at the cow lying in the center of the room. Fleetingly, she wonders why she can't find any teeth marks. But more than that, she wants to know how rabies could've taken hold so soon.

6

AMISS

- Central Colombia -
- Near the edge of the Amazon Rainforest -
-- Eight days before it starts --

Shaded by the dense foliage overhead, a jaguar emerges from the jungle and walks silently toward the small crater lake. Crouching low, it laps at the water.

Suddenly, the big cat's pupils grow round, and its ears tilt back. The hair along the creature's spine stands on end. It lets out a low growl. A trickle of tiny bubbles rises to the surface of the liquid. The jaguar's dark nose twitches as it sniffs the air.

Turning swiftly away from the water, the jaguar slinks back into the dense, green vegetation and vanishes.

7

CAPTIVE

- Eastern Missouri -
-- Day 8 --

"Aaron?" Nathaniel rolls onto his side. He yawns. His tongue feels sticky and bitter in his mouth.

Lifting his hand into the air to stretch, Nathaniel gasps as the movement sends a burning pain racing through his palm and up his arm.

A clock on the wall ticks loudly in the quiet room, and the bed squeaks as Nathaniel sits up and swings his legs over the side. The movement sends the room spinning. His vision goes dark at the edges. He sits motionless, closing his eyes and listening to the steady *tick, tick, tick* as he waits on the vertigo to pass. When he finally reopens his eyes, he looks down at his hand. A thick layer of white gauze is wound around it. Brow wrinkling, he stares down at the bandage. He can't quite remember what happened or how he got here. Or where "here" is, for that matter.

Nathaniel stands up slowly, bracing himself against the post that holds up the upper bunk. He looks around. A few streaks of sunlight come in through the gaps in the blinds, but not enough to clearly see his surroundings. He can make out the shape of several more bunk beds, some storage cabinets, and a few chairs.

Sliding his hand along the wall, Nathaniel moves toward the door until he finally locates a row of small switches in the middle of a wide metal plate. Flipping the first one, the fluorescent lights on the left half of the room buzz and click to life. He squints. As his eyes finally adjust and he can see clearly, he scans the room. His gaze lands on something hanging from one of the bed posts—a firefighter's helmet and coat—and suddenly, all of yesterday comes flooding back to him: *The fight, the injury from the knife, Aaron finishing off the zombie before vomiting all over the floor... Aaron rushing over, pouring alcohol over Nathaniel's sliced hand, packing and wrapping the wound... Aaron struggling to walk Nathaniel up the stairs as Nathaniel keeps sliding in and out of consciousness... Aaron maneuvering Nathaniel down onto the bed and throwing the blankets over him.*

Nathaniel turns, looking around the room again as if Aaron will magically appear out of thin air. No luck. He thinks this door next to the light switches is the one that leads downstairs—at least, that seems to fit with his foggy recollection of the previous night. Standing with his back to the stair door, he looks at the other walls. Along the righthand wall near the beds, there's a series of tall windows covered with black mini blinds. Some cabinets line the lefthand wall, along with a door at its center. Directly across from Nathaniel is a third door. He decides to try that one first.

Opening the door a few inches, Nathaniel peaks through the gap and calls out softly, "Aaron? You in here?"

No response.

Nathaniel slowly pushes the door open. In the lifeless room, the soft squeaking of the hinges sounds loud enough to wake the dead. He winces. With his undamaged left hand, he reaches in and feels along the wall until he finds the light switch and gives it a flick. These lights silently flare to life. Pushing the door the rest of the way open, he slowly steps inside.

The door clicks closed behind him, and Nathaniel jumps at the sound. He chuckles. Looking around, he realizes he is standing in the middle of a large dining room. To his left is something like an oversized living room. To his right is a large kitchen.

Spotting the refrigerator, Nathaniel rushes over and opens it up. Most of the food in there is a bit questionable at this point—who knows how long it's been there?—but there are plenty of canned and bottled drinks at the ready in the cabinets. Grabbing a bottle of water, he closes the fridge. He walks a few steps away and opens the pantry. He beams at the sight. The shelves are filled with rows upon rows of boxed and canned food.

As he pushes the cabinet door closed, Nathaniel tucks the bottle of water between his ribs and his arm to twist the cap off with his good hand. Then, lifting the bottle to his mouth, he tips it back. The cold liquid feels heavenly against his parched tongue. But as soon as it reaches his throat, he can sense it going down the wrong pipe. He chokes and doubles over at the waist as he's taken over by wracking coughs.

Still hacking, Nathaniel turns to set the bottle down on the table. He nearly jumps out of his skin at the sight of someone standing a few feet away. His eyes widen, but he recognizes Aaron's bowed head and the fingers twitching nervously at Aaron's side. Clutching his chest, trying to calm his spasming lungs, Nathaniel pulls in air and slowly releases it. Rasping and breathless, he calls out, "Aaron?"

Nothing.

Nathaniel puts the bottle on the table and swipes his sweaty palm across his shirt. He takes a few steps closer. "Come on, man. Is this some kind of prank? You're freaking me out." A nervous chuckle slips out, underlining the tension in the air. Stepping close to Aaron, Nathaniel taps him on the shoulder.

"No!" Aaron suddenly twists around and shoves Nathaniel away.

Nathaniel stumbles backward, whacking his injured hand

against the side of the table as he falls. He lands hard against the floor, and his vision goes dark at the edges. He sucks air through his teeth. Looking down, he watches as blood starts to soak through the center of the bandage. By the time Nathaniel looks up again, Aaron is nowhere in sight. Only the distant echo of footsteps gives any indication of where Aaron went. Nathaniel pushes himself to his feet and quickly retreats back to the bunk room.

Grabbing a chair, Nathaniel slides it across the room and jams it underneath the knob for the kitchen door. Then he does the same for the other entryways. Now barricaded in the room, he slips into the firefighter's coat and helmet. Nathaniel wraps the oversized coat tightly around himself, backs into a corner, sinks to the floor, and hugs his knees to his chest.

- Eastern Missouri -
-- Day 9 --

Bright morning sunlight peeks into the room, broken into thin strips by the rows of mini blinds. Nathaniel—still curled up in the corner with his head resting on his knees—slowly opens his eyes. He sits up. He'd gotten hot in the night and sleepily discarded the protective gear; now, the firefighter's coat lays crumpled on the floor with the helmet on top of it.

A sharp pain through his palm draws his attention. He looks down at it. The bandages are now dark brown, caked in a thick layer of dried blood. The skin underneath its thick wrappings feels warm and stiff. He knows that's not a good sign. He needs to tend to his hand, but the first aid kit is likely still downstairs. Unfortunately, that's not his most urgent concern.

He needs to deal with Aaron. He's just not sure how. Best-case scenario: the man is stressed and overwhelmed by this whole apocalypse thing, and eventually, he'll return to his old self. Worst-case scenario, he's been bitten.

Slipping back into the heavy coat and helmet, Nathaniel pushes himself to his feet and looks around the room. Plenty of things are in the room, but nothing that could realistically be used as a weapon.

Nathaniel groans. Moving quietly, he removes his helmet as he makes his way over to the exit that leads to the stairs. He presses his ear to the door, listening. It's quiet. He steps backward, slowly pulls the chair out from beneath the doorknob, and sets it aside. He leans his cheek to the door one more time, but still, it's silent. He straightens up, settles the helmet back on his head, and pulls open the door with his sweaty palm.

He moves through the doorway and onto the landing, scanning the room. Drawing a shaky breath, Nathaniel hurries down the steps and over to the nearest firetruck. He finds a wide compartment door on the side, twists the latch, and pulls it open to reveal its contents.

Nathaniel is still standing there, looking through the ample storage space when he hears someone running toward him. His breath catches in his throat. He grabs an axe and spins toward the sound. He lifts the axe up to his shoulder, but the heavy, two-handed device slips from his one-handed grip and clatters to the floor. His eyes go wide.

Nathaniel looks up just as something crashes into him and slams him into the side of the firetruck. The air flies from his lungs.

Aaron's face is inches from Nathaniel's. Aaron glares with black-streaked eyes. Nathaniel tries to shove Aaron away, but it doesn't work. Opening his mouth wide, Aaron roars. Nathaniel screams as he squeezes his eyes shut tight and pushes again.

Suddenly, the room is quiet, and Nathaniel realizes there's no more pressure on his chest. He opens his eyes. Aaron has moved back a step. For a moment, Nathaniel watches in wonder as Aaron's pupils contract and the black lines recede.

As his wits return, Nathaniel quickly sidesteps away until he's past the front of the firetruck with his back pressed against the large garage door. "Keep the hell away!"

"Nate, I... I'm so, so sorry, man." The color drains from Aaron's face, and he sinks to the cold concrete floor. He tilts his head down, presses his palms against his temples, and then looks up again. "It was... It was like I was just watching a movie; I didn't have control over my own body. It... Whatever this thing is took over, and I couldn't stop it."

Nathaniel looks at him sideways, unsure what he should say right now. "Why were you finally able to stop then?"

"It... I don't know, it just... It didn't *want* to attack you anymore."

"Uh-huh." Nathaniel finds the response less than adequate but can't exactly contest it. Instead, he moves on to his next question. "So, when did you get bit? I know my memory of that night is hazy, but I don't remem—"

"I didn't."

"Aaron, it's obvious you're infected. I just want—"

"I *didn't*! Aaron digs his fingernails into his calves as he shouts the response.

Nathaniel's eyes go wide, and he tenses up.

Aaron inhales, then exhales slowly, lowering his voice as he starts again. "I did not get bitten. I'll let you inspect me for bite marks if that'll make you feel better, but it wouldn't change anything, even if I was lying. You're right. I am infected. But it was *not* because of a bite. What do you remember from the first night we got here?"

"Well, I fought it and got hurt, then you stepped in and killed it. You threw up afterward, and then you came to bandage me up. Next thing I knew, I was waking up alone in the bunkroom."

"Right." Aaron slowly stands up. Seeing the look on Nathaniel's face, he quickly puts his hands up as if surrendering, then turns and walks toward the steps to sit there. "Well, I threw up because I got some of that zombie blood in my mouth."

"Okay. What..." Nathaniel gasps as he realizes what Aaron is saying. "Oh, shit."

"Yeah. So, now what?"

The pair stare at one another for a long time before Nathaniel finally responds. "I think I have to tie you up. Maybe we'll find a cure, or your body will fight it off eventually."

Aaron chuckles humorlessly at the optimism.

"I know it's a long shot, but what other choice do we have here? I mean, even if..." Nathaniel pauses, unable to put into words the dark thoughts that they both have running through their minds, "well, I still can't just let you run around infecting others."

"Fine."

Nathaniel nods and sends Aaron up the steps to wait in the bunkroom. Then, Nathaniel retrieves a bundle of rope from the firetruck. He looks down at the bandages wound around his hand. He needs to rebind the wound, but right now, if he wants to tie a rope, he needs to use his fingers. He unwinds the bandage, tosses it aside without paying much attention, and then hurries up the steps.

Aaron is waiting on a bunk bed at the far end of the room.

"Put your hands around the bedpost and turn away."

Aaron does as he's told. Nathaniel hurries over and ties Aaron up just as quickly as Nathaniel's damaged hand will allow. The scabs that line his palm break and fall away with the movement, and he leaves a pool of blood on the corner of the bed. He ignores the bleeding and finishes up. Hurriedly stepping away, he clutches his bleeding hand to his chest.

Aaron turns to face Nathaniel. Aaron's pupils start to grow, and the black slowly begins creeping across his eyes. Grinning, Aaron speaks in a voice much deeper than usual. "I won't hurt you, you know."

Sweat starts to bead up on Nathaniel's forehead. "I know you don't want to. But I really—"

"You don't understand. I won't hurt you. I realize now there's no point." Aaron's black eyes look pointedly at Nathaniel's wounded hand. "You were already infected."

- Eastern Missouri -
-- Day 10 --

The sun won't be up for at least another hour, but Nathaniel can't sleep. He sits down at the kitchen table with a bottle of water and lifts the container to his lips to take a drink. As soon as the cold liquid slides past the back of his tongue, his throat constricts. He chokes. The water flies from his mouth, soaking his shirt and pants.

He hurls the flimsy plastic bottle across the room. It crashes against the wall. Nathaniel stands up in such a rush, his chair topples over backward. He storms over to the refrigerator, yanks the door open, and starts grabbing food containers. He hurls them across the room one by one and watches as they explode against the walls.

When the last food container is destroyed, Nathaniel stands there, red-faced and shaking. He closes his eyes, slowly inhales, and then noisily exhales. He focuses on breathing for several long minutes until he finally reaches something near calm. Removing another water bottle from the fridge, he gently closes the door, walks back to the table, rights his chair, and resolves not to get up again until he's drunk the water.

The sun is well above the horizon as Nathaniel tips the last water droplet into his mouth. With a concentrated effort, he manages to force it down his throat. Standing up, he smashes the plastic bottle against the table before turning and walking away.

Stopping in front of the pantry, Nathaniel pulls it open and looks around. For a moment, he toys with the idea of forcing himself to eat something, but his stomach churns at the thought. Deciding that the victory over the water was enough battle for the morning, he figures food can wait.

Nathaniel opens up the first aid kit. Clenching his teeth, he pours alcohol over the wound on his hand, pats it dry, and then rewraps his palm with fresh gauze. Once the pain fades to a dull ache, he grabs another water bottle and heads back to the bunkroom. "Aaron?"

Aaron's back is turned toward him. If it weren't for the subtle movement of his shoulders with each breath, he could easily be mistaken for dead.

"Hey, man, I brought you some water."

Nathaniel walks closer. As soon as Nathaniel is within range of Aaron's peripheral vision, Aaron's head snaps toward him. Aaron's lips are chapped and cracked. His pupils are wide and rimmed only by a thin sliver of blue. The jagged black lines on the sclera are now so abundant, so dense, it's like looking up into the moonless night sky.

Aaron stares at Nathaniel for a few seconds, but deciding that Nathaniel is not a valid target, he soon loses all interest and turns away.

"You gotta drink this." Nathaniel steps up close to the bed and lifts the bottle toward Aaron's mouth.

Aaron jerks his head to the side, as far away from the bottle as he can get, and struggles against his restraints. He kicks wildly, nearly knocking the bottle from Nathaniel's hands. Nathaniel hurriedly steps back. Aaron calms down, returning to that creepy, death-like stillness.

Nathaniel sinks onto a bed across from Aaron. "Aaron?"

The black-eyed creature doesn't reply.

8

BREAKING NEWS

- Southwestern Kansas -

-- Day 9 --

Charlie pulls the truck up alongside the sidewalk and sets the brake as a rusted, old car speeds past. She turns and glares at the reckless driver. The vehicle bounces hard as it hits a deep pothole, but the driver doesn't slow down. As the car finally disappears around a bend in the road, Charlie climbs out and walks up the concrete steps to the shop's entrance. Just as she places her hand on the door handle, a second car comes tearing down the road, swerving around the hole, then speeding up as if trying to catch up to the first car. Scowling at this driver as well, she mumbles to herself, "Damn idiots. Gonna get someone killed driving like that."

Tsking noisily, Charlie turns back toward the door and pulls the handle. The door doesn't budge. She furrows her brow as she pulls again, then tries pushing instead. Still nothing. Taking one last drag on her cigarette, she takes it out of her mouth and stomps it out on the sidewalk. Peering in through the glass, Charlie raps her knuckles against the pane. "Melvin! You forgot to unlock the store again."

Stepping back, she waits, scowling at the door and muttering under her breath. "Come on, you old coot. Open the damn door."

Moving close to the door again, Charlie knocks louder. "Melvin! Just coming to tell you you'd have your money by the end of the week."

Melvin suddenly rushes out of the back room and unlocks the door. "What the hell are you doing? Get in here."

Charlie steps through the door, glowering at the man before her as he closes and relocks the door. He barely spares a glance at her before hurrying off. Melvin grabs a large cardboard box and returns to the back room.

"I'm headed to the bank to see about a reverse mortgage..." Charlie's words trail away as she watches Melvin run around the room, haphazardly tossing things into the box. She folds her arms across her chest. "Melvin, just what on God's green earth are you doing?"

At last, Melvin stops and looks at her as if the woman has grown a second head. "Wow. You weren't kiddin' when you said you don't pay attention to the news."

Melvin turns back toward the shelves to continue his packing as he talks. "To be fair, I didn't believe it at first. I still didn't believe it, even when all the TV stations quit broadcastin' the news. In fact, I didn't really buy it at all until last night when Rob Johnson forced his way in here, tryin' to bite me."

Charlie guffaws at the absurd statement. Melvin doesn't smile, though. And for the first time, Charlie notices the blood droplets that speckle the front of Melvin's shirt. Her laughter quickly fades away.

"See for yourself." Melvin tilts his head, gesturing toward the back corner of the building. "Take a gander at his eyes."

For a moment, Charlie stares in confusion. Then, she goes down the aisle and turns. Her eyes go wide, and her jaw drops.

There by the wall, lying on the floor in a pool of blood, is Robert Johnson. The shelves nearby are

practically barren as their former contents lie in lopsided piles around the body. Dented cans and smashed boxes show where the fight culminated. Next to the corpse is a blood-soaked hatchet. Robert's eyes are frozen wide open, nearly black as coals.

Charlie slowly wanders back over toward Melvin. "What..." She blinks at him. Her voice refuses to form any more words.

"They'd been talking about those rabies outbreaks, you know? Now they're saying it's somethin' new altogether. Acts kinda like rabies, but it starts showin' symptoms a whole lot sooner. Drives people over the edge when it gets in 'em. The news is calling the infected folks 'zombies.' I don't know about that, but whatever it turns 'em into, they're not humans anymore."

Melvin tosses a few more items into his cardboard box and then turns to face Charlie.

"Whole town's evacuating. I am, too, soon as I get these last few things loaded up in my truck. I'd suggest you do the same, but I know you, Charlie. I doubt anything short of God himself could get you to abandon your farm." Melvin's mouth turns up in a slight grin. "Take whatever you need. I'm picking up my son, and we're leaving."

Rooted to the spot, Charlie stares as Melvin approaches the door. With one last wave, he opens the door and disappears.

Charlie turns around. Her eyes travel across the store and its mishmash of random items before her gaze lands again on the black-eyed corpse in the back. Still in disbelief, Charlie leaves the store and climbs in the pickup. Robotically, she pulls a cigarette from its pack and places it between her lips as she stares blankly off into the distance. The lighter flicks. After touching the little, orange spark to the tip of the cigarette, she tosses the lighter into the seat and drives slowly back to the farm.

- Southwestern Kansas -
-- Day 10 --

Charlie rises with the sun after a long, restless night. And since she'd never been one to worry long or mope about things she couldn't change, she resolves to pull herself together. It's time to face this new—and bizarre—reality.

Quickly dressing and brushing her teeth, Charlie enters the tiny kitchen of the one-bedroom house. She walks up to the stove, twists the knob, and listens to it *click, click, click*. She turns it off and tries again. *Click, click*, but still no flame. Reaching into her pocket, she pulls out her lighter, puts it close to the burner, and flicks the trigger. At last, a blue ring of fire appears on the stovetop, and she puts the lighter back in her pocket. Setting a frying pan on the burner, she pours a dollop of oil and then walks over to look out the window. With the clear, blue sky and birds chirping in the trees, it's hard to believe anything is different today than just a couple weeks ago.

She returns to the stove and quickly scrambles up a couple of eggs. Pouring the food onto a plate, she turns off the burner and slides into a chair at the kitchen table to eat and think.

Melvin's gotta be wrong. Zombies and all that ain't real. Can't be.

Taking a bite of her breakfast, she shakes her head and chews slowly. *If it was rabies, my cow probably wouldn't've showed symptoms for a couple more weeks at least. Them coyotes did turn my cow awful quick.*

She scoops another forkful as her thoughts return to Melvin's store yesterday. *If it ain't true, how'd you explain Rob attacking Melvin? If he'd been bit by a rabid animal, he'd've known to get that vaccine. A rabies bite likely wouldn't've turned him sick in just a few days, neither.*

And them black-streaked eyes? Rabies sure don't do that.

Shivering at the recollection, Charlie polishes off the last few bites of the eggs and sets the plate and fork in the sink. *There weren't no bites on my cow and calf. I'm sure of that. Didn't see none on Rob neither. Course, I wasn't lookin' for any on him.*

For a fraction of a second, Charlie worries if she may have gotten herself infected since bites didn't seem to be a requirement for transmission. But then she shrugs the thought away. *Can't do nothin' about it now if I did.*

Charlie walks to the front door. She slips into her rubber boots, denim jacket, and ball cap, then heads out the door.

Before long, the pickup stops near the chicken coop, and Charlie steps out, feed bag in hand. Walking carefully across the yard, she tosses handfuls of the feed onto the ground. In a flurry of clucking and cackling, the chickens rush out from the small building and yard, surrounding the woman and truck as they peck at the food.

With the birds thoroughly distracted by their breakfast, Charlie places the feed bag back into the pickup, then steps into the coop to refill the waterers. That done, she bends down, looking around for eggs.

Midway through her task, Charlie bolts upright as a roar pierces the air from somewhere outside. The roosters scream in response. Charlie darts outside, nearly trampling several squawking hens as they rush into the protective shelter of the building. Still more of the birds run across the pasture, fly up onto the roof of the shelter, or dash underneath the pickup.

Charlie spins around amidst all the chaos, trying to see where the sound came from. She stops as her eyes land on the man standing just beyond the fenceline, underneath a tree with a thin, orange cloth tied around its low-hanging branch. The man's black-streaked eyes lock onto her. He tries to charge at her, but he's brought to an abrupt halt as his foot is caught in the trap.

The man bends down and grabs the trap, yanking hard against the anchor stake. It won't hold long. Charlie hurries over to the truck, pulls out her shotgun, and loads it. Lifting the gun to her shoulder, she turns to face the man and yells, "You need to get off my property! I won't warn you twice!"

"Five..." Charlie moves closer to the trespasser. "Four... Three... Two..."

She points the gun at the tree next to the man and fires. Bark and wood fragments go flying; bits of debris graze the man's face and leave deep gouges across his cheeks. Unflinching, he roars again and pulls harder against the foothold trap.

"One."

She aims, then fires again. The slug catches the zombie in the left shoulder and tears through, leaving a jagged, bloody hole. As blood pours down his side and his left arm hangs limp, the man bends down and uses his good hand to grab hold of the anchor stake. He pulls as Charlie takes aim for a third time.

Charlie squeezes the trigger, and the slug bursts through the lower part of the man's chest. The stake comes free from the ground, and he rights himself. He stands there, blood pouring from the open wounds. Charlie gapes at him as he glares back at her, still wholly unfazed by the damage.

The man opens his mouth wide in a roar, but no sound comes out this time. Charlie's eyes go wide. The man charges at her. She snaps out of her stupor, pulls some new slugs from her jacket pocket, and shoves two of them into the gun. The attacker is coming up fast. Charlie lets the remaining ammo fall to the ground, lifts the gun, holds her breath, and fires. This one finds its mark—straight through the center of the man's face—and he falls in a mangled, bloody heap just feet away from her.

Making her way back to the pickup, Charlie opens the door and plops into the driver's seat. She slides the cap off her head and uses her sleeve to wipe the sweat from her brow as she looks at the man she'd just killed. Her eyes slide down to his lower back, where his shirt has ridden up. A scabbed, half-healed wound sits there, just above his hip bone.

Well, she thinks as she sits there catching her breath, *no doubt about whether that one got bit. But those teeth marks sure don't look like they're from an animal.*

9

WAITING

- Southeastern Oklahoma -

-- Day 8 --

"So, you've seen at least, what?" Jake turns away from the window to look at his sister. "Three of them right around the house here?"

"Four..." Abigail pauses for a moment as she thinks back. "Wait, five. I forgot about that one near the road yesterday."

"Damn. So many, way out here in the middle of nowhere."

"Okay, get serious, Jake. I know you always say this is '*the boonies,*' but we're only two miles from the town line here. Just because there's some trees and a pond doesn't mean—"

Grinning, Jake holds his hands up in surrender. "Alright, I give. I've just gotta pick on you while I still can."

"Jake..."

Walking over, Jake kisses the top of Abigail's head and gives her shoulder a quick squeeze before he starts to pace across the room. "So, there are too many of those zombies here. We've got to find somewhere else to go."

"Agreed." Abigail drums her fingers on the tabletop. "Maybe we should just go to Mom and Dad's house. We can always go somewhere else later, but we really need to find out if they're okay."

"I think we need to get farther away than that, but..." His voice trails off as he stops in front of the window to look outside again. He finally turns back toward his sister. "Yeah, alright. Let's go there first. We'll figure out our next step from there."

Jake sits down at the table as Abigail grabs a sheet of paper and a pen. Together, the two begin to plan a list of supplies they'll load into the SUV. A few minutes later, feeling like they've covered the basics, Abigail starts rounding up all the items on the list.

Meanwhile, Jake takes Abigail's phone and checks the trail cam footage. Knowing what might be in store, Jake holds his breath as he taps play on the first video. The screen changes to show the outside of the house. Something moves just at the edge of the view. Jake leans forward. Suddenly, a doe pops out next to the bushes. She saunters across the lawn and disappears out of frame. The video ends. Jake's shoulders relax, and he chuckles.

Jake taps the other video from earlier in the day. This time he doesn't have to wait long, as the action starts right away. Just before the sun had fully risen, a trio of raccoons had tried to get into the trash can outside. Eventually, they ran away, and that video ended just as anti-climactically as it had started.

Informing Abigail of the mundaneness of the videos, the pair agree it's probably as safe as it's going to get. They each grab an armful of supplies and head outside. After a quick look around, Jake sets down the box he's carrying and leans the baseball bat up against the SUV's bumper. Abigail sends him back inside to grab the next box while she starts to load things up.

Right after the screen door clicks shut, Abigail hears something off to her left near the bushes. She freezes. She's already mentally kicking herself for staying outside alone, but she forces her thoughts back into the moment.

Without turning to look toward the sound, Abigail slowly reaches for the baseball bat that's leaning against the bumper. As soon as it's in her grasp, she spins to her left. A zombie is barreling toward her. Abigail's heart leaps into her throat at the sheer size of the monster heading straight for her. Her palms grow sweaty. She tightens her fingers around the bat's handle. She steps back, clenches her jaw, and raises the bat to swing.

Suddenly, Jake rushes out of the house and throws himself between his sister and the zombie. Jake leans forward and rushes, shoulder first, at the attacker. He hits the zombie square in the stomach. The air hurriedly leaves the attacker's lungs, and he falls to the ground.

Before the zombie can get to its feet, Jake shoves Abigail into the SUV, pulls the bat from her hands, and slams the door closed. Abigail blinks as her gaze bounces back and forth between the attacker and her brother. The zombie glares at Abigail. *Only* at Abigail. Jake walks in between the two of them, but it's almost as if the zombie sees right through him.

Without warning, the zombie leaps to his feet and rushes at the vehicle. Jake lifts the bat and swings it full force into the man's nose. The zombie stumbles backward as his broken nose drenches the front of his clothes with blood. He pauses for a second, swaying a bit. Then he charges again.

Once more, Jake swings the bat into the crazed man's face. A loud *crack* sends another spray of blood, along with a few teeth. The man falls backward and lands hard on the ground. In a blink, he's up and running again, this time with his jaw dislocated and hanging limp. He roars.

Jake rears back with the bat, but the man feints to the side. The swing of the bat misses its target as the man pivots around Jake and makes his way toward Abigail, now unimpeded. Recovering quickly, Jake swings again. This time he hits the man in the back of the head, the spot where the skull meets the spine. The attacker's knees buckle this time, sending him sprawling to the ground. Jake stands there, tensed and waiting to strike once more. But the assailant no longer moves.

At last, the blood-covered bat falls from Jake's hands. Breathing hard, he doubles over and rests his hands against his knees.

Abigail opens the door and slides out. Her heart still races. She takes a deep breath as she rests a hand lightly on her brother's back. "Are you okay?"

Jake, still out of breath, nods.

"I shouldn't have made you—"

Straightening up, he shakes his head at her. "I'm already bit. What are they going to do to me? Double infect me?"

Abigail snorts at his absurd response.

Grabbing his sister by the arm, Jake heads back inside and locks the door behind them. He peeks out the window at the gory corpse. "You said that one on the video didn't really react when it was shot in the face, right?"

Abigail confirms that's what it looked like on the trail cam.

"This one didn't seem to mind a metal bat to the face either. Seems like the only thing that stopped him was that whack to the brain stem."

"I think you're right. But..." Abigail pauses as she takes a look out the window as well. "How did he get past my cameras?"

"I really don't know. That had to have been intentional." Jake's eyebrows knit together as he looks at his sister. "You stay in here while I finish loading the car. He didn't care about me at all. I think he could sense that I'm already infected."

Abigail stays put and doesn't mention the tiny specks of black that are starting to form at the corners of her brother's eyes.

- Southeastern Oklahoma -

-- Day 9 --

Rain pelts the outside of the house as thunder rumbles somewhere off in the distance. A bright, colorfully striped test pattern lights up the TV screen. At Abigail's side, a radio crackles with static. She scrolls on her phone, looking through social media and news sites over and over, but most of the information is useless or simply speculative. Turns out, when the apocalypse happens, formally writing up the news isn't exactly top of anyone's priority list. But from what she can piece together, the infection can take hold in about a week, sometimes less. Who knows? Maybe it can take longer in some cases too, but there just hasn't been enough time to find that out yet. Worst of all, there isn't a cure, and with the speed that this thing is taking over, there isn't likely to ever be a cure.

At the sound of footsteps on the stairs, Abigail sets down her phone and turns off the television. She lets the radio continue to crackle in the background.

"Hey, Jake." Abigail turns to face him, but he seems to be a million miles away.

"Hello? Jake?" Abigail stands up and places herself directly in front of her brother, poking him in the shoulder. "Earth to Jake!"

Abigail takes a step closer and gasps as her eyes meet his. His pupils are dilated more than they should be under the bright overhead lights. The hazel irises have nearly been swallowed up. Jagged black lines branch out across the whites. A shiver runs down Abigail's spine, and she takes an involuntary step backward.

"Um... Jake?"

Finally, he blinks. The trance is broken. He holds a hand up to his brow, blocking the light as he stands there, waiting for his pupils to shrink to their appropriate size. The dark lines recede to the edges of the whites and leave barely more than a dark speck on each side.

Lowering his hand at last, Jake looks at his sister and blinks at her. He turns and looks back at the stairs, then with deep lines etched across his forehead, he turns to face Abigail again. "How did I get down here?"

"So, what does it feel like when the disease—or virus or whatever it is—takes over?"

Jake sighs. He looks down at the table as he answers her. "Sometimes, it's like I'm asleep. Someone might be using my body, but I don't know. It's like I'm not there at all. I just 'wake up' at some point, and I'm somewhere else..."

Abigail reaches out to put her hand on his, but Jake jerks away before she can touch him. He scoots his chair back a few inches and then folds his arms across his chest. Then, still refusing to look at her, he continues. "A couple times, it's felt like I'm watching as someone else controls me. I can see what they're doing, but my muscles just won't listen to me. It hasn't happened often. And so far, none of those spells have lasted long, but..."

"Earlier, when you came down the steps, you were 'asleep?'"

He nods.

For a long time, Abigail sits with Jake, and she answers his questions. Sometimes she has to repeat the answer over and over before the words will finally sink in. She might as well be speaking to an advanced dementia patient. But ultimately, his mind seems to wake up, and he can remember what was happening.

With Jake finally reoriented, Abigail makes cinnamon toast for the both of them and slides back into her seat at the table as she starts to eat.

"So, I know we were planning on leaving first thing this morning, but I, uh... I got an email earlier." She pauses to take a large bite, then stares intently at the toast as she chews.

Jake slides away his untouched breakfast. "And?"

"Do you remember my friend Suzanne?"

"Yeah."

Abigail finishes her food and then narrows her eyes at her brother's uneaten food. She opens her mouth to comment on it but decides against it. Instead, she continues her story. "So she was emailing me this morning. I don't know where she's been all this time, and the email was pretty brief. Anyway, she wants to go with us to Mom and Dad's. She can't make it until tomorrow, but I, uh..."

Tensing up, Abigail braces herself for the argument she's sure will ensue. "I told her we'd wait for her."

"Okay."

With one eyebrow raised high, Abigail stares at her brother. "Really? You're... Not gonna fight me on that?"

"No," he says with a half-hearted chuckle. "But I'm sure you'll fight me on what I've got to say."

Abigail leans forward as she scrunches up her face at her brother. Making a big show of it, she reaches out and places a palm against her brother's forehead as if checking for a fever. Finally, she pulls back and glares at him. "Who the hell are you, and what have you done with my Jakester?"

Jake laughs loudly this time, putting a smile on Abigail's face as well. As his laughter dies, he explains, "I'm not going to object because... Well, I'm not going with you."

Abigail's smile quickly turns to a frown as she opens her mouth to protest, but Jake shakes his head and gives a firm "no" before she can find the words.

"I can't, Abby, and you know it." Reaching out, Jake clasps his sister's hands in his own. He softens his voice as he continues. "You saw how I was this morning. It's only going to get worse. I honestly don't think you'll be safe if I go with you. At least if you have Suzanne, you won't be completely alone."

Abigail glares at her brother as tears threaten to spill from her eyes. Jake stares back, unfazed and thoroughly confident that he's made the correct decision. At last, she folds her arms across her chest and sticks out her lower lip like a pouting little kid. "Fine. Did I ever tell you how much I hate it when you're right?"

Jake chuckles, stands up, and pulls his sister into a tight hug. Abigail grins at the fact that she made him smile. But the angry, sad, anxious tears start to spill down her cheeks all the same.

10

OUT OF TOUCH

- Central Colorado -

-- Day 13 --

"Dad!" The 10-year-old Evie stretches the word out as she tries to get her father to pay attention to her. "Please! I don't—"

"Evie," Leland stops and finally turns to face the girl. Placing his fists against his hips, he looks down at his daughter. "What did I tell you before we came out here?"

Evie sighs and folds her arms across her chest. She rolls her eyes before looking at her father again. "You said, 'We use too much tech in this house. We're getting a break from all of it this vacation.'"

"So knock it off!" Leland's fingers slowly clench into fists at his sides. His voice deepens a notch as he speaks again. "Now, where's your brother?"

"Dad! Would you just stop and listen to me for one minute, please?! I hate fishing, and that's all we've done for two stupid weeks! You won't hike or make smores or do anything I want to do! You even said I could pick a trail to hike, but you lied! It's just fishing, fishing, fishing! Why can't I just have my phone back? I don't wa—"

"Knock it off!"

The little girl quails at the angry voice. Tears start to form in her brown eyes. She steps backward and turns her eyes toward the ground, realizing she may have pushed it too far. Again.

Leland takes a deep breath and slowly releases it. Uncurling his fingers, he quickly jams his hands into his pockets, closes his eyes, and counts backward from ten. Finally, he opens his eyes. Forcing his voice into a quieter tone even as he speaks through gritted teeth, he starts over. "I said no. You will get your phone back when we head home."

"When are we leaving?" This time, her voice is tentative, barely audible over the sound of the wind in the trees.

"Tomorrow," Leland growls the word. He'd rather never go back to the real world. But the supplies he'd packed are nearly gone by now, and rent is past due. Even once they get back, there's no telling how long it will take for him to find a new job. He can't keep delaying their return. "For now, Eric and I are going fishing. You can knock off the damned waterworks and join us, or you can stay by the tents and entertain yourself. What'll it be?"

Evie sniffles loudly and swipes a hand across her face as she tries in vain to stop the tears from falling. She opens her mouth to respond, but the lump in her throat makes it hard to find her voice.

Spotting Eric a little way up the path, Leland picks up the fishing poles, walks around Evie, and starts toward the boy. "You know where to find us if you quit with this bratty attitude."

Behind Leland, a timid voice mutters, "You always like him more."

Leland stops and grinds his teeth together. Without a word, he continues down the path with long, quick strides.

Eric comes bounding up beside his father. "Hey, Dad! I found a big lizard over there under..."

Leland marches past, and the child's voice fades away as he

hurries to keep up with his father. Eric looks up toward Leland and then stops to look back at the camp. He rushes to catch up again. His twin sister is nowhere to be seen. "Wait, where's Evie?"

"Not coming."

"Why not? I thought she..." The boy's words stop once more as he notices the fishing poles in his father's hands. "We're fishing again? But the last couple nights, you told Evie we'd go on that trail before—"

Leland shoots a glare at the boy, then turns his eyes back to the path. Eric opens his mouth to protest again but thinks better of it. Pressing his lips together, he follows his father to the lake.

Evie sits on the muddy ground beside the tent and hurls a small rock at a nearby tree. Its impact sends a tiny chunk of bark flying. Grabbing the bottom edge of her pale yellow t-shirt, she swipes the fabric across her face to remove the last traces of her tears. For a moment, a row of dark purple bruises is visible across her belly. The marks disappear from view again as she pulls the edge of her shirt back into place.

Pushing herself to her feet, Evie stands there and looks around. She's made up her mind. She marches down the hill to the rusting, silver minivan and opens the passenger door. A moment later, she retrieves her phone from the glove box and presses the power button. The battery is more than half-drained, and the signal is non-existent. With the device in hand, the girl marches back up the hill, over to the trailhead, and disappears.

The sun has started to sink low in the sky, and Eric has long since wandered away from the water to sit in the shade and look for bugs. His fishing pole sits abandoned in the small wave-worn rocks by the water's edge.

Leland stands on the dock with his hook in the water. Half a dozen empty beer cans sit on the dock at his feet while the cans from yesterday float on the water's surface below him. He looks out across the lake, shielding his eyes against the bright, setting sun. His brow furrows. For the first time, he realizes just how quiet the entire trip has been. The camping spot had always been relatively private, but he'd never been here so long without seeing at least a few other campers. He leans forward to peer around a tree at the water's edge.

All of a sudden, there's a tug on the line. Leland quickly reels it in. Just as the hook appears above the water's surface, the fish breaks free and falls, quickly swimming away and disappearing into the depths of the lake. Leland curses under his breath and tosses the fishing pole onto the wooden dock. He stomps away, stumbling ever-so-slightly, as he searches for his son.

"Eric!"

"Over here." The boy pops out from behind a bush and waves.

Leland heads over toward Eric. "Let's go. Might as..."

The man's voice trails away as he notices movement behind some nearby plants. Slowing his pace, he keeps moving forward, stooping down and trying to see what's behind there. Eric also notices and turns his attention that way, following a few steps behind his father.

"Hello?"

Another slight rustle comes from the bush. Leland stops. He reaches out with one hand and slowly pushes aside the leafy branches. There, crouched in the weeds and hidden by shadow, is a woman. Her black-streaked eyes meet his wide-eyed stare.

She opens her blood-encrusted mouth. As she leaps up, she lets out an eardrum-shattering, shrill roar. She lunges toward Leland.

Eric's eyes go wide. He screams and sprints back toward the camp.

Leland blinks and stumbles backward. The black-eyed woman swings at him. Her long nails tear into the flesh of his arm and break through his stupor. He rushes forward, slamming his fists into her chest and sending her staggering back.

Pivoting on his heel, Leland sprints back toward the water. His heart hammers against his chest as he looks for anything he can use as a weapon. Footsteps pound behind him. He skids to a halt next to the water, snatches up Eric's fishing pole, and spins around. He stumbles to the side and blinks quickly, trying to force his eyes back into focus.

She gets close. Leland swings the pole, and it whips through the air, landing against her neck with a loud *thwack!* The rod snaps in two, and the end of it dangles now from the clear line.

The attacker is thrown off balance, and her ankle twists underneath her. She stumbles forward and falls to the ground. Roaring, she leaps up again and spins back toward Leland.

Leland rushes forward with a yell, holding the broken rod out in front of him. He drives the fishing pole into her stomach. Blood spews out and runs down her front and over his hands. The crazed woman's heels dig into the ground, but Leland overpowers her. He shoves her backward until she falls into the murky lake water. She flails, trying to find her footing. Leland turns and runs.

Rounding a bend in the path, Leland hears the sound of a horn honking. Eric is sitting in the passenger's seat, wide-eyed and waving frantically. From somewhere at Leland's back, a roar rings out and turns his blood to ice.

Leland rushes down the hill, pulls open the silver door of the minivan, and flings himself into the driver's seat. Shoving one hand in his pocket, he fishes for the keys.

"Dad!"

Leland looks up just in time to see the woman barreling down the hill. She's dripping wet, and blood gushes from the open wound in her stomach. His heart leaps into his throat. He finally catches the keys, yanks them free, and jams them in the ignition. She's only a few steps away.

He throws the gear shift into reverse. Gravel goes flying as the minivan picks up speed. The woman gives chase but can't keep up. Leland twists the wheel, hits the brakes, and switches to drive. The black-eyed woman disappears into the rearview mirror as they make their way down the road.

"Are you alright?" Leland tears his eyes away from the road long enough to look at his son.

Eric nods. "Are you?"

Leland glances down at the deep gashes that line his forearm. Blood drips from the wounds, leaving dark stains on the blue seats of the minivan. He turns his eyes back to the road. "Yeah. I'll be fine."

Eric's face crumples. "Dad, what..." His voice breaks as he tries to form the question. "What about Evie?"

11

SUPPLIES

- Southwestern Kansas -
-- Day 12 --

The windshield wipers move noisily across the wet glass, and Charlie peers up at the overcast sky. So far, it's only released a fine drizzle, but the thick layer of dark gray looks like it's ready to start a downpour any minute. She hopes it'll hold off until this evening, but she's grateful that she was able to feed all the animals and check over the cattle for any signs of infection before the weather turns worse. Even more than that, she's glad the cows all seem fine.

Pulling up next to the sidewalk and tossing her cigarette out the pickup window, Charlie looks at Melvin's abandoned store. The large pane of glass along the front wall was fine last time; now it has a long, jagged crack running down its length. The door is open only an inch or so. The shelves inside have been looted and now sit half-empty. The floor is littered with spilled feed and ripped boxes.

Charlie curses at herself for not stocking up before the looters and the vandals got to the place. She sighs loudly. Reaching down to the brown, leather holster at her hip, Charlie pulls out the pistol and checks that it's loaded. Then, sliding the gun back into place, she opens the pickup door and climbs out. Her right hand rests on the pistol grip as she makes her way to the entrance.

Listening intently, she moves slowly toward the unlatched door. Walking up the concrete steps, she stops outside the doorframe and calls out, "Hello?"

After a few moments of silence, she slowly moves inside and pulls the glass door shut behind herself.

She takes a step and then stops as the smell of decay hits her so abruptly that it nearly knocks her off her feet. She swallows hard. Charlie inhales deeply, knowing that if she can hold out for a little while, her nose will stop telling her about the horrendous odor. She clenches her eyes shut as she breathes. Charlie's stomach churns. Her throat tightens, and she swallows hard again before taking another deep breath through her nose. Several excruciatingly long minutes later, the nausea subsides, and the smell of decay fades into the background.

From the back of the main room, Charlie can hear a low buzzing. She edges around the long row of shelves until she gets a clear view. The corpse of Robert Johnson still lies there, covered in wriggling, yellowish-white maggots. A black cloud of flies swarms around him, filling the room with the steady hum of a thousand tiny wings.

Making her way quickly through the whole building, Charlie confirms she's alone before finally relaxing enough to let go of her pistol. She returns to the main room and sets to work, checking for anything worth salvaging there.

A few bags of chicken feed lean against one wall. She grabs one in each hand, carries them out to the truck, and then returns inside. Some cans of food—beans, corn, peas—still sit near the rotting body. Carefully stepping around the carnage and avoiding any cans with dried blood spatter on them, she grabs the few remaining cans and sets them by the door in a cardboard box. A couple flashlights, some batteries, and a dozen candles go in the box as well.

Charlie searches for ammo, but that shelf has already been picked clean. She pauses to look around. Noticing a couple traps still tucked away at the back of a shelf, she walks over and scoops them up.

Thunk-thunk!

As Charlie spins around at the sound of something hard suddenly hitting the glass, the traps slip from her hands and clatter loudly against the tile floor as she reaches toward the holster at her hip. She stops before she can pull the weapon free. The man on the steps just outside the closed door grins as he stands there with his own gun already aimed at Charlie.

Looking unblinkingly into the man's eyes, Charlie slowly lifts her hands into the air.

For a time, neither of them moves, but Charlie's mind is racing. She could try to run, but where? The front door—and the direct path to her pickup—is blocked by the man. The back door probably wouldn't work either since he could just follow her through or even be waiting outside for her. She could try to draw her gun and shoot him first, but she doubts she has the speed to pull that off.

At last, she has an idea. "What do you want?"

"Food, meds. Whatever else—"

"What?" Charlie leans toward the closed door, keeping her left hand aloft and slipping the baseball cap from her head so her white hair is on full display. Cupping her right hand around her ear, she calls out, "My hearing ain't too good these days."

The man huffs loudly. Shaking his gun emphatically at her, he calls out again, "I want food. Medicine. Any—"

"You're gonna have to come in here." She touches her ear again. "My ears just don't work like they used to."

The man's lips pinch together as he glares at her. His gun hand twitches. He opens his mouth but quickly closes it again as he reaches for the door handle.

With the gun still trained on Charlie, the man steps back and uses his free hand to yank the door open. The man's short hair swishes in the sudden breeze created by the door's movement. At the same time, that air—that putrid, death-filled, decaying zombie air—hits his nose. The color drains from his face as he clamps a hand over his mouth. As the gun slips from his fingers, he turns and rushes back out onto the sidewalk, gagging and choking.

Charlie hurries over and retrieves the man's gun, engages the safety, and then stuffs the weapon into her waistband. Taking her own gun in hand, she follows the man outside. After thoroughly emptying his stomach onto the sidewalk next to Charlie's truck, the man straightens up and turns to face her again. He wipes one of his sleeves across his mouth.

"Now, what was it you was needing?" She looks steadily at the man. She keeps the gun ready and well within his view, but it's pointed away from the stranger. She hopes they can resolve this without bloodshed. "No reason we can't be civil and share here."

The man narrows his eyes and looks Charlie up and down. "All of it!"

He charges at her. She swings the gun toward the man and pulls the trigger. The bullet tears a strip of flesh from his arm. He lets out a yell. The man slows but keeps coming. As he gets close, she folds her arm, steps forward, and rams her elbow straight into the man's nose. Blood pours from his face, and he stumbles back, staring wide-eyed at Charlie.

"I tried bein' nice." Charlie slowly raises the gun and points it toward the center of the man's chest. "Next time, I won't miss."

The man glares at her as he clutches his broken nose and steps backward a half dozen paces. Finally, he turns and runs away.

Charlie returns into the store, grabs her last box and the foothold traps, then hurries back to the truck. She grins to herself as she sets the truck into motion. She may look every bit of her sixty-seven years, but she can still hold her own.

. . .

- Southwestern Kansas -
-- Day 14 --

Charlie steps out onto the porch with one hand resting on the pistol at her hip. The shotgun hangs from its sling across the chest of her overalls. She looks out across the fields toward the north, east, and west sides of the house. Then she steps forward and peaks around the corner at the south side. All is calm.

As the tightness in her shoulders relaxes, she moves back up near the front door and leans back against the wall. She puts a cigarette between her lips, lights it up, and takes a long drag. She watches the shadows slowly move across the ground as the clouds drift across the blue sky.

A few minutes later, she drops the cigarette butt on the porch floor and stamps it out with the toe of her rubber boot. She pulls her baseball cap from her overalls pocket, pushes her hair out of the way, and slides the hat onto her head.

Climbing into the pickup, Charlie heads over to the barn for hay and feed. Within a matter of minutes, she's taken care of the cows and chickens, and she's gathered up all the eggs.

Charlie returns to the pickup, drives up next to the fence, and climbs out. She walks over, bends down, and steps through the gap between the barbed wires.

Moving slowly and cautiously, she creeps forward into the woods. Between each step, she pauses to look around and listen. At last, she makes it to the strip of orange cloth. Grabbing a long stick, she gently clears away the leaves that hide the steel trap. Then with that same stick, she presses down on the center of the trap until it slams closed and snaps the narrow bit of wood in half.

With one hand, Charlie grabs the bolt cutters from the tool loop on her overalls. She squats down. Finding the chain that holds the trap in place, she cuts a single link. Using the bolt cutters, she pries against the newly broken bit of metal, bending the link until she can pull it free. As she picks up the trap and stands back up, a roar rings out from somewhere far off in the distance. Her heart begins to beat faster. She puts her hand on the butt of her pistol and turns toward the sound to stare off through the gaps in the trees.

The hairs on the back of her neck stand at attention. She swears she's being watched. But there's no sign of movement, no sign of eyes peaking at her through the forest.

Deciding it's time to go, she makes her way back to the truck. Her pace is faster now, and she keeps glancing back over her shoulder. She's still scanning her surroundings for danger, but she doesn't completely stop until she's back in the pasture by the barbed wire fence. She tosses the trap into the truck bed and takes a deep breath. Closing her eyes momentarily, she exhales loudly as she opens the pickup door.

She gets back in the truck, drives across the field, and repeats the process until she's collected all the foothold traps. These times, the process is entirely uneventful. As the last trap goes into the pickup, she returns to the driver's seat and drives back to the barn.

Parking once more in front of the decrepit structure, Charlie gets out, opens the barn door, and steps inside. She stops and grins. The gray cat has found his way inside again.

"Hey, Tom." Stooping down, Charlie gives the furry critter a good scratch behind the ears. "Glad I didn't scare you off."

Tom lifts his head up to look at her. Then, purring loudly, the cat closes his eyes and returns to his nap.

Straightening up, Charlie goes over to the narrow workbench along the side wall and begins rifling through the drawers. She pulls out a spool of thin, straight wire and a pair of wire cutters, then shoves them both into her pockets before turning her back on the workbench.

Charlie stands there, surveying the room. She spots a half dozen wooden pallets stacked in the far corner. Hurrying over, she picks up a couple of them and carries them out to the pickup bed.

She goes back inside. She heads over to the far corner, brushing aside cobwebs as she goes. A few minutes later, she returns to the truck with a spool of barbed wire.

Making one last trip into the dim interior of the barn, she grabs a hammer and crowbar from their hooks on the wall and picks up the jar of nails from the workbench. Moving to the door and reaching down, she gives Tom a few more pats. Finally, she goes outside and gets back into the driver's seat.

Arriving back at the house, Charlie exits the truck and lowers the tailgate. She pulls out the pallets and crowbar and, before long, has the pallet boards dismantled on the ground. Setting the boards aside, she picks up the traps, grabs her spool of straight wire, and then sets off toward the back of the house.

Stepping between a pair of close-set old oak trees, Charlie wraps the end of the thin wire around one of the trees. She walks three paces over to the adjacent tree, pulls the wire taut, and cuts it long. The new end is then fastened tightly around the second tree. She moves backward to look. Even knowing it's there, the neck-high wire is nearly invisible. She quickly adds another strand of wire closer to the ground.

She moves close to the pair of trees again and anchors a trap to the left of the two trees. Another trap goes on the right. Each one is covered with a layer of leaves and twigs. Charlie steps back and takes another peek. Nodding at the setup, she picks up the rest of her supplies to repeat the process at another spot.

Heading to the pickup again, she grabs the barbed wire and begins unrolling it as she walks. She goes across the yard to the west, moves a few steps south, then winds back toward the east. A couple passes, then she repeats the process around the next side of the house. She keeps this up, making her way back and forth, letting the wire fall into the grass where it's nearly invisible. Leaving a two-foot-wide gap around the house's exterior and one narrow passage that runs diagonally away from the front door, she manages to cover a significant portion of the yard.

Charlie knows she can't cover every inch of the place with traps and wires. But she can at least cover the areas where someone would be more likely to sneak in. As for the rest, she'll have to hope she can get a clear view of them coming and a chance at a clean shot.

With the traps all in place and the wire used up, Charlie returns to the truck. Tucking a stack of loose boards beneath her arm, she grabs the jar of nails and heads around the back side of the house. Two boards get nailed across the kitchen window.

Taking a step backward, she looks it over. She thinks, *It ain't much, and it won't keep 'em out forever. But if one of 'em tries to get in, I'll know it anyhow.*

She turns. Her eyes land on the neglected garden. For a moment, she wishes Isaiah were still here. He was always better at growing things than she was. And truth be told, she's tired of being alone in this house full of memories. But she quickly chases away the self-pitying thoughts. This end-of-humankind is not something she'd want him to see. She gives herself a shake and promises she'll get the garden tended to soon.

Picking up the stack of boards again, she moves on to the next window and does the same thing. Slowly, she makes her way around to every window on the house.

When the last window is boarded up, she pulls the cap off her head and brushes back her sweat-dampened hair. As she gathers up the final few boards, Charlie turns and looks at the horizon and the sun that's just starting to disappear. Deciding that's all she can manage for one day—and her stomach loudly reminds her that she hasn't eaten since breakfast—she heads inside.

Charlie sets her guns down and locks the front door. Then, taking one of the remaining boards, she props it diagonally from the underside of the doorknob to the carpeted floor. She wedges another board against the back door.

Going into the narrow kitchen, she absentmindedly uses her

lighter to light up the stovetop, quickly fries a few eggs, and then slides them onto a plate. Just as she sits down and pierces the first egg with her fork, a roar sounds from outside. She freezes. It's closer now than this morning.

Picking up her plate, Charlie goes over and grabs both guns, then turns off the lights. She hurriedly shovels the food into her mouth and sets the plate aside. She moves the wooden rocking chair across the room, puts the pistol on her lap, and takes the shotgun in hand. Watching intently as the evening light fades away, she sits facing the door and waits.

12

SEARCHING

- Central Colorado -

-- Day 14 --

The previous night had gone by in a blur.

Eric sat in the passenger seat, begging to go back as Leland had sped down the road, searching for a phone signal. When he'd finally gotten one, Leland swerved onto the shoulder and hit the brakes. He'd tried calling the park ranger station, but it went to voicemail. His call to 911 had gone unanswered. His phone refused to establish an internet connection, so he couldn't find the local police station's number. In growing desperation, he'd punched in the number for his car insurance company. No answer.

Jabbing a finger at the radio, he had scanned through the different stations, half expecting a news report about an insane asylum escapee. Rather unhelpfully, though, none of the stations offered anything more than lifeless static.

As frustration, anger, and fear had overwhelmed Leland, he slammed the phone into the steering wheel and let its shattered remains fall to the floor. Eric had gasped loudly, then clamped a hand over his mouth. The boy had then wordlessly climbed from the front into the middle row of seats and curled up into a ball, letting the silent tears continue to fall until he slipped into sleep.

Now, as the new day dawns, Leland leans his head against the steering wheel, staring out the driver's side window toward the horizon. He hasn't gotten a wink of sleep as his thoughts keep returning to that woman's eyes. Her dilated pupils were surrounded by a thin sliver of green. The whites were marred by an abundance of dark, zig-zagging streaks. And the blood caked on her lips and down her shirt...

Drugs? Meth or maybe bath salts? For the millionth time, he racks his brain, trying to find justification behind the attack. *That might explain the violence, but I don't know of any that would do that to your eyes.*

Some kind of mental illness? I suppose some of them could cause violence too, but what about those damned eyes?

Maybe her eyes were tattooed or dyed somehow? Maybe contacts? But why did she attack us? And we couldn't have been the first either since she was already covered in blood when we first saw her.

Was she part of some weird cult? Was she possessed? Leland shakes his head and shoos away the absurd ideas.

His thoughts start to veer from the confused wonderings about what they'd been through. Other ideas start to creep in instead—questions that he doesn't really want the answer to. Sitting there, he wishes he had a drink. Something to calm the aching in his head and slow the racing thoughts. But what few cans he had left are still back at the campsite.

Leland forces his mind back onto that endless loop of trying to explain what they'd been through. Anything is better than thinking about why he hasn't gone back to search for his daughter: deep, unbridled terror of that... Black-eyed *thing* back there by the lake.

Eric stirs as the sun begins to creep into view. Leland turns and glances back at him. But as soon as Eric's eyes open, Leland twists forward again, unwilling to meet his son's gaze.

"Dad? What's..." His voice trails away as the memories of yesterday come back to him. He sniffles. Wiping his nose on his shirt sleeve, he looks out the window. In a tear-choked voice, he starts again. "When are we going back to look for Evie?"

"I don't... I..." Leland looks into the rearview mirror. Seeing those wide, brown, tear-filled eyes staring at him, he looks away and sighs. As he starts the engine of the minivan, a shiver runs down his spine.

"Evie!" Leland waits, scanning the area on each side of the dirt path that runs between the dense trees and plants of the forest. His tire iron is gripped in his hands, and he holds it near his shoulder, ready to swing. After a few moments, he moves ahead and then stops to call out again.

Eric follows a few steps behind his father, twisting side to side as he looks for signs of his sister or the woman who attacked them yesterday.

"Dad? Evie wanted to check out that one trail kinda over by the tent. Maybe we should see—"

"Have you ever tracked down a lost kid?" Leland spins around and grabs hold of his son's arm. He squeezes tightly as he glares at the boy. "If you know all about it, why don't you take the lead?!"

Eric shrinks back, shaking his bowed head. Leland clenches his teeth together and exhales loudly before letting go and turning back around to resume his search. The kid's logic makes sense, and somewhere deep inside, Leland knows it. But right now, as terror holds him tight, all reason and sense vanish.

"Evie!" Leland stops, and his eyes widen. Over his shoulder, Leland whispers, "What was that?"

Eric's palms slicken with sweat. Goosebumps break out across his skin as he turns and looks around.

For the space of several rapid heartbeats, all is calm. Then, far off to their left, a piercing roar sounds out somewhere in the forest. Father and son both turn that way and stare. It's *her*. That frighteningly familiar sound is etched into their memories. They're both unexpectedly reliving the previous afternoon.

From somewhere to their right, there's a deep, bellowing roar. A flock of birds takes flight, and the pair realize that this second creature is much closer than the first. They can hear twigs snapping. Its feet pound against the dirt, bringing it rapidly closer.

Leland's tire iron falls from his grip as he spins around. Grabbing hold of Eric's wrist, he starts running down the trail. Eric struggles to keep up, and before long, he's far too winded to protest.

At the fork in the path, Leland turns left, still dragging the boy behind himself.

Yanking open the sliding door, Leland tosses Eric into the minivan and slams the door. Sprinting around to the driver's seat, he jumps inside, starts the minivan, and speeds off toward the road.

Eric's chest aches as he tries to catch his breath. Turning around in his seat and watching helplessly out the back window, the campsite disappears behind them for the last time.

13

GOT IN, GET OUT

- Southeastern Oklahoma -

-- Day 11 --

Abigail paces across the kitchen to the living room and back again. Suzanne hasn't appeared yet, and Abigail's anxiety is growing by the second. She waited restlessly all day yesterday with no word. Cell service is virtually non-existent now, and of course, Abigail had gotten rid of her landline phone years ago. Emails to Suzanne are going unanswered. Abigail knows she needs to leave sooner rather than later, but she's trying to hold out a while longer.

If she's not here by tomorrow... Abigail tries to push the thought aside and hold out hope that her friend will be here any minute now.

"Abby!"

Abigail hurries up into the attic to find Jake.

Turning off the radio, Jake turns around to face his sister. "Finally found a working station. Well, if I stand next to the window and hold onto the antenna, anyway. They're saying the army is trying to do some kind of quarantine in the areas with the worst outbreaks. Barricades and roadblocks have started popping up on the roads leading out of the more heavily impacted cities. Some people are able to make it out of the area, but a lot of 'em can't."

Nodding, Abigail begins to chew on her thumbnail. She carefully steps over the plate of untouched eggs and the coffee next to Jake and moves to the window to watch for her friend.

After an entire day of worrying, pacing, and worrying some more, Abigail decides it's time to retire to her attic hideout. She grabs a couple unopened cans of soup and two spoons and heads up the steps. At the top, she sets everything down in front of Jake, then turns back to fold the ladder up and latch it in place.

"Steak and potato or chicken noodle?" Abigail takes a seat on the floor next to her brother.

Jake stares off into the distance and shrugs.

"Okay then. You get..." She twists the can around to read the label. "Chicken noodle. Here."

Obediently, Jake takes the unopened can from her. He looks down at it as he rolls it back and forth from one hand to the other, refusing to meet her gaze. "Abby."

"Hmm?" She chews her bite quickly and sets the can down on the floor as she waits for Jake to continue.

Turning to the side, Jake sets the unopened can on the floor at the end of the cot. Abigail finally notices this morning's coffee and eggs still sitting there as well. Behind that is a fully intact peanut butter and jelly sandwich. A dozen ants have already gathered and begun to carry away the feast.

"You haven't been eat—"

"You need to leave tomorrow."

Abigail's brain takes a few seconds to switch gears. She blinks at him. "But Suzanne—"

"You leave tomorrow, Abigail Jane. Now, I'm done discussing this." Jake abruptly lays down on the cot and turns his back toward her. "Good night."

Stunned, Abigail gawks at the back of his head for a long time. Finally, she pushes aside her half-eaten can of cold soup and turns off the light. Curling up in her pile of blankets on the floor, she clenches her eyes shut and hopes sleep will come quickly.

A faint squeak from Jake's cot draws Abigail's attention, and she turns around to see his silhouette sitting upright in the dark.

"Wha—"

"Sh!"

Abigail raises an eyebrow at her brother—not that he can see it in the dark room—and waits for an explanation. When she realizes one isn't coming, she grabs her phone and types a message: "What's going on?" She turns the bright screen toward Jake's face so he can read it.

Jake squints at the screen, snatches the device from Abigail's hand, and types, "Listen!"

Together, they wait in silence. Abigail starts to type another message but stops suddenly. She hears it now, too: the floor downstairs creaking softly as if someone is tiptoeing across it. The seconds drag by with the sounds growing ever closer until, at last, they stop. Then a soft *tap... tap... tap...* The plywood pieces that are holding the ladder in place bob up and down in time with the taps.

Abigail slowly scoots over, grabs hold of the anchoring plywood, and starts to pull. Jake covers her hand with his. He's close enough now that in the faint moonlight, she can clearly see him silently mouth the word "no."

Yanking her hand free from his grip, Abigail grabs her phone again and types, "What if it's Suzanne?"

Jake glares at her. He snatches the phone back and types his response: "WHAT IF IT'S NOT?"

Abigail's blood runs cold as she realizes he could very well be right. In fact, the more she thinks about it, the more convinced she becomes that he is. *Surely Suzanne would make her presence known. She wouldn't let them think she was an intruder. Right?*

Holding out her hand, Abigail gestures toward the phone. He passes it back. She types out, "Well, damn, you don't have to YELL."

Jake rolls his eyes, but even now, she can see the hint of a smile behind the gesture. He mouths the word "smartass" at her.

She sticks out her tongue briefly and then types out a new message. "We can't yell out in case it's not her. But if it IS her, we need to let her in. If it's a zombie, I think we're going to have to get rid of it. I don't think it'll go away on its own. Got a plan?"

One board has been pulled free from the ladder; Jake has it in his hands as he stands near the top step. Abigail is at the other end, ready to pull the second board out as soon as her brother gives the signal.

Jake holds up three fingers and drops them down one at a time. *Three... Two... One... Go!* Abigail yanks the board free. A second later, there's a tug from below, and the ladder unfurls toward the floor. Jake hurries down the stairs, the plywood board in his hands held high, ready to swing. Abigail bites her lip and hesitates as the guilt gnaws at her for listening to Jake's instructions and letting him go down there alone. But after a few seconds, she gives in and follows Jake's one and only instruction: hide.

With bated breath, Abigail counts the seconds as they drag by. She strains to hear anything from downstairs, to get any clue of what is happening. Her heartbeat pounds in her ears and she thinks that surely the intruder can hear her.

The interminable waiting threatens to drive her mad.

Thwack!

Abigail jumps at the sudden noise from downstairs. It seems as if all hell has broken loose. Her mind races, trying to identify the sounds and decipher whatever must be happening on the floor below.

Plywood slamming into a doorframe. Roaring. A body crashing into the wall. A loud groan. Swooshing air, the plywood board missed its mark. Fist to the jaw. A body falls. Feet shuffling, trying to stand. Plywood to the back of the skull once, twice, thrice. A body thuds limply against the floor. Jake gasping for breath. Something large being dragged. The back door opens. Silence.

Long, tense minutes pass before footsteps start to ascend the stairs. Dusting the cobwebs from her clothes, Abigail stands up. Then, as she makes eye contact with the man who is decidedly *not* her brother, she freezes.

The zombie lets out a shrieking roar. Breaking from her stupor, Abigail grabs a book from the nearest box and hurls it at the monster's face. He dodges, and the book sails harmlessly past. But still near the top of the ladder, his foot slips off the edge and through the opening. He tumbles off-balance, his arms flailing madly as he tries to break his fall. Several *thumps* and one loud *crack* later, silence returns.

Abigail moves to the top of the steps and looks down. The zombie lies sprawled on the floor below, his head twisted at an unnatural angle. Downstairs, red splotches slowly run down, leaving uneven, red stripes along the cream-colored walls. Thick red streaks coat the floor from the kitchen to the back door.

Now, Jake—covered in a thick coat of blood—comes back into the house. Breathing heavily, he walks to the bottom of the steps and looks up at his sister. Then he looks back at the corpse on the floor. "Where the hell did *that* one come from?"

Abigail shrugs as Jake steps over the body to make his way back up into the attic.

. . .

- Southeastern Oklahoma -
-- Day 12 --

"Hm?" Abigail groggily rolls over. Jake had mumbled something she couldn't quite make out, and she had been reluctantly dragged from sleep. She rubs eyes as she turns toward him. "Jake? What's going on?"

"Get downstairs!" He bellows, "Now!"

Abigail's eyes go wide. She leaps up. With shaking hands, she pulls the plywood boards from beneath the ladder. Jake is breathing heavily behind her, still facing away from her. Abigail tosses the boards aside, extends the ladder, and hurries down. Turning back, she watches as Jake wordlessly retracts the ladder and fastens it back in place.

Still staring up at the ceiling, Abigail takes a step toward the dining table. Her foot catches on the zombie corpse and sends her stumbling to the floor. She's tired, scared, confused, angry, alone—so utterly alone—she can't hold any of it anymore. She opens her mouth and screams.

Up in the attic, her brother doesn't respond.

Abigail walks through the house, double-checking the locks on the windows and doors. Nothing broken, nothing out of place. She's genuinely baffled at how those zombies had gotten in. When she finally peaks out the front door, the mystery is solved. The empty magnetic box that usually stays underneath her car is laying open on the front porch. The spare key from it is still in the door's lock. She shivers at the realization. Abigail spends the next few hours blocking windows and barricading doors.

At last, the creaking of the attic ladder draws Abigail's attention. From the far end of the house, she walks back to the kitchen. Jake stands at the base of the steps with his eyes closed and his jaw clenched. Both his hands are balled into fists so tight that his knuckles are turning white.

Taking a tentative step closer, Abigail tries to speak, but her voice gives out. All that comes out is a whispered "Jake?"

Through gritted teeth, he hisses, "Get out."

"What do you mean? What's going on?"

Reaching out, Abigail places one hand gently on her brother's forearm. Jake jerks away from her touch. His breathing is shallow and quick, and he's beginning to quake. He still has his eyelids clamped shut.

"Get. Out. NOW!"

Abigail shivers but doesn't go. She clears her throat and tries again to reason with her brother. "I was waiting on Suzanne. R-remember?"

Suddenly, Jake's eyelids pop open. Abigail gasps and stumbles backward into the wall. Jake's pupils are so large, the sclera so streaked that from where she stands, his eyes appear to be solid, unbroken blackness.

Watching helplessly, Abigail's eyes fill with tears. She knows she should run, but sorrow and terror keep her rooted to the spot. Jake is shaking, panting. He bristles with restrained energy as every ounce of his willpower goes toward keeping himself away from his sister.

"O-okay, Jake." Abigail's voice cracks. "Just let me grab my stuff, and I'll—"

"NO!"

Jake charges toward Abigail. Tensing up, she braces herself for the attack and the bite that's sure to come. Instead, he grabs her by the shoulders and forcibly hurries her to the front door.

For the first time, Jake sees the pile of furniture and junk that Abigail had piled there just this morning. He releases her and roars that ear-shattering, shrieking, animalistic roar—the one that feels as though it rattles the walls and freezes the blood in her veins. Abigail's breath comes in shallow gasps. As she stares wide-eyed, tears pour down her face.

Now a mass of unbridled rage, Jake begins hurling away the obstacles of the barricade as if they weighed nothing. Abigail's own thoughts are too disjointed, too fast to make sense of. She cowers in the corner of the room as her brain jumps frantically from one idea to the next: flee - hide - fight - run - bring Jake back.

The barricade now gone, the wild-eyed man yanks the door open and turns around. He storms over to Abigail, picks her up, and tosses her haphazardly onto the front porch. Before Abigail can react, the man that was her brother slams the door shut and throws the deadbolt into place.

Scrambling to her feet, Abigail wraps her arms around herself as she stares at the door. The key that had been in the knob just moments ago is now gone. She spins around, looking frantically at her surroundings. She's completely lost. She could take shelter in the car and lock its doors, but she can't go anywhere without keys. Walking is an option, but she'd be alone and unsheltered with only what she can carry in her arms.

Still deliberating between her few and terrible options, the door suddenly swings open. Abigail's phone and a single key come flying at her. As they land in the dirt beside her, the door slams shut and locks again. The crazed man leers at her through the glass in the door.

Snatching up the phone and the key, she backs toward the SUV. Swiping the tears off her face, she swallows hard, then shouts, "I love you, Jake!"

For the briefest moment, the black in his eyes recedes, and her brother returns. Tears fill his eyes. Jake nods. Then the blackness comes back again, and Jake is gone.

Abigail turns and throws herself into the driver's seat. She starts the ignition, slams it into gear, and speeds out of the driveway. Loose gravel goes flying in her wake. She takes one last glance into the rearview mirror to watch as her big brother, her home, and her entire life all disappear into the distance.

For almost an hour, Abigail drives. She stares intently at the road and lets it lull her into a half-trance, trying to quell the horrible thoughts that gnash at the edges of her brain. Finally, as rain begins to patter against the windshield, she can't keep her mind hushed anymore. She turns into the driveway of an old, long-abandoned farmhouse and parks.

At first, she stares blankly off into the distance. But soon, a stray thought occurs to her: *I obviously needed the car key to leave. But why did he go through the trouble to get my phone to me as well?*

Abigail pulls the device from the passenger seat and looks at the now-cracked screen. Her heart hammers as she lights up her phone. An unsent text message sits there, one that she never wrote.

"Love you always ab be safe"

Grief crashes into her like a tidal wave, and the phone slides from her grip. Abigail screams and pounds the steering wheel until her throat aches and her hands are red and tender. Tears stream down her face unfettered, soaking her dark green hoodie and leaving her eyes red and sore. At last, she's too exhausted to think anymore, too dehydrated to shed another tear. She slumps back into her seat and lets the sound of the pouring rain soothe her into a deep, dreamless sleep.

- Southwestern Missouri -

-- Day 13 --

Blinking in the pale light of early dawn, Abigail takes a bit to get her bearings. When she finally remembers where she is and the horrors of the past couple of weeks, her emotions threaten to overwhelm her again. She closes her eyes and draws in a long, shaky breath as she wipes her sleeve across her face. She exhales. Another deep inhale—this time much steadier—then opening her eyes, she exhales.

Abigail flips down the visor and looks at herself in the mirror. Her hair is a tangled mess. Her eyes are bloodshot, and her eyelids are swollen and red. Dried tears coat her cheeks with a white crust. She can't help but let out a sarcastic chuckle as she thinks, *I couldn't blame someone if they looked at me right now and thought I was one of those monsters.*

A loud rumble from Abigail's stomach breaks through her thoughts. She reaches for the door handle then pauses, at last deciding that stepping outside in the dim light in this unfamiliar terrain is too risky. She verifies that the doors are all locked. Then she twists around and awkwardly climbs through the interior toward the back. Plopping down in the back seat, she begins searching.

The water bottles are easy enough to find. Abigail grabs six of them and tosses them into the front passenger's seat. She resumes digging. A few moments later, she's located the granola bars and tossed a handful of them into the passenger's seat as well.

She starts up one last search.

Quite a while later, Abigail clambers back into the driver's seat, victorious. The fanny pack clutched in her hand already holds her toothbrush, toothpaste, and a few tampons. She crams several of the granola bars into the main pouch as well. One water bottle goes into the elastic-banded bottle pocket. She stops for a moment and stares at the bulging pack. Finally, using the elastic bands on the zipper pulls, she ties a loop around the neck of a second water bottle and lets it hang from the pouch. It's awkward, but she decides it'll have to do for now.

Lifting the bottom of her hoodie, Abigail clips the overly stuffed and uncomfortable bag around her waist. She pulls the fabric back down and looks at the supplies still in the passenger seat. Grabbing a couple more water bottles, she shoves them into the hoodie's front pocket. Picking up the rest of the granola bars, she looks down at the pockets of her jeans and rolls her eyes. The tiny little things might as well just be decorative. She looks down at the bars. Finally, she takes all but one of the remaining ones and shoves them up the baggy sleeves of her hoodie.

Abigail sighs. Her arms will crinkle as she walks. The water at her waist will jiggle and slosh. The bulk sitting atop her belly makes her look like she's put on at least 30 pounds since this whole hellish ordeal started. Her face still looks red and puffy, as if she's recovering from a fight with a bee. She sighs again and reminds herself, *The apocalypse is no time to worry about sex appeal.*

Another loud growl from her stomach, and Abigail thinks back, wondering when she last ate. More than a day ago, she'd had half a can of cold soup. Her eyes grow misty as she realizes that it will be the last meal she ever shares with her brother.

Blinking quickly to force the tears away, she grabs a bottle of water from the seat and promptly chugs half of it. Then, she grabs the one granola bar that's still out. The food seems to vanish before her eyes as she hungrily devours it.

When the meager meal is complete, Abigail pours some water into her palm, washes the tear stains from her face, and then drinks what's left in the bottle. Her stomach grumbles again, but it's somewhat less intense this time. Abigail would love to keep eating, but since she'd also like to keep it all down, she decides to give her stomach some time first.

Leaning her head against the window, Abigail stares off into the distance and waits.

Abigail pulls into her parents' driveway and puts it in park. With the engine still running, she sits and watches. No signs of movement. She honks the horn and waits. Still nothing.

Taking a long, deep breath, she twists the key and pulls it from the ignition, then shoves it into her pocket. Abigail turns around in her seat. She grabs hold of her baseball bat, turns toward the front, and takes another long look at the surroundings. Exhaling slowly, she pulls the door handle and carefully steps out.

Abigail stops. Turning her head back and forth, she listens and watches for any signs of danger. Then, suddenly, she dashes up to the house. She quickly digs through a potted plant, retrieves the spare key, and jams it into the doorknob. Hurriedly unlocking the door, she lets herself inside.

The door squeaks loudly as she pushes it closed. A clock in the hallway ticks louder than it should. Otherwise, the place is silent.

Quickly and quietly, she makes her way through each room, searching for anyone at all. Fortunately, there are no zombies in the house. *Unfortunately,* her parents are also nowhere to be seen.

Abigail returns to the kitchen and finally notices the note on the small whiteboard by the fridge. In her mother's elegant penmanship, it says, "Went to George's." Relaxing a bit now that she has at least some clue of where her parents might be, she takes off her fanny pack and lays it on the kitchen counter. She decides she'll use tonight to gather whatever supplies she can find in the house. Then first thing tomorrow, she'll head over to her Uncle George's house.

As Abigail opens up the cupboard to look for something to eat, she jumps as her phone unexpectedly chimes in the still room. She pulls it out and looks at the notification. It has connected to her parents' wifi, and a new trail cam video is available.

Swallowing hard, Abigail stares at the phone screen. Her shaking finger hovers over the icon. She knows she shouldn't look, but she can't seem to ignore it either. She presses the screen, and the video starts to play. At Abigail's house, a woman with a purple pixie cut steps out of a car. A lug wrench is clenched in her hand.

Just at the edge of the camera's field of view, Abigail can see a man sneaking through the bushes, closer and closer. The woman hears a noise and turns to look, just as the man charges forward...

Abigail stops the video and promptly uninstalls the app from her phone. Whether Jake just attacked Suzanne or Suzanne killed Jake, Abigail doesn't dare find out.

- Southwestern Missouri -
-- Day 14 --

Yesterday, Abigail had moved her car into the garage and spent the day loading up everything in the house that might be useful. Then when night fell, she'd curled up in the driver's seat to sleep. She had decided that it would be the safest place to rest; if anything got into the garage, she could start the engine and simply drive away.

Now, after her second night in a row of sleeping in the driver's seat, her back and neck are not happy. Groaning loudly, she slides out of the SUV and stretches her back, then twists her spine from one side to the other. She tries massaging the tight, angry muscles, but it's no use.

Grabbing the baseball bat, she turns and walks back into the house and toward the kitchen. A nearly-empty cereal box sits on the top shelf. She grabs it, finds a bowl, and fills it up. Not trusting the who-knows-how-old milk in the fridge, she finds a spoon and eats the cereal dry. As she crunches into the hard, stale flakes and makes a face, reminding herself, *At least I don't have to kill my own food. Yet.*

When she's done, she walks over and sets the empty bowl in the sink. She can hear a noise outside. She pauses, leaning close to the window to listen but can't make sense of what she's hearing. Reaching across the sink, she lifts the glass pane up, turns her ear toward the opening, and waits. A distant *Thump! Thump! Thump!*

Abigail recloses and locks the window. Standing there, lost in her thoughts, she struggles to place that sound. She drums her fingers against the countertop while she thinks.

Finally, she remembers the storm shelter out back with the heavy steel door. *Someone must be trapped inside.* She turns and leans back against the counter, mulling over the situation. *Who is it? Are they hurt? Would they want to hurt me? Is it safe for me to go out there? If they're trapped, is there even anything I can do about it?*

After a long while, she sighs. She's not sure if it's the right thing as far as keeping herself safe, but she knows she has to at least go look; she has to at least try to help them.

She couldn't live with herself if she didn't.

Abigail picks up her bat, moves to the back door, and peaks through its narrow sidelight. The shelter is out of view, but it looks clear from what she can see. Opening the door an inch, she listens again. Everything seems calm. With her bat held high and ready to swing, she opens the door the rest of the way and steps out to the back porch.

She's just stepping into the unmown grass when she hears the soft *click* of the gate latch behind her. For a split second, she thinks of going on the offensive. But she'd rather find out what exactly she's up against.

As the gate begins to swing open, Abigail bolts off across the large backyard. Her heart hammers. Only a few beats pass before she can hear the pounding of footsteps behind her. Her lungs already ache. That bone-chilling roar sounds behind her, and she pushes herself even harder.

The fence is coming up fast. Abigail makes a hard left. Ready to double back across the yard, she leaps off the 10-foot tall retaining wall. The bottles of water slip from her hoodie pocket and fall into the dirt beside her. As she lands, her foot twists underneath her, and a sharp pain shoots through her ankle. She gasps. She collapses to the ground. Quickly crawling away, she rolls over to see where the attacker is.

The zombie's eyes are fixed on its prey: her. He's reached the edge of the retaining wall. He jumps. Coming down, his foot lands on top of a water bottle. It rolls out from underneath him. Falling forward, his left knee makes contact with the ground first, and his leg lets out a sickening *crack*. Abigail gags even as she pushes herself back, away from the monster.

He catches himself with his hands and tries to push himself back upright. As he puts weight on the injured leg, it buckles beneath him, and he falls back to the ground. Abigail stares, wide-eyed and thanking her lucky stars. It's over. She may have sprained her ankle, but he definitely can't chase her with that shattered leg.

Abigail carefully stands up as the zombie starts to drag himself toward her. She hobbles past him. Before he can twist himself around again, she lifts the bat high and swings it hard into the back of his neck. His entire body goes limp. Abigail stuffs the water bottles back into her pocket and limps over to the concrete retaining wall. She leans her sweaty forehead against the cool surface as she catches her breath.

Thump-thump.

Straightening up, she uses the bat as a makeshift crutch and moves cautiously toward the noise in the concrete and steel shelter. She gets close and notices the handle has been removed from the steel door; the bolts that had held it in place look like they were removed from the inside. Her chest begins to feel tight.

"No, please..."

Slowing down even more, she sees that the air vent at the top of the concrete box has been broken off, leaving a six-inch wide, circular hole in the roof. The metal vent tube is lying on the ground. Next to it is a power drill that looks like it had been chucked out through the newly made hole.

"No, no, no..."

With bated breath, she takes the last few steps to the shelter and looks down through the hole in its roof.

A lump forms in her throat. "Dad?"

The zombie turns its face up toward her. Large pupils and

black-streaked eyes look up at her from her father's face. His hand darts out through the opening, trying to grab hold of her. He lets out an ungodly screech as Abigail turns away and slowly returns to the house.

Robotically, Abigail walks to her childhood bedroom, picks up a long-forgotten teddy bear, and clutches it to her chest as she sinks to the floor. The tears will come eventually. But for now, she just feels numb.

14

RUMBLINGS

- Central Colombia -
- Near the edge of the Amazon Rainforest -
-- Three days before it starts --

A nearly imperceptible rumble runs through the ground. One small patch of the lake's water seems to sizzle as a small flurry of bubbles race to the surface. A small bird—unfortunate enough to be perched inches above the escaping gas—shrieks, then falls lifeless into the frothing liquid.

As suddenly as it started, the lake stills, and the forest returns to normal.

Residents of the nearest village—almost three miles away—go about their lives, completely unaware.

15

THE REFLECTION

- Eastern Missouri -
-- Day 15 --

Nathaniel manages to choke down half a piece of toast, one tiny morsel at a time. Next, he completes his daily water ritual. His stomach gurgles painfully, and his lips are cracked, but it's already noon, and he just doesn't have the willpower to try any more today.

Flies buzz around the kitchen, zipping from one pile of rotting food to the next. Nathaniel ignores them and sits down at the table, entirely unbothered by the growing odors in here. Under normal circumstances, the stench might've been to blame for his lack of appetite, but he knows it doesn't matter now.

He gets up from the table and slowly enters the bunkroom.

"Aaron?"

Aaron's back is turned. He doesn't respond.

Nathaniel walks up to the side of Aaron's bed. Aaron's head hangs limply against his unmoving chest.

Drawing a slow, shaky breath, Nathaniel walks up and places a hand on Aaron's shoulder to shake him. When there's still no reaction, Nathaniel presses his fingertips against the side of Aaron's throat.

Nothing.

Nathaniel turns and walks into the bathroom. For the first time in over a week, he forces himself to face his reflection. Two tiny, jagged streaks of black mar his right eye.

16

PRIORITIES

- Eastern Colorado -
-- Day 17 --

"Dad?" Eric unbuckles his seatbelt and scoots up to the edge of the seat. The video screen on the gas pump loudly plays a cheery commercial just outside the minivan's window. "Is anyone looking for Evie?"

Leland slowly turns around. Sweat clings to his brow, and his eyes are half-closed. "What?"

"Are the police or somebody looking for Evie?"

"What?" Leland gives his head a quick shake to wake himself up. The movement makes him groan in pain, and he presses his thumbs into the sides of his head, massaging slow circles on his temples. "Why would..."

As his words trail off, Leland squeezes his eyes shut tight and groans again. He reaches into his pocket and pulls out his wallet. He grabs a credit card, flings it toward Eric, and re-pockets the wallet as he climbs out of the minivan. "Fill up the tank."

Eric slides the door open and gets out. He swipes the card and puts the nozzle in the tank, then watches between the pumps as his father disappears into the building. Quickly swiping away the tears, Eric folds his arms across his chest and leans against the minivan to wait, exactly like he's done a million times before.

The building's clear glass door slowly closes behind Leland. He spots the coolers on the far side of the room and he heads over. Pulling the door open, Leland closes his eyes and lets the cold air wash over him. He shivers. When he opens his eyes again, he grabs a case of beer and carries it up to the checkout, plopping it down on the counter. His hand shakes slightly as he pulls out his wallet. Leaning over and resting his folded arms on top of the beer, he waits impatiently.

Minutes pass in silence. Leland looks around. On the counter is an opened newspaper dated two weeks ago with the word "Zombie" in bold text above a photo of someone with black eyes, just like the woman at the lake. He stares for a moment in awe. If he hadn't seen it himself just a few days ago, he would've assumed this was just another cheap tabloid.

He looks up. On his left, there's a large food warming case, still filled with hotdogs that spin slowly across the rollers. The meat is now so dark it's nearly black. Between the color and the shriveled, wrinkly appearance of the food's outer layer, they look like overgrown raisins.

Leland turns away from the counter. "Hey!"

Wincing again at the pain in his head, Leland tears open the cardboard box, pulls out one of the cans, and takes a long drink. Placebo or not, he can already feel the fog in his brain starting to lift. He looks around once more. Throwing back the rest of the beer—spilling some past the side of his mouth and down his chin—he feels the shakiness in his hands start to subside.

"Hello!" Setting the empty can down on the countertop, he wipes the beer from his face and turns toward the entrance to the employees-only room. "Anybody here?"

Deciding at last that the place is abandoned, Leland grabs the case, hurries outside, and puts it in the back of the minivan. Once it's stowed away, he heads back toward the building.

"Come with me."

Eric slides out of the minivan and silently follows his father inside and over to the cooler. He pauses to look around. "Everyone's gone here too?"

Leland ignores the question. He grabs two six-packs and shoves them into the boy's hands. "Set those in the front seat and get back in here."

"Can I get some food? I'm starving."

"Go!"

Eric rushes outside to do as he's told, then walks back inside just as Leland goes out. Leland grunts as he lugs two stacked cases of beer through the narrow doorway. A bottle of whiskey lays on top, tucked awkwardly beneath the man's chin. Eric glances at his father, then darts back inside. Grabbing a few jerky packets, he hurriedly shoves as many as he can into his pockets. A few small bags of chips and a pack of cookies are soon stuffed inside his shirt. As the front door swings open again, Eric dashes over to the cooler, grabs two more six-packs, and disappears back to the minivan.

After several trips by each of them, the beer cooler is nearly empty, and the minivan is almost full. Eric has managed to sneakily fill the section of floorboard below his seat with snacks, juice, and water. He climbs inside, careful not to damage his provisions, then slides the door closed behind himself as Leland gets back into the driver's seat and starts the engine.

Eric tears into a bag of chips, hungrily savoring the familiar, salty flavor.

Leland cracks open another beer, takes a long swig, and then drives away.

17

ON THE HUNT

- Southwestern Kansas -
-- Day 15 --

Charlie wakes with a jolt as the pistol slides off her lap and clatters against the wooden frame of the rocking chair. The gun comes to a rest on the carpet by her feet. Reaching down, she winces as her stiff neck reminds her of last night's terrible, slumped-over sleeping posture in the hard, straight-backed chair. She rubs the back of her neck with one hand and picks up the gun with the other. Standing up, Charlie's back also makes its soreness known. She groans. Her entire body seems to *crack* as she stretches.

The sky is still dark, but the clock shows half-past-seven. Leaning forward, she takes a second look outside. The sun is up but hidden behind a thick layer of dark gray, ominous clouds. It's not raining yet, but she has no doubt that it will before the day is through.

Charlie sets down the pistol and the shotgun and yawns, stretching again. This time, it's only her back that loudly *pops* and *crackles*. She lets out a grumble.

Turning around, Charlie puts her hands on her hips and glares at the rocking chair as if it's somehow the chair's fault she chose to fall asleep there. She huffs as she turns away. She can't handle another night like that.

She wanders off, quickly prepares for the day, then returns to the front door. She throws the shotgun sling over her shoulder and holsters the pistol. Pushing the board away from beneath the knob, Charlie pulls the door open and steps out onto the porch.

The damp air hits her in a small gust, raising goosebumps along the wrinkled and age-spotted skin of her arms. She buttons her denim jacket, pulls her baseball cap onto her head, and sets off toward the gravel road. With any luck, she'll find that zombie she heard last night and put a swift end to it.

Regardless, she won't be sleeping in that chair again.

Charlie strides off the porch and across the yard, then stops in the middle of the road to look around. After a few moments of internal debate, she turns and begins moving quickly southward. It's not much to go on, but she's confident she'd last heard it somewhere off this direction, maybe a few hundred yards away.

Coming at last to a wide gap in the trees that line the road, she stops. She turns east and, with slow and cautious footsteps, begins to tread into the overgrown foliage.

Charlie slowly winds her way back and forth for nearly two hours, searching for any sign of the black-eyed creature: a torn bit of clothing, a trail of blood, a bone-chilling roar. Anything that might lead her in the right direction. She's just about to give up when she spots a deep imprint of a large sneaker in a patch of half-dried mud.

Turning in the direction of the shoeprint, Charlie begins to veer northeast. A few raindrops plop onto her jacket, leaving round, dark splotches as they seep into the fabric. Distant thunder crackles as the temperature starts dipping. She ignores the worsening weather and continues onward. A cluster of broken twigs on a tall bush show that she's most likely still headed the right way.

The wind starts to pick up, and quick gusts whistle through the gaps of the tree branches and set them swaying. The rain is falling harder now. Charlie finds another footprint and presses onward.

A bright flash tears diagonally across the sky. It's followed soon after by a deep rumble that shakes the ground beneath her feet. Charlie keeps going.

A roar cuts through the air.

Charlie spins toward the sound. The wind violently rips the hat from her head and sends it sailing away. She watches only for the briefest of moments before a noise draws her attention. She turns to her left. A zombie appears from behind a tree and charges at her.

The driving rain plasters Charlie's hair across her forehead. She swipes one hand across her face, but the wet strands stick to her skin and cling to her eyelashes. The attacker is closing in.

Charlie takes aim and fires. The shot goes low. The slug erupts through the zombie's wrist, shattering the bones and tearing through the flesh, leaving a ragged stump. His hand hangs limply from a few thin strips of flesh. He doesn't slow down.

The gun jams. Before Charlie can react, the zombie crashes into her. Her breath rapidly exits her lungs as the zombie's shoulder slams into her stomach. Her feet slip on the wet ground. Charlie and the zombie both fall backward. Water splashes up around them as they crash into the ground and the shotgun slips from her hand.

Dazed and winded, Charlie lies there. Lightning flashes. The ground shakes with thunder. The zombie drags himself upward and clamps his jaws around Charlie's left shoulder. She looks over at him, entirely unsure what to do. As her senses and breath finally return, she yanks the pistol from the holster and slams the grip into his temple. A thin ribbon of blood flies out and paints a line across Charlie's face. His teeth slide off her and falls to the side.

Charlie tries to right herself. The zombie is faster, though. He rolls into a crouch and then springs forward tackling her again. Charlie raises the gun and fires. The bullet finds its way through the center of the zombie's skull, and a spray of blood and brain matter comes raining down on her, soaking nearly every inch of her torso and face. The zombie falls half across her, pinning her to the ground.

It takes all her strength, but Charlie finally manages to roll the zombie off herself and stand up. He begins twisting and contracting as though he's about to leap up and attack again. Charlie leans close and fires the pistol into the skull three more times until his head is wholly unrecognizable. At last, the zombie quits moving. Other than a few, minor twitches, anyway.

Charlie's hair, face, and clothes are all drenched with a dark mixture of blood, gray matter, rain, and mud. But she grins as she notices that his teeth couldn't puncture through the tough denim of her jacket.

Turning to look up at the sky, Charlie lets the pouring rain wash the vile taste of the zombie's blood off her lips as another streak of lightning cuts across the sky.

- Southwestern Kansas -

-- Day 17 --

Opening her eyes, Charlie rolls onto her side and pushes away the faded, blue and green quilt. At the same time, she glances over at the clock to see it's just past seven. Sunlight shines brightly through the narrow gap in the curtains next to the bed.

With a loud yawn, Charlie sits up and rubs one hand across her eyes. She stands up. Raising her arms toward the ceiling, she stretches and listens as her back and knees crackle and pop with every movement. She pulls back the ruffled, blue window coverings and looks through the glass, between the wooden boards that are nailed to the outside of the wall. There's barely a cloud in the sky. A rabbit hops across the yard while a bird merrily sings out from one of the nearby treetops.

Taking the three steps across the narrow room, Charlie picks up her overalls from the back of the wooden rocking chair, quickly changes into them, and lays her nightclothes across the bed. Sitting down, she pulls on her boots. Dressed for the day, she heads into the kitchen and closes the bedroom door behind herself.

The drowsiness begins to fade as Charlie makes her way over to the cupboard. She pulls out two glass jars, one filled with something golden-yellow; the other filled with something deep red with little, dark specks inside. She sets them on the counter, looks from one to the other, from the honey to the strawberry preserves, and back again. At last, she makes her choice. She puts the honey back and closes the cupboard door.

Moving to the freezer, Charlie takes out a couple slices of frozen, whole wheat bread and tosses them into the toaster. Soon, the toast is done and smeared with a thick layer of the sweet, red substance. Charlie slowly nibbles at it. She manages to get through a few bites of the first piece before deciding she's not as hungry as she thought. She pushes the plate away, most of the toast left untouched. Taking a small sip of water, she walks over and sets the cup next to the sink.

With the meal abandoned, Charlie heads to the bathroom and pulls the door shut. In passing, she glances at the mirror above the sink and wonders if that tiny black speck had always been there near the corner of her left eye.

By the time she's gotten ready and the bathroom door opens again, Charlie has a plan for the day.

Sliding the ball cap onto her head and slipping into her jacket, she walks to the front door. The shotgun strap goes around her shoulder, and the pistol slides into the holster at her hip. Turning away, she walks to the closet to retrieve her fishing gear. Moving back to the front door once again, Charlie uses her toe to pry loose the board that's jammed beneath the doorknob, then steps out into the early morning sunshine. The air is still.

Charlie takes a look around, searching for any sign of danger. Other than a few chirping birds in the trees and the chickens clucking in the distance, it's quiet.

She turns to the southeast and sets off. Her progress toward the pond is slow—there are fences in the way and thorny branches that grab her clothes. And of course she stops regularly to listen to her surroundings. But at last, she makes it to the edge of the murky pond, finds a fallen log she can use as a seat, shrugs out of her jacket, and baits her hook. Making herself comfortable as the sun begins to warm her skin, she casts her line into the water and settles back to wait.

As the sun sits well past its apex, Charlie pulls the filled net from the water. Then she kills and cleans the fish with quick and practiced movements before tossing them in her small cooler and gathering all her gear.

She's about to start the trek back home when she realizes she won't be able to quickly access her guns without dropping—and likely spilling all the contents of—the cooler. She stands there a moment, thinking. Finally, she unhooks the shotgun from its sling and lays it on the fallen log. Picking up the cooler, she fastens the ends of the sling around the cooler handle, then slides the sling back into place. The cooler rests now at the center of her back with the sling hanging diagonally across her chest.

Satisfied with the arrangement, Charlie nods. Taking the shotgun in hand, she sets off. She doesn't go back the way she came, though. This time, she goes north. Instead of going straight home, she plans to walk out near the chicken coop. She'll scoop up the eggs while she's there and see how the animals are doing on food and water, then she'll head to the house from there.

Charlie winds her way slowly through the trees. A shadow passes along the ground in front of her and she pauses to look. A turkey vulture flies through the cloudless, blue sky. Disengaging the gun's safety, she starts walking again. Just as she sees a glimpse of the chicken coop's roof off in the distance, she hears a low noise. She spins around and presses the butt of the gun to her shoulder. Twisting side to side and walking slowly forward, she scans for the source of the sound.

That deep groan comes again. Charlie pivots toward it. Her face is nearly unreadable—the only outward sign of her confusion is the slight deepening of the vertical line between her brows. The large shadow passes by again.

Charlie takes another step.

The sound comes a third time, closer now. She turns. At last, she sees the source. The no-longer-human creature lies sprawled on the ground and glares up at her with his black-streaked eyes. One of his hands stretches toward her as he tries in vain to push himself up off the ground. He opens his mouth. A feeble attempt at a roar comes out. That sound—the one that had once been loud and primal and bone-chilling—now comes out weak and almost pitiful.

Cautiously, Charlie walks closer until she's just beyond the zombie's reach. She looks down the barrel of her gun at him. A deep bite mark is visible on his shoulder. The skin around the wound is bruised; the teeth marks are clearly pus-filled and badly infected. Dried blood stains cover the zombie's shirt. His lips are cracked and flaky. His cheeks are sunken, and his arms look as though they're nothing more than skin and bones.

For a moment, Charlie wonders how this one could've gotten so close to the house without her noticing. And for that matter, when did it end up here? More than anything, though, what had made it so weak that it couldn't attack? At last deciding none of that really matters, she lets the wandering thoughts drift away. She moves back a few paces, takes aim, and puts the creature out of his misery.

With her ears still ringing from the blast, Charlie can't hear the sound of a truck moving slowly down the dirt road near the house.

18

ALONE

- Central Colorado -

-- Day 15 --

Evie's stomach growls loudly, reverberating off the damp cave walls. The chocolate bars and graham crackers she'd stuffed in her pockets before her solo hike had been eaten the first night as she sat alone and terrified in the dark. That was over a day and a half ago, and her stomach now angrily reminds her of this fact.

She presses the power button on her phone. It doesn't respond. Its battery had given up the last of its life yesterday when she'd tried to send those texts to everyone in her contacts list. Every last one had come back with the same, simple message: "Unable to send."

Shoving the lifeless phone into her pocket, Evie leans back against the wall as her eyes begin to sting. She'd already shed so many tears, though, and gone long enough without water that the tears will no longer come. Habitually, she blinks the non-existent tears away and tries to think. She'd always been taught that if you're lost in the woods, stay put until help comes. But the idea of spending another night alone, in the dark, scared, hungry, thirsty, and with absolutely nothing to do except dwell on her miserable situation? Well, she thinks she'd rather take her chances at getting more lost.

The girl creeps up to the mouth of the cave. Crouching down at the edge of the shadows, Evie shields her eyes against the bright light of the morning sun and looks out into the green of the forest. The memory of those sounds—those inhuman roars—wash over her, and she shivers. She nearly creeps back into the depths of the cave.

With her stomach loudly grumbling again, her resolve is renewed. Squinting, she crawls forward into the sunlight, ducking out of view behind a large shrub and stopping. She crouches there, listening and waiting for her eyes to adjust to the light. At last, she blinks a few times, then takes a long look around.

Evie plops down on the ground, unsure what to do next. She licks her dry, cracked lips. Again, her stomach tightens and lets out a long, deep growl. Laying a hand across her gurgling mid-section, she decides she has to return to the tent. Even if her dad and brother are out looking for her, food and water will be there at the campsite.

She takes a deep breath, stands up, and moves onto the trail. She takes a few tentative steps. Suddenly trembling, she stops and looks up and down the track. She feels far too exposed. Darting back into the untamed foliage, Evie ducks down. She inhales deeply, then breathes out, waiting for her heart rate to slow back to normal.

She knows it will take longer if she stays off the path. And she knows she'll make more noise crouching through the plants than if she were to remain on the dirt trail. But every instinct inside her tells her that the most important thing is to stay out of sight.

So, crouching in the tall weeds a few feet away from the well-worn path, she starts the long, slow journey back to camp.

Drenched in sweat, breathless, and exhausted, Evie finally spots the tent. She pops out from her hiding place and rushes up to it. The girl makes a beeline for the package of plastic water bottles and yanks one out, Evie twists the cap off. She brings it to her mouth and before long, half the bottle is emptied, either drank or spilled down the front of her shirt. She puts the lid back on the bottle and lowers it to catch her breath.

Evie is about to begin her search for food when she hears the crunch of gravel against a boot sole on the trail. She dives out of sight. A twig snaps underneath her, and the leaves of the bushes around her swish together at the sudden intrusion. Reaching out, she stops the movement of their shaking branches, then slowly retracts her hand and holds her breath.

Slow, steady footsteps get closer. Then, after an eternity, a woman steps into view.

The woman is twisted so that her back is turned toward Evie. Relief washes over her. She shifts forward, ready to come out and rush up to the woman and beg for help, but then the woman turns around. Evie sees the black eyes and the blood-stained mouth; she gasps. Evie clamps a hand over her own mouth and stares wide-eyed. Just then, Evie's stomach seems to think she's being a little too quiet and lets out another loud growl. But the woman stays still, oblivious to notice the noise.

Evie's brows knit together, and she tilts her head to the side as she watches. The woman takes a few more steps, stopping again to look toward both sides of the trail.

A pair of squirrels chase one another through the forest floor, trampling across the leaf-strewn ground with enough noise to wake the dead. Still, the woman doesn't acknowledge it.

Evie looks down at the water bottle. She carefully throws it across the trail behind the woman. The thin plastic crinkles as it crashes into the side of a tree before it tumbles down and rolls off into the weeds.

No reaction.

Again, Evie contemplates leaving her hiding spot. But, before the girl can move, the two squirrels dart out onto the trail in front of the woman and her eyes lock onto them. She roars and charges forward. The little rodents take off in opposite directions, and the woman sprints into the woods after one of them. Evie stares into the forest until the forest as leaves rustle and branches crack. Eventually, when all goes quiet again, Evie slumps back against a tree trunk with her hand atop her racing heart.

Shaking, the girl stands and turns around. With every intention of returning to the minivan to hide out and hopefully find some food, she crawls through the weeds to the top edge of the hill. When she can finally see the bottom of the slope, her heart sinks.

The minivan is gone. They left her.

Despair tries to take hold of her. If it weren't for the pains in her stomach, she'd stay here longer, lost in the deep hopelessness of her situation. But for now, all she can think about is that relentless gnawing in her belly.

Evie turns and slinks back to the tent. She tucks her t-shirt into the top of her jeans. Then, gathering up several of the water bottles, she drops them into her t-shirt.

Then, crawling inside the tent, she grabs a dark green sleeping bag. She climbs out and ducks back into the foliage with the sleeping bag tucked under her arm.

Moving hunched over through the greenery is difficult, especially now with the sleeping bag and the waters. But she keeps going alongside the trail until she finds a bear locker.

Evie darts over to the big steel box. She unclasps the door. As she opens it up, her shoulders relax. It's not entirely empty. She grabs the few cans and packages from there and shoves them into the sleeping bag without paying much attention to their contents. Removing the water bottles from her shirt, she tosses them in the bag as well.

With the heavy sleeping bag slung over her shoulder, she hurries out of sight and heads back toward the cave.

- Central Colorado -

-- Day 16 --

Yesterday afternoon, Evie polished off the small box of cereal. Then by the evening, she'd eaten the last few of the fig bars. Finally, as the sun had started to set, she'd ventured out of the cave, found a closer bear locker, and tucked the remaining food inside before returning to the cave for the night.

Now as the birds start to sing and the sun lights up the entrance to the cave, her stomach starts to softly rumble. She sighs. She's going to have to leave her shelter again. Evie walks to the cave entrance and pauses, listening for anything unusual. Eventually, she moves out into the sunlight. Staying hidden just off the trail, she heads to her small food stash.

Evie stops to listen again. Deciding she's still alone, she emerges from the shadows and walks up to the bear locker. She unclasps it, reaches in and grabs a random can, then refastens the doors.

As she quickly ducks down in the tall grass by a large tree, she looks down at the container in her hand. Refried beans. Not exactly what she'd prefer for breakfast, but she'll make do. Turning the can upright, Evie frowns. Up until now, she hadn't thought about how to open these cans.

Shoulders drooping, tears start to well up in her eyes as she glares angrily at the can. She lets it fall to the ground. She could check the other cans—maybe at least one has a pull tab—but if she can't find a way into the ones without it, then she's even lower on food than she'd thought.

Evie lays down in the grass and curls up into a ball. The ground beneath her face quickly soaks up her tears and leaves a thin layer of mud on her cheek and down one side of her long braid. For a long time, she lies there, simply letting the emotions take over.

At last, the tears slow. Dragging the hem of her shirt across her face, she sniffles loudly and pushes herself upright. She narrows her eyes at the can.

Turning slowly, Evie looks around until she finds a big rock with a sharp point on one side. Grabbing it, she crawls over to the can and slams the edge down onto the side of the metal cylinder. It rolls out from under the rock with barely a dent. Evie looks all around and waits, listening to her surroundings.

All is calm.

She scoots up close to the can and looks down at it. Leaning away, she grabs a few more rocks and jams them up against each side of the can. Then Evie takes another swing. The can rolls forward, and two rocks loudly smack into one another. Evie's eyes widen and she flattens herself out on the ground, scanning the area for movement.

Nothing.

Sitting up again, Evie checks the can. The dent is a little bit bigger now. She sets it between the barrier rocks again. Then, just for good measure, she places a few more stones around the perimeter of the can. She brings the sharp rock up over her head and slams it down. With a loud *crack,* it splits in two. Evie's face falls. But then she sees the hole in the side of the can. She giggles excitedly.

Evie gasps and presses her hand across her mouth as she ducks down in the grass. With racing heart, she waits. No rushing footsteps, no roars.

She snatches the can up off the ground and looks at it. Her lip juts out as she looks down at the tiny hole. It's not enough.

The girl stares at it for a long time until she suddenly remembers the house key on her necklace. She pulls the chain off and grabs the key. She shoves the blade of the key into the small hole and begins to drag it back and forth, letting the little metal ridges act like a saw around the circumference of the can. Frequently, she has to stop and wipe a layer of beans off the key and start again. It's slow and tedious work, but the can walls gradually give way.

By the time she's made it three-quarters of the way around the can, she's worked up a sweat. She wipes the key off one last time before putting the necklace back on. Then, holding her breath, she takes the can in her hands and bends the ends toward one another. She grunts with the effort. As the two cylindrical halves tear apart, Evie smiles broadly.

Carefully avoiding the sharp can edges, she scoops out some of the pale brown mixture and takes a bite. She chews slowly, savoring the salty food she'd fought so hard to obtain.

Once half of the can is emptied, she stops and sets the jagged, empty half on the ground and looks at the remaining portion. There were some plastic baggies in the bear locker, so she decides to save the rest for later. She heads to the locker, puts the half can of beans inside a bag, seals it up, and closes the door.

As Evie turns to move away from the locker, she hears something on the trail behind her. It sounds like a loose piece of gravel crunching against the sole of a shoe. She grabs the empty half of the mangled can, darts away, and ducks behind a thick patch of weeds.

Evie leans forward and peers out between the green stems. The sound is getting louder, closer. Footsteps are coming up the trail. From the sound of it, multiple sets, and they're just around the bend.

The girl's heart races. She bites her lip, looking from side to side. She's not very well hidden, but she's afraid she'll draw more attention to herself if she tries to move. Her breath comes in shallow gasps. Clutching the bottom end of the can, she waits as they get closer.

A man appears around the bend. His shirt is tattered and covered in dark stains. A moment later, another man and a woman come into view, and their clothes look equally bedraggled. Evie stares hard at their eyes, but the trees are thick, and she can't see much detail in the shadows.

Evie's heart hammers against her ribs so hard she's afraid they'll hear it. She holds her breath and slowly sinks lower into the weeds.

They keep coming. The first man walks forward and steps into the light.

Evie sees his eyes at last—no black!—and lets out the breath she'd been holding. She smiles.

The woman latches on to the older man's arm. "What was that?"

The younger man suddenly charges forward with a sledgehammer held up overhead.

Evie shrieks and leaps up as the half-can falls to the ground. "Don't hurt me!"

The younger man skids to a halt in front of her. He blinks at her momentarily as his face slowly transforms from fear to relief. He lowers his hand and lets the sledgehammer fall to the ground. Raising his empty hands in front of himself, the younger man slowly steps forward. "I'm sorry. I don't want to hurt you. We thought you were one of those zombies."

Evie stares at the three of them as she searches for something —*anything*—to say.

The younger man kneels down in front of her. "What's your name?"

She wraps her arms around herself. "Evie."

"Hi, Evie. I'm Brad." The man pauses and turns to wave the others forward.

The woman approaches first but stays behind Brad and nods.

"That's my girlfriend, Joan. And this here's my dad."

"Pleasure to meet you, Evie." The older man steps close. He rubs a palm over his chin and across the dark mole there before extending his hand for a shake. "You can call me Melvin."

19

DETOUR

- Southern Missouri -
-- Day 18 --

For days, Abigail didn't do much more than ice her ankle and sleep. But when this morning rolled around, she finally managed to pull herself together.

Now moving into the kitchen, she realizes the pain in her ankle has lessened to a dull ache. It's a bit stiff and tender, and she doesn't think she can run any marathons, but it's time to move on. She hurriedly chokes down a bowl of the stale, dry cereal. Then she equips her essentials-filled fanny pack, stuffs some new water bottles into her hoodie pocket, and climbs into the SUV. *With any luck,* she thinks as she starts the ignition, *I'll be at Uncle George's before noon.* She backs out of the garage and heads east.

Abigail puts her foot on the brake as the interstate traffic slows. Eventually, things come to a complete standstill. She winces as her sore ankle has to put extra pressure on the brake. She puts the SUV in park.

Rolling the window down a bit to let in some fresh spring air, she looks at the long line of cars in front of her. Up ahead, just before the bend in the road, she can see the barricades and the green camouflage uniforms. The National Guard had set up road-blocks several days ago. Last she'd heard, they were still letting people through as long as they didn't have symptoms. Now though, she's unsure if that policy still holds true. If it did, surely there would be some progress as people were allowed through the barricades.

Abigail nervously taps her thumbs against the steering wheel as she cranes her neck, trying to get a better look. But it's useless. It's too crowded and too far away for her to see exactly what's happen-ing. Reluctantly turning off the engine, she climbs out and starts weaving her way between vehicles and moving toward the barri-cades. She needs to find out what's going on; she might need to find a new plan.

Only a few car lengths from where she started, she freezes as someone screams up near the barricade. The air suddenly sounds like it's filled with thunder as a dozen guns start firing on the civil-ians trapped in their cars. Chaos erupts around Abigail. Horns honk, tires squeal, people scream. She turns and sprints back the way she came. Panicked onlookers tear past Abigail, slamming into her, nearly knocking her off her feet. She rights herself and runs until she finds her SUV and dives inside. In one fluid motion, she turns it on, slams it into gear, and jerks the wheel hard to the left. Stomping the gas pedal, the SUV jerks ahead and across the median. Soon, she's on the opposite side of the road, speeding west. Dozens of other vehicles do the same as gunfire continues behind her.

Whatever the reason for the screaming and the sudden shooting—regardless of whether they were opening fire on zombies or humans—she needs to get as far away from there as possible. She's sure all the main roads will be blocked. But they can't possibly block *every* road.

Going west now, she presses hard on the accelerator. The speedometer needle moves further and further to the right. Her pulse races as she goes faster than she's ever dared drive before. She weaves recklessly through the other speeding cars, swerving back and forth from the left lane to the right to the shoulder and back again. Before long, she leaves most of the other vehicles well behind her. Abigail speeds up a steep hill. As soon as she's on the other side—beyond the view of all those drivers behind her—she hits the brakes and takes a sharp left onto the first crossroad she finds.

She tears down this side road, kicking up a cloud of dust in her wake. When at last, she makes it down the hill and around a small bend, she lifts her foot off the gas.

Much slower now, the SUV bounces along the potholed dirt road. She starts to relax a bit. But then, as she comes to the top of a small hill, she can see a trio of green Humvees parked in the middle of the road. Uniformed soldiers stand watch, guns in hand. Even from this distance, she can see them react to her impending approach. They begin to crouch down and take aim toward her vehicle.

Abigail slows to a crawl. She looks to both sides of the road, hoping for some other path to reveal itself, but the trees are thick on each side of the ditch.

She swallows hard. Just as she's about to hit the brakes and throw it into reverse, she sees it. Off to her right sits a gravel driveway, hidden away amongst the trees and overgrown grass. Maintaining what she hopes looks like a casual, unworried driving speed, she turns into the long, winding driveway. With any luck, the soldiers will think she lives there and that she's just heading home.

She looks off to her left just before she gets to the tree line. A group of soldiers are pointing her way and climbing into one of the

Humvees. She holds her breath. Going slow, she waits until they're blocked from view, then slams her foot down on the accelerator.

Gravel flies up behind the SUV as the tires try to find purchase. At last, they do, and she launches forward. She speeds down the driveway and then around another bend. She goes straight for a bit, but then seeing the barbed wire fence, she jerks the wheel to the side and plows through it.

Speeding through the field, the SUV bounces up and down, side to side, shaking Abigail violently. She rolls the window down and strains to hear. As far as she can tell, the Humvee's tires are still crunching against the gravel of the driveway.

Abigail's eyes dart back and forth as she searches for somewhere to hide. She spots a gap in the middle of a group of trees. She drives up, its the brakes, and throws the vehicle into park. Leaping out, she looks at the spot. It's not hidden well, but it's the best she can do in the time she has available. She grabs her bat and takes off at a dead run through the trees. The rumble of the Humvee's engine is getting louder. Her legs burn. She can barely pull enough air into her lungs, but she keeps pushing. She doesn't have much time. Desperate, she ducks below an overhang in the mud of a creek bank and clamps one hand over her mouth to muffle the sounds of her ragged breath. She waits.

Somewhere not too far away, Abigail can hear the Humvee stop and turn off its engine. She hears the doors open and then close. She trembles. Two deep, masculine voices are talking, but she can't tell what they're saying. She hears the heavy footfalls moving through the weeds. More talking. A soft *hiss*. A moment later, the doors open and close once more. The Humvee's engine fires up, and before long, she can hear it fading into the distance.

She waits a long time before finally daring to peek out from her hiding place. The Humvee is already well out of sight. Something doesn't feel right, but she can't figure out what.

Ducking back down, she begins to weigh her options. *Now what? They'll see me if I go back the way I came. It's going to get dark soon, and I'm not really sure where to go from here. Besides, headlights would be a dead giveaway for my location. It's probably best if I wait until morning. I'd like to sleep in the car in case I need a quick getaway, but what if they come back?*

Abigail lightly taps her foot against a rock as she tries to decide what to do. She can't drive away, at least not yet. She can't run. Literally. What other choice does she have? Abigail looks at the big oak tree in front of her and sighs. Sliding her ponytail holder from her hair, she grabs her bat and uses the hair tie to fasten the handle of her bat to her belt loop.

Taking one last look around, hoping for any other options, Abigail shakes her head. She takes a moment to stretch her tired legs, then jumps up and grabs hold of a thick tree limb. Before long, she's several feet off the ground, and she settles onto the widest branch she can find. She slides her belt from its loops and throws it around the branch, strapping one leg to the tree. She's sure she won't manage to get any rest up here. But at least off the ground, she's not easy to get to. And the surrounding evergreens do a good job of shielding her from view. She settles back against the rough trunk and prepares to sit through a very long night.

- Southern Missouri -
-- Day 19 --

Abigail jolts awake and lifts her head. Sleep had finally come, and she'd begun to slump, tilting dangerously far over the side of the thick branch. Fortunately, though, her belt had done its job. Leaning back, she rests her head against the oak's thick trunk. She takes a deep breath and exhales slowly as she tries to ignore the stiff achiness in her back.

The sun is just beginning to peek through the needles of the pine trees. Yawning widely, she rubs the sleep from her eyes, then stretches as best she can given the circumstances. She leans over—

intentionally this time—and looks at the ground below her. Then, she scans the area a bit further out, all the way up to her abandoned SUV. No visible soldiers, no signs of zombies.

No more phones, no lights.

Abigail stops and half-heartedly chuckles. *At least I've still got a car.*

She removes the "seatbelt" from the branch and refastens it through her belt loops. Then, for the first time since she'd made the ascent, she tries to flex her ankle. She gasps. Between yesterday's exertions and the night's damp chill, the still-healing ankle had stiffened and now aches terribly to move.

Wincing, Abigail leans back against the trunk, grabs a granola bar from her trusty fanny pack, takes a bite, and begins to chew. She needs to get down and back to the car. But descending with this ankle is going to be tough. Polishing off the last few bites of the bar, she takes a drink and returns the bottle to her pocket.

Bending her knee, she draws her foot up close. She slowly extends the foot, bends it back, and twists it side to side while taking mental note of exactly which movements hurt. Then she slides her foot closer still and shifts forward until that ankle supports just the tiniest fraction of her weight. Tears sting at her eyes. She quickly leans back and takes her weight off that leg.

Frustrated, she growls. She can't stay up here. Taking off her belt yet again, she wraps it around her ankle and foot to form a makeshift brace. Unhooking the bat from her waistband, she tosses it a few feet away from the base of the tree and watches it roll to a stop. She turns and dangles her legs over the side of the branch.

Steeling herself, Abigail turns around and lies down so that her stomach is on the branch. She slowly stretches down toward the next large limb. Her biceps burn with the slow, unaccustomed movements, but she can't afford to rush. She finally makes it within reach of the next branch and is careful to put all her weight on the good foot. She sways a bit and has to lean against the trunk until she regains her balance.

Then, she repeats the entire process. Over and over again until, at last, she's back on terra firma. Winded, sore, sweaty, and weak, but finally on the ground. She hobbles over, picks up, the bat and leans heavily on it as she limps back to the SUV.

Coming into the clearing, she catches sight of her waiting vehicle. Something looks different, but she can't quite figure out what. *It's almost as if it seems shorter somehow.* As the truth sinks in, her jaw drops. It *is* shorter. That strange hiss: the soldiers had deflated her tires. They couldn't find her quickly, so they stranded her instead.

Abigail growls as she climbs into the driver's seat and slams the door shut. Gripping the wheel tightly, she stares through the windshield at the empty field before her. Then, in a fit of pique, Abigail reopens and slams the door a dozen more times. As the anger and frustration finally subside, she unclenches her teeth, leans forward, and rests her forehead against the wheel.

Slowly, Abigail sits up. She reaches into the glove box and pulls out an old map. It has sat there for years, unused and out of date. But now, with a dead phone battery and no access to its GPS, she has to go about it the old-fashioned way.

Finding her location on the faded paper, Abigail's eyebrows rise toward her hairline. She'd known she was close to her uncle's house but didn't realize exactly how close from the middle of this field. If she'd stayed on the main road, she would've had to go almost another twenty miles. But from here, if she cuts straight through the fields, it's only six miles.

No sense walking on this ankle any farther than I have to. Might as well drive as far as I can. Abigail starts up the ignition and lightly presses against the accelerator. At first, the deflated tires don't want to move the vehicle across the grassy terrain, but eventually they get her moving.

Five very slow, very bumpy miles later, the wheels finally get stuck in a deep rut. Sighing, even as she thanks her lucky stars that she made it this far, she grabs what little she can carry, leans on the bat like a crutch, and starts limping in the direction of her uncle's house.

Nearly an hour has passed by the time she finally spots the house, and she almost bursts into tears as relief washes over her. She picks up the pace.

"Abby?!"

Abigail's heart skips a beat. She stops, staring disbelievingly as the figure steps out of the house and comes running toward her. Tears fill up her eyes.

"M-mom?"

Marlene throws her arms around her daughter. Abigail stands rigid at first. But soon, she squeezes her mother tightly, burying her face in her mother's curly gray hair.

"Oh, honey. I thought..." Marlene's voice gives out as her eyes begin to burn with tears. She squeezes her daughter tighter still. Abigail can barely breathe in the tight embrace, but she can't bear to pull away.

At last, Marlene steps back. Reaching out, she pulls a few dried leaves from Abigail's tangled hair. A smile lights up Marlene's face as she wipes the tears from her cheeks. Throwing Abigail's arm over her own shoulder, Marlene beams as she helps her the rest of the way to the house. George is standing on the porch, smiling at the two of them. As soon as the women make it up the steps, he sets down his cane and wraps them both in a hug.

Finally, the trio wipe away their tears and head inside. Abigail collapses into the nearest chair. Marlene grabs another seat and slides it over close to her long-lost daughter. She reaches out and takes Abigail's hand. George stands at the corner of the wallpapered room.

"Honey. I... Your father locked himself in... He made me promise to... I mean..." Marlene presses her free hand against her mouth as she begins to sob.

Abigail closes her eyes as she squeezes her mother's hand. "I know, Mom. I... I went by the house. It's not your fault."

Marlene nods but refuses to meet her daughter's gaze. "Have you heard from your brother? He was going to come check on you, I think. But that's the last I heard."

Now it's Abigail's turn to fall apart. The tears flow rapidly, and her throat gets tight. She takes a deep, shaky breath. "Y-yeah. He was there, but he... He got bit. He tried to hold on long enough... To say goodbye to you and Dad, but he just couldn't anymore. He made me leave without him."

Abigail had thought her mother seemed broken when she spoke of losing her beloved husband. But if that was broken, this was shattered, pulverized, obliterated. Hearing that her firstborn was gone—that Marlene couldn't be there with him in the end, that she couldn't say goodbye—all the light goes out from her and she seems to shrink in on herself.

Marlene silently stands up. George hurries over and tries to put his arm around her, but she shrugs away from his touch and disappears from the room.

Abigail's shoulders droop. She sinks down in the chair and lays her head on the table.

"Hey, kiddo." George comes over and pulls his niece close.

Leaning into his warm embrace, Abigail soaks his plaid shirt with her tears.

20

TOLD YOU

- Southwestern Kansas -
-- Day 18 --

Charlie's eyes fly open. Her gaze darts around the darkened room, trying to make sense of what just pulled her from a deep, dreamless sleep. She pushes away the covers and sits up. Something—a noise from outside—had woken her, but her groggy mind can't quite make sense of what it was. Standing up, she goes to the window and moves the curtains back an inch to peek through the glass. The wooden boards block sections from view, and she has to bend down to look between the gaps. She can't see much, but none of the shadows outside seem out of place.

Picking up her pistol, she slowly creeps into the kitchen. She flicks on the porch light, and the yard is suddenly awash in its bright, yellow glow. Charlie stares out through the glass. Still, nothing seems amiss.

She moves through the house, checking all the windows.

From somewhere far off in the distance, Charlie hears a zombie roaring. Turning the lights off again, she returns to bed and promptly falls back into that deep slumber.

Charlie walks out of the bedroom and pulls the door closed behind herself as she steps into the kitchen. She moves across the small room and pulls open the squeaky pantry door to search for breakfast. Her stomach feels empty, but the longer she stands there, the more she realizes the thought of food holds no appeal. In fact, she's trying to remember when exactly she last ate or drank anything. Yesterday's barely-touched toast catches her eye. It's still sitting on the table, now becoming breakfast for a trio of houseflies.

Moving to the sink, Charlie fills a glass with water and lifts it to her lips. Her stomach churns at even the idea of swallowing the cold liquid. She tosses it down the drain, sets the glass in the sink, and turns away.

Leaning back against the countertop, her thoughts race. She debates about going into the bathroom to check her reflection in the mirror, but she already knows that the black speck in her left eye has grown. And, she assumes, that tiny spot has most likely started to stretch into thin, zig-zagging lines. Odds are, the right eye has its own black dot now too.

"Damn."

She stands there for a long while, her arms folded across her chest, lost in her thoughts. A deep and growing gloom waits at the edges of her mind, trying to grab hold, threatening to envelope her. But before the grim thoughts can take root, she shoos them away. She knows she can't change her fate any more than her late Isaiah, so there's no sense wasting time trying.

Charlie walks over to the front door. She pulls her denim jacket on, slides the shotgun sling over her shoulder, and tucks the pistol into its holster. Pushing away the board beneath the doorknob, she swings the door open and steps out onto the porch.

As she makes her way into the yard, Charlie pulls the cigarette pack from her hip pocket. She shakes one loose and places the cigarette between her lips before returning the pack where it belongs. Then she reaches into the overall's bib pocket and pulls out the little, green lighter. With the flick of her thumb, a flame appears, and she lifts it toward the cigarette.

"Hands up."

Charlie raises an eyebrow but otherwise ignores the sudden command from the nasally voice. She touches the flame to the cigarette, inhales deeply, then slips the lighter back into her pocket.

"I'm not kidding! Hands up!"

"Look," she takes a drag on the cigarette then grips it between two fingers as she exhales the smoke, "if I'm fixin' to meet my maker on this fine, sunny morning, I'm enjoyin' one last smoke 'fore I go."

The owner of the voice makes a few unintelligible noises and then goes quiet. A minute later, he jams the cold, metal barrel of a pistol against Charlie's spine. "Fine. You've had your damn cigarette. Now, hands up!"

Chuckling, Charlie drops the cigarette and stomps out the flame with her boot. She lifts her hands and starts to turn and face the man.

"I didn't tell you to turn around! Stay put, you old hag!"

She pointedly ignores him as she completes the turn and when her eyes meet his, Charlie grins. She looks pointedly from the blood-soaked bandage on the man's arm to the dark, purple bruises around the obviously shattered nose. "Well, look what the cat drug in! Didn't expect I'd ever see you again after I run you off at the store."

The man's teeth grind together as he glares at her. The pistol shakes in his hand. "Drop your..."

His voice trails away, and he quickly backpedals several feet away from Charlie. "What the hell? You've been bit!"

Staring at the man, Charlie leans forward and chomps her teeth together as if trying to bite him. His eyes grow wide as he backs himself into the wall, and he jumps at the sudden, unexpected contact with the structure. Charlie can't help but laugh at him.

The man's cheeks turn red as he glares at her. Shaking his pistol with every syllable, he shouts, "Drop your guns!"

Keeping her left hand raised, Charlie uses her right to unclip the shotgun from its sling and bends down to set it on the porch. With only her pointer finger and thumb, she grabs the pistol from its holster and gently places it on the concrete. Then she straightens back up and raises her right hand again.

"I damn near killed myself on all those wires out there last night." He pauses and forces a grin onto his face, no doubt trying to look menacing. "I thought you'd caught me when you started flipping on those porch lights."

Charlie notices the shallow, red gash across the man's throat and grins. "I s'pose that wire did its job then."

"Fuck you, bitch." The man hurries forward and kicks the guns away from Charlie, then quickly backs away, out of her reach. "Now, here's what's—"

A purple blur suddenly charges past Charlie, roaring. The zombie smashes into the man, tackling him and the pair fall to the ground with a loud *thud*. Charlie stands there, blinking at the abrupt appearance of the small woman in the purple dress.

The zombie and the man struggle against one another. The zombie is bearing down. Her teeth are inches away from his throat, biting at the air. He tries to push her away, but her fingers are already latched tightly on him, one around his bicep, the other around the back of his neck.

The man presses the pistol and his free hand into the zombie's chest. He shoves. The zombie's hand is wrapped around his neck and it slides up toward his face. She digs her nails into his throat, tearing deep gouges into his flesh.

He screams.

A shot rings out.

For Charlie, the world suddenly goes silent. She looks down. Blood is gushing from her stomach, drenching her clothes and making the concrete beneath her feet red and slippery. The bullet meant for the zombie had gone straight through the center of her purple dress and stopped deep within Charlie's belly.

Charlie clamps a hand against the gaping wound as her brain starts to register the pain of the shot. A wave of dizziness washes over her. Her vision goes dark around the edges. She stumbles up the steps, through the door, and into the little house. Blood pours between her fingers.

The pair on the ground continue their struggle. The man finally shoves the zombie hard enough that she loses her balance and rolls off him. He rolls the other way and leaps up.

The man runs inside the house, dripping with blood and guts that had once been inside the zombie. As soon as he's past the threshold, he turns, slamming his shoulder against the door as he tries to shove it closed. The zombie is already halfway through the doorframe, though.

She roars as she slams her body into the door.

The man stumbles backward into the house. Bringing the pistol up, the man swings it hard into the side of the zombie's head. She stumbles backward into the door, and it bangs closed behind her.

In the brief respite from the assault, the man notices a quiet little *click, click, click* noise coming from somewhere just a few feet to his left. He turns.

The man's eyes move toward the stove and meet Charlie's narrowed gaze.

"I told you I wouldn't miss next time."

As the zombie grabs hold and sinks her teeth into the man's neck, Charlie flicks the button on her lighter, and the entire house explodes in flames.

21

CHOICES

- Central Colorado -

-- Day 19 --

"You said," From the corner of her eye, Joan catches a glimpse of Evie. She slides across the seat, moving closer to Brad, and begins again, quieter. "You said it would only be for one night, and then we'd move on. We need to go. It's not safe here, and you damn well know it."

Joan tears off a bite of beef jerky and chews it as she narrows her eyes at Brad. He turns. Leaning forward, he looks past Joan to see Evie sitting beside his father at the lake. The young girl laughs brightly as the older man tells her one of his corniest jokes.

"I know, but..." Brad turns back toward Joan. "I mean, Technically, yeah, it's not safe here. Thing is, we don't know that it's safe anywhere else either."

Brad pauses. Joan looks unconvinced and ready to argue, so he quickly speaks up again. "And we can't just abandon a child here."

The pair sit in silence for a moment, and both turn to look at the girl. Finishing off the last few bites of the jerky, Joan wipes her hands on her jeans and then shoves the empty plastic wrapper into her pocket.

Brad lays his hand on top of Joan's as he speaks up again. "Maybe we just need to take her with us."

"No!" Joan jerks her hand away and abruptly stands up. Her gaze darts toward the child for a moment, but neither Evie nor Melvin seems to have noticed Joan's outburst. Placing her fists on the table, Joan leans down to look at Brad now. Lowering her voice yet again, she continues. "Why do you think that man left his own kid in the first place? She's probably been bit!" Joan slams a palm on the top of the wooden picnic table. "Let's leave her and go!"

This time, Melvin and Evie both turn to look back at the others. Melvin distracts the girl again and quickly ushers her farther away from the argument.

"You can't mean that." Disbelief is written across Brad's face as he turns his attention back to Joan again. "Even if she has been bitten, she's just a kid, Joanie. I can't just leave a scared child here all on her own."

"You'd put us *all* at risk for some kid you didn't even know existed just a few days ago?"

The pair sit motionless, glaring intently at one another as time slowly ticks by.

At last, Joan huffs. Her expression softens. Sliding back onto the bench, she reaches out and takes Brad's hands in hers, gently caressing his fingers. "Look. Let's just say for a moment that we did take her with us. What if her daddy comes back looking for her after we leave here?"

With a deep frown, Brad looks at Evie again as he slides his hand out from Joan's. Off in the distance, Evie is up now, bouncing around and regaling Brad's father with some lively story. Melvin's deep laugh rings out.

"If he hasn't come back by now, I really doubt he's coming back at all. But if he did..." The tiniest glimmer of doubt crosses Brad's expression. "But we can't just abandon her here."

"Damn it, Brad!" Joan's eyes dart over toward the girl once more. Evie and Melvin have wandered further down the bank. "We can't take care of a kid! We're barely getting by with just us three! And besides, do you know the first thing about taking care of a child? Especially one that's just going to turn into one of those—"

"What the hell has gotten into you?! It's not as if she's a baby! She's half-grown. I think she can handle bathing and feeding herself. And honestly, we have no reason to believe she's sick." Brad rolls his eyes at Joan. "And you know what? Before the world went to shit, you never would've suggested something like this!"

"Well, the world *has* gone to shit. So yeah, things are a bit different these days. Now—"

"Enough, Joan!" Brad abruptly stands up. "I'll ask her whether she wants to stay or go. But either way, I am *not* leaving her here alone!"

Brad turns and walks swiftly away from the table. Joan follows closely behind.

"Hey, Evie."

Evie stops in the middle of whatever she is saying to Melvin, and the pair turn to Brad.

"I've got something I want to ask you. I promise you can pick whichever option you want. It's totally up to you. Okay?"

"Um," Evie's smile fades, and a row of wrinkles appears across her forehead. She licks her lips. "Okay."

Brad sits on the ground, hoping the kid might feel more comfortable if he's not towering over her. "So, before we came here, Dad and Joan and me were thinking we were only gonna stay here for a night or two and then keep moving on. But then we ran into you and..."

Evie's eyes fill with tears. Seeing the unnecessary apology forming on her lips, Brad hurries to reassure her. "We're not mad at you about that! I promise, Evie. Really, it's alright."

Joan lets out a "hmph" from behind him. Brad does his best to ignore it and keeps talking to Evie. "It's just something that happened. It's nobody's fault."

Brad smiles at Evie. She nods, but her eyes still shine with the unshed tears and her lip trembles ever-so-slightly.

"So I want to give you a choice. Do you want us to stay here with you? Or do you want to hit the road with us?"

"Y-you'd take me with you?"

Brad nods at her.

"What if..." Evie blinks quickly, swallows the lump in her throat, then starts again. "What if my brother is still out here too?"

Evie pauses for a moment. Brad can tell she has more to say, though, so he waits patiently. When Evie speaks again, her voice is barely more than a whisper. "What if my dad comes back and I'm not here?"

"Well, Brad thinks y—"

Brad twists around and glares at Joan until she stops talking. He softens his features as he turns back to Evie again. "That's why it's up to you. We can wait with you, or you can come with us."

"I..." Evie's eyes dart between the three of them. She looks at Brad again. "I want to wait a little longer."

"Alright then." Brad nods. "That's what we'll do."

Evie stares for a moment. As the tears start to spill down her cheeks, she blurts out, "You're really not going to leave me?"

Brad leans closer and looks into her wide eyes. "Never."

Stepping forward, Evie throws her arms around Brad's neck. He smiles, returning the hug as a tear rolls down his cheek as well.

- Central Colorado -

-- Day 20 --

"Brad!" Joan hisses the name. When he doesn't respond, she grabs him by the shoulder and shakes him. "Brad! Wake up!"

Brad awakens with a jolt. He grabs the handle of his sledge-hammer as his wide eyes turn toward Joan. He can't make out much more than her silhouette in the dark corner of the cave, but the panic in her hushed voice is clear as day.

"Wha'sit?" His tongue is less than awake as he hisses his response to her.

"There's something outside."

Evie rolls over in her sleeping bag along the far wall and quickly sits up.

Melvin had spent the night propped up against a large rock with his blanket wadded up behind his back. Now, with all the hushed whispers around him, he begins to stir.

Sliding quietly out from her sleeping bag, Evie hurriedly crawls over beside Brad. "I heard it too. There's something out there."

"Alright." Brad pushes himself to his feet and lifts the sledgehammer to his shoulder as he faces the cave entrance. The morning sunlight is just beginning to light up the floor at the cave's opening, but the group is still cloaked in deep shadows. "Joan, go wake Dad up."

Giving Evie a wide berth, Joan hurries over toward Melvin. She wakes him and quickly whispers to him about the noises outside. Grabbing his shovel, Melvin uses it like a cane to push himself up off the ground, then moves over to Brad's side.

"Dad, you stay..." Brad trails off as he notices Joan's silhouette move so that Melvin stands between her and Evie. He shakes his head and continues. "Stay here with the girls. I'm gonna go look."

"Keep your wits about you."

Brad nods, then tiptoes forward. Just before he steps into the light, he moves over to the wall and presses his back against the rough, damp stone. He creeps sideways toward the entrance. When he's finally made it close enough, he slowly leans forward and peaks out.

Breath catching in his throat, Brad ducks back inside the dark interior and quietly hurries back to the others.

"Is it..."

Their shapes seem even more formless now that he'd just looked out in the bright morning sun. He turns toward Joan's whispered voice. "No. It's a bear. A mother with a couple of cubs.

Looked like the mother might've been chewing on some kind of food can."

Evie gasps. "I'm sorry! I didn't mean to leave that refried bean can out on the ground—"

"I told you that kid was going to get us—"

"Joan!" Brad hisses her name. "Not the time!"

Melvin leans over and whispers to Evie but loud enough for the whole huddled group to hear. "Not your fault, Sweetheart. We *all*," he pauses to let the words sink in, "knew you had dropped that can when we surprised you that first day. None of us remembered to pick it up, neither."

Straightening up again, Melvin returns his attention to Brad. "So what do you think, son?"

"I guess the first option is to fight. But we don't have enough firepower to take on a bear. Definitely not an angry bear with cubs to defend. Much less one that's just come out of hibernation and now associates our area with food. So, I think that option's out."

The other three nod their agreement.

"Second option is to stay put and see if they move on soon. If they do, we can head out and find somewhere else to hide. But who knows how long they might stick around. Problem is, do we really want to risk them backing us into this cave with no way out?"

He takes a deep breath and exhales slowly. "They can probably smell us and possibly even hear us, but I don't want to test the theory that they're just okay with our presence and that we're not going to startle them into attacking. So anyway, that brings us to what I think we need to do. Option three: try to sneak out of here."

No one responds. The group barely even dares to breathe.

"Dad?"

"Well, I'm not too keen on any of those options, to tell you the truth. But I think you're right. Sneaking out is our best bet."

"Alright. Evie?"

"I... I, um..." She gulps. "I guess sneak out."

"Joan?"

"Oh, do I get a say now? Sure. Let's go."

Brad rolls his eyes but keeps his retort to himself. "Dad, keep a tight grip on that shovel. I'll be keeping the sledgehammer too. If worse comes to worst, we'll want some kind of weapons. Everything else, though, we need to just leave here. We'll move slower and make more noise if we try to carry a bunch of crap. We can come back for it later if we have to.

"Those bears are off to the right, over close to that bear locker. So, we're gonna go up to the cave entrance and tiptoe around to the left, hugging that cliff wall for as long as we can. Make for the truck; we'll figure out what to do from there. Go slow, and don't talk. Dad, you'll take the lead. I'll bring up the rear and keep my eye on the bears. I'll start swinging if they get close. Everyone got it?"

Taking the tense silence as confirmation, Brad nods. "Let's go."

Melvin moves to the cave entrance and waits until Evie stands close behind him. He steps out and disappears around the corner. The others soon follow.

They move slowly. Melvin keeps the shovel raised. Evie whimpers softly every time they hear the bears grunt behind them. Joan looks back over her shoulder between each step forward. Brad moves sideways with his back to the cliff so he can watch behind them.

The group has made it a few dozen paces when suddenly, there's a high-pitched, bone-chilling roar behind them.

Evie shrieks.

A second roar, louder, closer.

Brad spins toward the sound.

Joan gasps loudly, then takes off running. She knocks Evie to the ground but doesn't slow as she disappears toward the trail.

The shovel slips from Melvin's hands.

With wide eyes, Brad gawks past the animals. On the other side of the family of bears is a zombie. The zombie sprints between the trees, coming straight for the mother bear.

The bear lays her ears back and charges. She clears the distance in a heartbeat, rears up on her hind legs, and swings a black paw through the air.

The zombie lets out another roar, but the bear's swing connects, and the sound cuts off abruptly. Spinning through the air like a rag doll, the zombie lands with a dull *thump*. The bear rushes over and takes another swing. When she lifts her claws, they're coated in blood, flesh, and strips of tattered cloth. Another swing, and another, and another until the zombie no longer moves.

The mother bear steps back and then sits down on the ground as she starts to lick the blood from her paws. The cubs bound over to the zombie and begin to sniff.

Turning toward the others, Brad motions for them to hurry.

Melvin grabs his shovel and helps Evie to her feet. The three start jogging to the trail, now compromising between speed and stealth. As soon as they've rounded the bend in the path, they all break into a run.

When they finally spot the truck, they turn and sprint across the graveled parking area. Joan slides over in the seat, and the others rapidly clamber inside.

Melvin jams the key into the ignition and throws the truck into gear. Gravel goes flying behind them as he speeds out toward the road.

"I'm sorry, Evie." Brad puts an arm around her shoulder. "I don't think we can stay here any longer."

Evie whimpers and sinks low in the seat. "What if my dad comes back? I'm gonna be in so much trouble for leaving."

"What?" Brad pulls her close to his side. "Your dad would understand. It wasn't safe to stay there."

Teary-eyed, Evie looks up at him. She opens her mouth to respond but clamps it shut again as she turns to look out the window.

"Evie," Brad hesitates, unsure how much to share with her. At last, he goes on. "I don't think your dad is coming back."

Her head whips back toward Brad. "He's not?"

Brad looks down at her, expecting inconsolable sadness. Instead, he finds hope shining in her eyes. His heart breaks for her, and he hugs her tight. "No, he's not."

"What about my brother?" The hope disappears, and a deep anguish takes its place.

"I'm so sorry, Evie. I don't know what happened to your brother. I don't..." Brad draws a shaky breath. "I don't even know where to look."

Evie buries her face in Brad's shirt, quietly soaking the fabric with her tears.

Swallowing the lump in his throat, Brad turns to his father. "You think that bear is gonna turn into one of those things?"

Melvin glances over before turning his eyes back to the road. "I don't really know. But I'm not planning on sticking around long enough to find out."

22

GONE

- Eastern Missouri -
-- Day 19 --

Sitting at the dining table, Nathaniel stares at the empty plastic bottles before him. His clothes and the table are thoroughly drenched, and he can't manage to force more than a few drops down his throat this morning. He stands up. Just as he turns to walk away, he feels himself disappearing again.

When awareness returns, Nathaniel is standing downstairs on the concrete floor with the firetruck at his side, still dressed in the firefighter's coat and helmet. His pulse is racing. Sweat drips from his forehead. Everything around him seems slightly blurred and overly bright. He closes his eyes and focuses on his breathing as he struggles to make sense of what just happened.

At last, he opens his eyes. He blinks a few times, then looks around the room to get his bearings.

When he does, he heads into the downstairs bathroom and turns to face the mirror. He stands there, watching his reflection, fascinated by the strange, black lines in his own eyes. Water drips from the faucet. The tiny, repetitive *plink* of droplets against the ceramic basin echoes off the walls, and he lets it lull him into a trance.

As he waits, unmoving, his pupils dilate, and the black lines slowly spread and branch toward the center of his eyes. Again. Then, Nathaniel disappears before leaving the room, heading out the front door into the street, and starting to walk.

23

BEGINNING OF THE END

- Central Colombia -
- Near the edge of the Amazon Rainforest -
-- Day 0 --

The ground trembles ever-so-slightly. Animals around the lake dart away, disappearing into the dense undergrowth. Plants along the forest floor shake and twist as all the small creatures hurry to safety. Soon, the entire area around the lake is abandoned. The leaves go still as the tremor fades away, and the place is left in eerie silence.

Another rumble, more violent this time, runs through the ground. Overhead the canopy shakes, and dozens of leaves break free and flutter to the forest floor. The entire body of water fills with bubbles and turns the lake into a muddy, frothing, churning mess. Waves crash against the shoreline. What once was quiet stillness transforms into cacophony as the gas breaks free from its liquid barrier. A small fraction of the gas vanishes up through the gaps between the tree leaves where the wind carries it away.

But the vapor is escaping from the water too quickly, and the trees are too dense. The remainder of the mixture is trapped by the thick veil of leaves above and funneled directly toward the nearest civilization.

Moments later, residents of the small, nearby village begin to collapse as the air is replaced by the noxious gas. Most die quickly; a few simply pass out. As the poison in the air finally dissipates, something microscopic and horrifying remains. Some bacteria or virus—something unknown since prehistoric times, something long since buried and trapped deep beneath the ground's surface—has been shaken free from its earthly prison and carried by the toxic vapor.

The portion that does manage to make it through the thick tree canopy is rapidly carried off by the wind and flung out into the far corners of the world.

As the few survivors awaken, their pupils dilate, and the whites of their eyes become streaked with jagged black lines.

24

RIGOR MORTIS

- Southern Missouri -
-- Day 23 --

For days, Abigail laid in bed and rested—*really* rested—for the first time since the world ended more than three weeks ago. She hadn't seen a zombie in days, and she felt safe here. She knew that it couldn't last forever, of course. But the lazy days had done wonders for both her morale and her sore ankle.

This morning, as the sun peaks through the gap in the curtains, Abigail slowly opens her eyes. Pushing herself upright, she swings her legs over the edge of the couch. She stands, stretches, and then makes her way to the kitchen.

"Mornin', kiddo."

Grabbing the canister of oatmeal, Abigail pours some into a bowl. "Hey, Uncle George."

"Coffee's ready."

"Thanks." Abigail adds water and a scoop of sugar to the bowl, quickly stirs it, then sticks the mixture in the microwave. A few minutes later, she returns to the table with her coffee mug and bowl. "Is mom still in bed?"

George nods as he takes a sip of his coffee. The steam rising from the mug fogs up his glasses, concealing his dark brown eyes behind the haze. Sliding the glasses off, he lays them on the table beside his empty bowl.

"So," Abigail takes a bite. "Do you still have that 4-wheeler thingamajig?"

George chuckles. "The UTV? It's out back. Why?"

"Mind if I borrow it? When I abandoned my car, there were quite a few supplies still inside. I want to go back and grab what I can."

"No."

George and Abigail both jump at the unexpected voice from the doorway.

"Mom, I just—"

"Absolutely not, Abigail Jane." Marlene crosses her arms and glares at her daughter. Her eyes are puffy and red, and her voice is hoarse and low. "You are not going out there again."

Abigail hurries over and wraps her arms around her mother. "Mom, I understand why you don't want me to go. I really, honestly do. I know the news about Jake broke your heart. And I know you're scared it'll happen to me too. But the stuff we have here—the food and medicine and all that—well, it won't last forever. If I go back to the car, I can get the stuff I brought, and it'll help us last quite a while longer. It's only about a mile. I can be there and back in less than an hour."

Marlene's face crumples, and the tears begin to fall again in earnest. "Sweetie, please don't go out there."

"I'll be okay, Mom. I swear. I'll be back before you know it."

"Fine. Then I'm going with you."

"Mom, I don't—"

"Abigail Jane!" Marlene straightens up her shoulders and looks her daughter in the eyes. "I couldn't be there for Jake when he needed me. Don't you dare tell me I can't be there for you now!"

Abigail sighs. "Alright, alright. If it means that much to you. But at least eat something first. You've barely eaten anything or even moved in days." With that, Abigail guides her mother into a chair, prepares another bowl of oatmeal, and sets the food in front of her.

Together, mother and daughter speed through the field on the dirty UTV. Each of them wears gloves and a thick layer of duct tape around their arms and legs.

As Abigail's abandoned vehicle comes into view, Abigail looks over at her mom in the driver's seat. Marlene looks as though she has aged twenty years overnight. But she sits up straight with her jaw firmly set. She is resolved to see this through.

"Okay, Mom, don't forget our deal. If we see a zombie, you try to let me deal with it, alright? I know you don't want to see me hurt, but I'm faster than you are, and I've actually had to deal with several before now." Abigail didn't bother to mention that most of her encounters had involved her running or hiding from them. Even that was significantly more experience than her mom had with these creatures.

Marlene glances at her daughter before refocusing on the drive. "I still don't like this, Abby."

Abigail ignores the protest that she's already heard a million times in the last half an hour. "If you have to defend yourself against one, try to go for the brainstem."

Nodding as they stop next to the SUV, Marlene turns off the engine. She picks up a wooden cane—courtesy of George—and holds it up, ready to swing as necessary. "Let's get this over with."

"Keep your guard up." Abigail quickly scans the area, looking for any signs of movement. Satisfied they're alone in the nearly empty field, she jumps out and hurries to the waiting SUV.

Hustling back and forth between the vehicles, she piles boxes onto the bed of the UTV. On the third or fourth trip, as she reaches in to grab another box, the hair on the back of Abigail's neck rises. She freezes.

"Abby!"

Abigail spins around, and the supplies fall from her hands. She sprints back to the UTV as her mother turns on the engine. From off to their right, they see it. A redheaded zombie is barreling toward them. Marlene slams the UTV into gear and takes off.

It doesn't take long to leave the zombie behind in their cloud of dust. But as their heartrates start to return to normal, Abigail notices something else up ahead. She leans forward, squinting at the shape off in the distance.

"Mom, do you see that? Over there, by that fallen tree?"

"Yeah. I can't tell what it is, though."

"I think it's a person. Pull up there. We can see if they need help."

Marlene opens her mouth to protest. *What if it's a trick? What if it's a zombie trying to lure us closer?* But then changes her mind, knowing she'd hate herself if she knew she left a helpless person to those things. She nods and drives over toward the motionless body. Pulling up close, she turns the UTV off and picks up her cane again. With a wave of her hand, she sends Abigail over to investigate as she stands guard once more.

Keeping her bat held high, Abigail walks slowly toward the person. Whoever she is, she's lying flat on her back, completely still. "Hello? Are you okay?"

No response. Abigail takes a few more steps. Close now, she taps the woman's foot with the end of her bat. Still no acknowledgment. Abigail leans over her and looks at her face for the first time. Dried blood coats the woman's chin. Her eyelids are wide open.

And her blue irises are almost entirely swallowed by the swollen pupils and the jagged black lines. In fact, from where Abigail stands, it's hard to tell there's anything bright or colorful left in those eyes. Abigail gapes down at the rigor-mortised face. After a moment's hesitation, she grabs the woman's shoulder and rolls her over onto her stomach. She shifts the woman's hair aside, and Abigail stares at the back of the skull. It seems to be completely and utterly undamaged.

"Abby."

Turning back toward the UTV, Abigail sees it off in the distance. The redheaded zombie is still sprinting toward them.

"We have to get goi..." Marlene's words trail off as she suddenly looks toward the ground with wide eyes. She drops to her knees and begins rifling through the weeds and dead leaves. "No, no, no, no. Shit, no."

"Mom?"

"I dropped the key! Get over here and help me find it!"

Abigail rushes over, drops to her knees, and starts frantically searching. Her heart races, and her palms begin to sweat inside the thick gloves. The zombie is getting close. Abigail grabs her bat and leaps up. She moves between the redhead and her mother and shouts over her shoulder, "Keep looking!"

Marlene's breath comes in quick, shaky gasps. Tears blur her vision, and she fights to blink them away. Finally, she spots the bit of silver metal. The gloves and duct tape make it difficult to grab, so in desperation, she snatches the key up with an entire fistful of dirt and grass before spinning back toward the UTV.

"I found it!"

Abigail rushes back and clambers into the UTV. Her mother does the same as she rapidly sifts through the debris in her gloved hands. She fires up the ignition, pops it into gear, and hits the gas just as the redheaded zombie lets out that shrill, horrifying roar only inches behind them. Abigail clamps her hands over her ears.

Marlene's skin breaks out in goosebumps, and her heart leaps into her throat.

From somewhere behind the redhead, another roar. Abigail spins around in the seat to look. A zombie emerges from the woods at the edge of the field; he's dressed in a firefighter's coat and helmet, and his hand is wrapped in gauze. Close on his heels is yet another zombie, this one in a blue and white striped sweater.

Abigail twists back toward the front just as Redhead leaps forward. Redhead's hand grabs hold of Marlene's arm. Marlene screams as the cart swerves to the side. The cart rocks violently as Marlene yanks the wheel back in the other direction. Redhead's foot finds its way onto the cart, and she finds the leverage to pull against Marlene's arm. Redhead roars.

The UTV swerves again, and Abigail uses one hand to grab the steering wheel. With the other, she reaches for her mother, but her fingers only find empty air. Marlene is thrown out the side of the still-rolling cart with the zombie still gripping her bicep. The pair tumble across the field in a tangled mess of flailing limbs.

Sliding into the driver's seat, Abigail yanks the wheel hard to the left as she smashes the accelerator. Marlene and Redhead have finally stopped rolling. Dizzy and disoriented, they clamber to their feet, looking like a pair of drunks. Firefighter and Stripes are gaining on them now, and Redhead seems to be finding her balance.

The UTV closes in. Abigail grabs her bat, twists the wheel hard to the right, and leaps out. Her feet hit the ground, and she stumbles but keeps going. Redhead turns toward Abigail and reaches out. Abigail swings the bat into the zombie's arm. A loud *crack* bends the arm the wrong way and throws Redhead off balance. Abigail brings the bat around again, this time hitting Redhead across the jaw. Teeth fly through the air, and the jawbone hangs loose on one side. The zombie falls.

"Run!" Abigail brings the bat down hard against the base of Redhead's skull.

Marlene takes off and jumps into the passenger seat of the cart. Abigail throws herself into the driver's seat and slams the gas pedal against the floor.

Chest heaving and sweat trickling down her face, Marlene looks back over her shoulder as Firefighter and Stripes disappear into the distance behind them.

25

SKINNED KNEE

- Southern Missouri -
-- Day 26 --

Abigail slowly opens her eyes. The room is still dark, with only a thin sliver of moonlight creeping in through a gap in the curtains. Pressing the button on the side of her watch, she squints at the bright, glowing numbers. There are still a couple hours to go until sunrise, so she rolls to her other side and pulls the covers up over her shoulder. As she closes her eyes again and wills sleep to return.

Just as she starts to drift back into dream, she hears something from the kitchen again. A tiny *squeak*, like damp rubber on a shoe, moving against the linoleum floor.

Throwing the covers off, Abigail quietly rolls over. She sits up, wincing as the sheets swish and the bed springs creak, seeming much louder than they should in the still room. She waits. Seconds tick by in silence before Abigail dares to breathe again. She stands up, tiptoes across the room, and presses her ear against the door.

Squeak.

Abigail steps back, staring at the doorknob. Her heart begins to race. She wipes her damp palms across the bottom edge of her shirt and draws in a long, deep breath. Exhaling slowly, Abigail turns toward the other side of the room. She sneaks over to the dresser, retrieves the baseball bat leaning against it, then returns to the door. There she waits, quietly listening again.

Twisting the doorknob, she pulls the door open an inch.

"Mom?" Abigail hisses the word toward the dark kitchen. She's not sure why she's whispering, but somehow it feels safer. "Uncle George? Hello?"

A chill runs down her spine as the dark house swallows her words and returns nothing but silence. Abigail takes a deep breath and pulls the door open. The bedroom door creaks behind her. As she steps out into the hallway, she tightens her grip on the bat and tries to swallow her fear.

Squeak.

Her breath catches in her throat. Abigail freezes. An eternity passes in silence before she forces herself to continue creeping forward. The floorboards groan, her ankle pops, her heart hammers inside her chest; every sound feels amplified a thousand-fold. She slowly tiptoes on until she reaches the end of the hallway. She stops, takes a deep breath, and tightens her fingers around the bat's grip. Stepping forward, she flips on the light switch and turns.

Abigail gasps. She's face to face with Firefighter. The doorway is too narrow for her to swing the bat. Instead, she brings the handle forward and slams it into the zombie's collarbone. He roars as he lunges forward.

Abigail shrieks.

Firefighter slams his bandaged fist into her stomach. Her voice goes silent as all the air leaves her body. The bat slips from her hands, and she falls backward, gasping for air. Firefighter drops to his knees, straddling one of her legs. Abigail tries to push herself away, but he's stronger and heavier than her, and he's latched onto the end of her shirt.

Dragging Abigail across the wooden floor, he roars again.

Abigail tries to kick with the leg that isn't trapped beneath her attacker, but that leg is pinned between him and the doorframe. With her heart beating a million miles a minute, she throws her arms across her face and clenches her eyes shut.

As his teeth sink into the flesh of her forearm, she finds her breath and screams.

Thwack!

Abigail howls as Firefighter's head is jolted to the side, and his bite rips her flesh. Tears pour out beneath her clenched eyelids.

Firefighter raises up and twists backward. Another *thwack* as something slams against the side of his helmet again. The helmet flies off across the hallway and crashes against the wall before it clatters to the floor.

The zombie starts to roar. The sound is cut off with a loud *whack!* Then, *Whack! Whack!* in quick succession, and Firefighter slumps over as his entire body goes limp. He falls on top of Abigail's chest. She finally forces her tear-filled eyes open as she struggles to push him off herself. A moment later, George kneels beside Abigail, and together they roll the corpse away.

George helps Abigail sit up, and through a sheen of tears, she finally takes a look around the room. Blood coats the walls, the floor, her hair. More red trails down the door frame, along with chunks of skin and bone. Abigail swallows hard, trying to force the contents of her stomach to stay there.

"Are you alright?"

His words somehow feel distant and muffled, even though he's only a few feet away from her. Abigail presses a hand to her arm, trying to hide the severity, but the blood rapidly leaking between her fingers gives it away. Her arm feels as though it's on fire. She tries to nod at her uncle even as the tears continue to flow and all the color drains from her face.

George looks down at Abigail, worry etched deep across his forehead. Utterly lost for words, he pats her knee. Slowly turning around, he grabs the door frame and grunts as he pulls himself to his feet.

"Marlene? Are you okay?"

George is unsteady without his cane, but he slowly makes his way over to his sister's side. Laying a hand on Marlene's shoulder, he gently shakes her. She's drenched in blood. It drips from her hair and chin. Her clothes are soaked. It's all over her mouth and eyes. Wide-eyed and trembling, Marlene stares at the corpse.

"Mom?" Abigail's voice comes out weak, barely more than a whisper. Her own injuries are temporarily forgotten as she looks at her mother. Abigail's voice cracks as she speaks again. "Mom? Are you alright?"

"Marlene?"

Without a word, Marlene walks past George, steps over Abigail, and goes down the hallway and into the bathroom. The door clicks shut, and the unmistakable sounds of vomiting can be heard from in there.

"That one," Abigail sniffles loudly as she pauses to tilt her head toward the dead zombie on the floor, "is one of the ones that chased us the other day. Did it… Follow us here?"

George sinks into a chair as he stares at the mutilated body. He lifts his hands in a shrug, shaking his head. "I really don't know. But kiddo, I'm so sorry we didn't make it in here sooner. I'd heard something outside. Your ma and me was checking it out."

Abigail nods. She can no longer speak past the lump in her throat. Voiceless, she mouths the words, "It's okay."

George pushes himself back up and hurries over as quick as his frail body will take him. Breathing heavily at the effort, he pats Abigail on the top of the head. "Come on, Kiddo. Can you stand up? We need to get you cleaned up."

Suddenly, Abigail feels like a child again, waiting for Uncle George to patch up a skinned knee and distract her from her pain with a sweet treat. The tears flow ever faster at the memory. Before long, she's shaking as she sobs loudly at the thought that this time, a hug and some chocolate ice cream can't make things right.

- Southern Missouri -
-- Day 28 --

The bite on Abigail's arm burns, dragging her yet again from her light sleep. She rolls over on the couch and looks across the room at her uncle. He's scrunched up on the loveseat beneath a thin, green sheet, and one foot hangs at an awkward angle off the edge of the cushions.

Moving her blankets aside, Abigail sits up and rubs the sleep from her eyes. She then stands up and quietly makes her way to the fridge. Pulling the door open, she stands there, unmoving, blindly staring at its nearly-barren shelves. It doesn't matter, though. Her appetite is nowhere to be found. She closes the door and walks away. Just as she sits down at the table, a silhouetted figure appears in the doorway.

"Hey, Uncle George. Couldn't sleep?"

"Not with you sawing logs over there."

Abigail grins, but the smile doesn't reach her eyes. "Very funny."

George flips on the light and sits down across from Abigail. He's slightly winded from the effort of walking through the house without his cane. "How are you this morning, kiddo? Were you able to get any sleep last night?"

Abigail shakes her head. "Not much. My arm feels like it's been dragged through a poison ivy patch and lit on fire."

"I wish there was something I could do for you." Reaching out, he places his hand on top of hers and gives it a light squeeze. "You seen your ma at all since you got up?"

"No. Looks like she's still holed up in the bathroom."

George sighs. Standing up, he ambles across the room, grabs

the first aid kit, and returns to the table. "Let me put a new dressing on that wound."

"Why bother? It's not—"

"Abigail Jane," George tilts his head back and narrows his eyes at her. His voice deepens into a tone that brooks no argument. "You don't know what the future holds any more than I do. You do not get to give up until the end. You hear me, young lady?"

Right now, on the brink of a deep, all-consuming depression, Abigail finds there's an odd sort of comfort in being spoken to like a child who has gotten out of bed for the dozenth time after being tucked in. She leans forward. Silently, she extends her arm out and lets him bandage it.

As George finishes up, he pushes the first aid kit aside. "Now, there's something I've been thinking about."

"Okay..."

"It's not safe here anymore. There's just too many of 'em around here now, and they're starting to find the house. So, I..." George hesitates. He squeezes his eyes shut and takes a deep breath before continuing. "I think you and your ma need to get out of here. Find somewhere—"

"What?! No way, I'm not leaving you!"

"Kiddo, it's admirable that you feel that way, but—"

"But nothing! I am not leaving you! What the hell happened to that bullshit you just rattled off to me about not giving up?"

"Abb—"

"You're coming with us! If anyone should stay here, it should be me!"

"Abby, you—"

"No, damn it!" Abigail stands up so abruptly that her chair nearly topples over backward. She begins quickly pacing through the kitchen. "I'm not leaving you! We can all go and find somewhere better. How could you expect us to get by without you? You actually know how to trap and skin animals! Mom and I can't do that, and we're going to need to eventually. And besides, what if I turn and attack mom? You have to be there to stop me!"

Abigail swallows hard as tears begin to sting her eyes. She struggles to make her voice form the words to go on. Finally, she chokes out, "Don't do this, please. Don't send me away like Jake did. I can't go through that again. I just can't..."

"Hey there." George uses the table to push himself to his feet. He shuffles over, wraps his arms around Abigail, and gently strokes her hair. "I love you more than anything, Kiddo. I'm so sorry for this. I hate seeing you in pain, but I really think it's the only way."

"Why?"

"It's not safe here. You can agree with that much, right?"

Abigail nods.

"Look at me. I can barely get through the house without my cane. I can't run, and I can't fight, so I'd only be slowing you down. And to make matters worse, I'm nearly out of my medications. I'm only going to go downhill from here. That all means that you need to go and leave me here. And before you say it again, no, I'm not giving up. Me sending you and Marlene away? Well, that's my best hope for the future. For you two to find your way, even if that's without me."

"But what if I..."

"What if you bite your ma? She hates herself for not being there with Jake at the end. I think she'd rather take that chance with you than never see you again."

"But..."

"I know, Kiddo. I love you. But this is..."

George leaves his thought unfinished as they hear the bathroom door creak open and footsteps start down the hallway. They both turn to look. Marlene appears in the doorway. Her head is tilted toward the floor, and she's breathing heavily. George takes a step forward, and Marlene jerks her head upright. She looks past him entirely, as if he's not even there. Instead, she glares at Abigail with her black-tinged eyes.

"What's going on, Marlene?" George reaches a hand out toward her.

Marlene snaps her head toward him. Her teeth are bared, but she hasn't moved from the doorway. Suddenly, Marlene starts laughing. Then, just as abruptly, the sound stops. She clenches her eyes shut and presses her palms against her temples.

"Hey, kiddo. Your ma and I both love you, but—"

Abigail and George both jump as Marlene lets out a low growl. Her fingernails dig into her scalp, but her eyes are still tightly closed, and she hasn't left the doorway.

"My keys are on the hook by the door." George tosses the words over his shoulder without taking his eyes off Marlene. "Take my car and get out of here."

"No." The word comes out as a half-sobbed whine.

"You need to go. Now."

Abigail backs up. Seeing the first aid kit on the table, she grabs it and tucks it under her arm. She stands there, torn by indecision. Fear pushes her to leave, but loyalty keeps her feet rooted to the floor.

"Go!"

As George shouts the word over his shoulder, Marlene's eyes pop open, and she lunges forward.

Abigail runs toward the door. She snatches the keys and a jacket off the wall hook and bolts outside. Her uncle's scream reaches her as she jumps into his car. Abigail starts the ignition just as the zombie that has taken over her mother's body runs out the door. Terror chases sentimentalities away. She throws the car into reverse and speeds backward down the driveway. The zombie chases after the car. Abigail turns the car around, shifts into drive, and slams the accelerator.

As the car flies down the road, Abigail watches as the house becomes a tiny speck in the rearview mirror.

26

GET HELP

- Western Kansas -

-- Day 25 --

Leland lies sprawled out on the ground, snoring loudly. His head is propped awkwardly against a tree, and a half-empty whiskey bottle is clutched in his hand.

Eric sits on a fallen log, throwing pebbles into the campfire. Once in a while, a cluster of sparks breaks away, and he watches them flutter like fireflies as they get swept away by the evening breeze. His stomach growls noisily. He'd been hoping to ration the last of his food, but his belly is beginning to ache, and his earlier resolve is slowly fading. If he had something—*anything*—to do besides sit and think about food, he might've been able to ignore the hunger.

Groaning inwardly, Eric stands up, tiptoes past his father, and slowly slides open the minivan door. He grabs the last pack of beef jerky, a small bag of chips, and a candy bar, then returns to his seat on the fallen log.

"Hey." Leland sticks out his hand expectantly as he slurs his words at Eric. "You got food? I'm hungry. Give it here."

"But, Dad..."

Leland pushes himself up so quickly that Eric steps back and stares wide-eyed. Swaying slightly, Leland leans down and deepens his voice. "Don't make me ask again."

Eric hesitates for a moment before finally placing the small food packages in his father's hands.

Leland looks down at the meager rations as he settles back onto the ground. "Sour cream and onion? Gross." He tosses the bag over his shoulder. It lands in the dirt behind him.

Clenching his jaw tightly, Eric walks around his father, grabs the discarded bag, and returns to his seat to eat his piddly snack in silence.

"What else we got to eat?" Leland noisily chews on a thick piece of jerky as he looks at Eric.

"More sour cream and onion chips." The lie comes easily. It's true enough that the only thing left is chips. But Eric doesn't know —or care—which flavors they are. He angrily shoves a chip into his mouth.

"Hmph." With his teeth, Leland rips off another large chunk of jerky and begins chewing it as he leans back against the tree.

"We've got to get to a store or something. I'm out of water and—"

"Shut the hell up! I can't take your damn whining!" Snatching up an unopened beer can, Leland hurls it at Eric. The can hits the fallen tree just inches from Eric's knee and bursts open at the side. Leland snarls, "There, drink that."

Eric recoils, gaping at the ruptured can. Then his stomach rumbles again. Any fear is quashed by the gnawing in his stomach. He straightens his spine, pours the last few chip crumbs into his waiting mouth, chews, and swallows. "And we need more food."

Leland—caught completely off guard by the fact that the boy

dared to respond at all—just stares. Silent, tense seconds tick by as the two meet each other's eyes. Finally, Eric looks away.

"Did you know I played football in high school?"

Eric's eyes dart back to his father. "What? What does—"

"Not that you can tell it nowadays." Leland pats his round belly. "I was pretty good back in the day, though."

"I don't understand." Eric's eyebrows fold together until they nearly meet in the middle. "Why are—"

"That's how your mom and I first met. She was in the marching band. Did I ever tell you that?"

Eric slowly shakes his head from side to side, still completely lost on the point of this conversation. But since his words seem to be falling on deaf ears, he stops bothering to reply. He barely even remembers his mother. She'd died six years ago from cancer they hadn't caught in time. Ever since then, Leland hadn't been the same. And up till now, Leland had flat-out refused to talk about her.

"Prettiest trumpet player I ever met." Leland stares into the distance, a soft tenderness shining in his eyes. "Don't know what she ever saw in me, though."

Leland pauses long enough to toss back another mouthful of whiskey. "Ever since the world went to hell in a handbasket, I've been thinking a lot about her. I... I think if she was still here, I might've managed to be a decent person."

The bottle slips from Leland's hands, and he lets his eyes flutter closed. He continues faintly. "It's not right. It should've been me that got sick and died, not her. I'm sure as hell glad she didn't have to see the world come to this, though."

In a matter of seconds, Leland's muscles relax, and he resumes his snoring.

Eric gets up and grabs the half-eaten package of jerky from the ground. He takes it to the minivan, slides the door closed behind himself, and slowly chews the food as his father's words swim through his head.

. . .

- Western Kansas -
-- Day 26 --

Leland stops the minivan at the side of a large grocery store, kills the engine, and steps out onto the sidewalk. He takes a few steps and looks into the front of the store. The lights are off inside the building, and the overcast sky offers little light through the building's tall windows.

Leland returns, sits back in the driver's seat, and polishes off the last few drops of his beer. "Hey." When there's no response from the middle row of seats, Leland twists around to look.

The boy is leaning awkwardly to one side with his chin against his chest, breathing slowly. His eyelids are twitching ever-so-slightly. Even in his sleep, his stomach growls noisily.

With a low growl, Leland throws the empty beer can at his son, hitting Eric in the chest and startling him awake. Eric's eyes open wide, and his head jerks upright as he blinks wildly. It takes Eric a few seconds to understand what happened and for his heart to quit hammering inside his chest. When the sudden shock finally wears off, Eric slumps back against the seat again, staring at his father.

"Go in there and scope it out."

"What?!" Eric's eyes bug out as he looks between his father's face and the store's dark interior. "By myself?!"

"Someone's gotta be ready with the getaway vehicle if things go south."

"Wh... I..." Eric's chest is tight. His palms start to sweat, and he struggles to keep the panic from his voice. "C-can I at least have a flashlight?"

"Sure." Leland cracks open another beer, then turns to face forward again.

Eric blinks at the back of his father's head. His stomach gurgles loudly again. "Where is it?"

Leland shrugs.

Rain starts to lightly fall. The view through the windshield slowly blurs as the tiny droplets begin to dot the glass.

There's a long, tense pause. Finally, Eric finds his voice again. "It's too..." He pauses, drawing in a shaky breath. "It's-it's too dark. I can't tell if it's safe. Let's go somewhere else. Or wait till the sun comes back out."

"You want food and water?" Leland points at the building, turns toward Eric, and growls, "it's in there!"

"But..." Eric's stomach gurgles loudly. He presses a palm against his empty belly as he looks at the front of the store, then glances back at his father. Clenching his teeth, Eric yanks the minivan door open and steps out into the drizzling rain.

Water droplets cling to his short hair and soak into his shirt as he slowly approaches the glass doors and stops next to the entrance. Cupping his hands around his eyes, he leans close and peers through the glass at the dark, shadowy interior. Nothing seems to be moving. He steps back as the sky lights up in a quick, bright flash. Taking a deep breath, he reaches out, grabs the door handle, and pulls.

It doesn't budge.

Eric yanks harder this time and nearly falls backward when his hand slips off the damp metal handle. To make sure, he leans his shoulder into it and pushes. Still nothing.

Eric turns around and runs back toward the minivan. Meeting his father's eyes through the windshield, he shrugs and mouths the words, "it's locked."

Leland rolls his eyes. Grabbing an empty whiskey bottle from the floorboard, he climbs out and closes the minivan door as thunder rumbles softly in the distance.

"Move."

Eric hurries out of the way. Leland stomps over to the entrance, lifts one arm up to cover his eyes, then throws the bottle through the door. Glass rains down across the sidewalk and floor. Leland turns around and, with a jerk of his head, he signals for Eric to go inside.

Gritting his teeth, Eric obediently walks up and steps inside. Glass crunches beneath his shoes, and he slips as the pieces shift underneath him. He grabs a nearby shelf to break his fall, rights himself, and moves slowly onward.

Leland stands in the doorway, hesitating to come inside.

Eric goes to the left, speeding up as he gets to the decomposing produce section, trying desperately to get past the foul air as quickly as he can. But he nearly breaks into a sprint as he has to cross the area filled with rotting piles of packaged meats.

Finally, at the far end of the store where he can halfway breathe again, Eric stops and looks back over his shoulder. His dad is nowhere in sight. He shrugs. Turning his attention back to the shelves, Eric tears open a bag of trail mix and hungrily pours it into his mouth, sighing as the sweet and salty mixture reaches his belly. He looks around while he chews another large mouthful and spots an abandoned cart at the end of the aisle. He grabs it and hurries along, filling it with food and drinks.

Once the cart is on the verge of overflowing, Eric hurries up to the front of the store. His father is still nowhere to be seen.

"Dad? Where are you?"

Lightning flashes. Half a moment later, a loud, rumbling boom comes from outside. Eric jumps at the sudden noise, then he laughs nervously at his own jumpiness.

"Dad!"

After silently waiting a few seconds, Eric sighs and unlocks the shattered front door. He pushes the glassless door open, steers the cart through the doorway, and turns onto the sidewalk. Then he halts in his tracks.

Eric's jaw drops, and his heart begins to race. He should be able to see the minivan from here; its front end should be poking out beyond the corner of the building. But it's not. He struggles to breathe as he stands in the rain, feeling the tears sting his eyes. He can't help but wonder if Evie felt this same hopelessness.

Trembling, Eric lets go of the cart. He slowly lowers himself onto the wet sidewalk and buries his face in his hands.

At the sound of footsteps, Eric gasps. He doesn't have a weapon, and he knows he could only outrun one of the creatures for a little while. He jumps up and spins around, rapidly blinking as he tries to clear his vision, but the tears flow faster.

Glass crunches against the floor.

Breathing heavily and swiping at his eyes, Eric steps back.

The dark shape moves across the dark room, closer and closer, glass crunching under its feet. The monster reaches out, steps up to the doorway, and then...

"Knock that shit off, boy."

Eric gasps as he realizes it's his father stepping out of the shadows of the building. Leland has a case of beer tucked beneath his left arm, another case in his left hand, and his right clutches the handle of a basket filled with various brown and green bottles.

The terror written across Eric's face vanishes. He begins laughing wildly, even as the tears continue to spill. Overwhelmed by this confusing mixture of emotions, Eric walks up and throws his arms around Leland's waist.

"What's gotten into you?" Leland stares down at the boy before using his elbow to shove Eric away.

Eric's laughter vanishes as he stumbles back, crashing loudly into the shopping cart and wincing from its impact against his upper arm.

Leland growls and turns away. He walks past the cart and, for the first time, notices the empty parking space at the side of the building. "What the..." His voice trails away as he gawks.

Breaking into a jog, the liquid in the bottles sloshes noisily as Leland heads to the side of the building and disappears around the corner. Eric grabs the cart and follows a few paces behind.

The minivan sits there, thirty feet away from where they'd left it, its back bumper smashed against the corner of a big, green dumpster.

Letting out an incomprehensible shout of frustration, Leland marches down the sloped lot to the driver's door, drops the beer cases on the ground, reaches inside the minivan, and furiously shoves the gearshift from neutral into park. Eric knows what's coming. He leaves the cart behind and rushes around to the far side of the minivan, then ducks down out of sight. He clamps his hands over his ears.

Leland bellows a string of curses and a heavy, glass bottle slams hard into the side of the dumpster. The metal lets out a loud, rumbling boom from the impact, sounding like a violent crack of thunder right on top of them. As the bottle cracks open and hits the ground, the liquid oozes out, flows underneath the minivan, and coats the bottoms of Eric's shoes.

Yelling again, Leland throws another bottle, and another, until they're all lying cracked or shattered on the blacktop. His anger slightly mollified, Leland turns and stomps back into the store for replacements.

A quick flash lights up the entire sky.

Eric creeps out from his hiding place. He grabs the cart and hurries over to the waiting vehicle with it, quickly tossing his supplies inside. Once the cart is empty, Eric climbs inside the minivan. He moves past his usual spot in the middle row and sits down in the back row instead, well away from where the driver can reach. Buckling his seatbelt, he looks up in time to see his father stomping his way back. Eric crouches low in the seat, hoping his father won't notice him for a good, long while.

- Southwestern Kansas -
-- Day 28 --

It's been nearly forty-eight hours since Leland's outburst at the grocery store, and his temper has finally cooled somewhat. In that time, though, Eric has been trying to stay quiet and out of his father's sight. Leland's ever-present rage continues to simmer just below the surface.

The minivan speeds over a small pothole in the road, jostling Eric from his sleep. He sits up, rubs his eyes, and looks over the top of the middle row of seats and out the windshield. A thick layer of fog covers the world. Other than the trees that line each side of the road, there's nothing to see out there but white.

Uninterrupted static softly plays over the radio.

Leland takes a drink. Setting the half-empty can back in the cupholder, he looks into the rearview mirror and catches Eric's gaze. "You finally awake back there?"

"Yeah." Eric unconsciously runs a hand across the deep purple bruise on his upper arm. Deciding that his father's mood seems stable enough at the moment, he dares to ask a question. "Where are we going?"

"East."

"Oh." Eric waits, but no elaboration is given. "Where are we right now?"

"Somewhere in Kansas." Leland rubs a hand across the dark stubble that lines his chin, then turns to look back over his shoulder. "You still got any of them peanut butter crackers back there?"

"Uh," Eric pauses to look through the plastic sack in the floorboard by his feet. "Yeah, two bags left. You want 'em?"

Leland turns his focus back to the road. "Yeah, bring them up here."

Eric grabs the two snack-sized bags, unbuckles his seatbelt, and stands up. Hunching over slightly as he moves, he squeezes through the narrow gap at the side of the middle row.

"Here."

Leland twists to the side, looking back over his shoulder as he reaches for the crackers.

"Look out!" Eric shrieks the words as he twists around, fumbling for the nearest seatbelt.

Leland whips his head toward the front. Seeing the figure in the middle of the road, he slams the brakes and jerks the wheel to the side.

The tires screech.

With a loud *thud,* the vehicle collides with the person. The body launches into the air, slamming into the windshield and shattering the glass before the body rolls across the roof.

The minivan begins to spin out of control, tossing Eric hard into the door. He cries out as his already-bruised arm collides with the hard plastic.

All their bottles, cans, and food come loose, rolling or flying through the vehicle's interior.

Eric tries to move, but the force of the spin has him pinned against the wall. His stomach churns. The spiraling momentum of the minivan goes on and on and on until suddenly...

It stops.

Eric is abruptly flung to the other side of the minivan. His forehead collides with the window. He sinks into the floorboard as his vision goes black.

A few seconds pass before Eric slowly opens his eyes. His head throbs, and a streak of blood runs along his eyebrow and down the side of his face. Pushing himself upright, Eric slides open the door and scoots to the opening to put his feet on the ground. He tries to stand but a wave of vertigo sends him tumbling forward onto the grass. As his stomach rolls again, Eric leans over, but he manages to fight back the nauseous feeling with a few long, deep breaths.

He grabs the minivan door and slowly pulls himself to his feet. The world seems to spin around Eric. Moving slowly, cautiously, he makes his way around to the front of the vehicle. As he moves, he finally sees what brought them to such a sudden halt. The front end of the driver's side is smashed, wrapped halfway around a large tree.

Eric quickens his pace, and keeping one hand on the vehicle or the nearby trees as he moves, he walks around to the driver's door. He grabs the handle and pulls, but it won't budge.

"Dad!"

Leland doesn't move.

"Dad!" Eric pounds on the window. Just as he's about to return to the passenger's side door, Eric notices movement from within. He pounds against the glass again.

"Hmm." Leland groans as he opens his eyes. He turns toward the window. For several seconds, he stares, not fully comprehending what's happening. At last, Leland reaches out and turns the crank to roll down the window.

"Are you okay?"

Leland blinks slowly before shaking his head no.

Eric leans in slightly through the window. He can't see any blood or any obvious injuries. "What's wrong?"

"I... I can't move my leg. My head feels awful, but..." Leland squeezes his eyes shut and groans loudly again as the pain washes over him. "But it's my leg I'm more worried about."

Turning his head to the side, Eric looks toward the floor. The vehicle's structure around the pedals has completely caved in, trapping Leland's feet beneath the dash.

"I don't..." Eric steps back, looking at his father with wide eyes. "What do I do? I don't know what to do."

Leland reaches out, grabs the door handle, and pushes. It still won't move. He groans again as he slumps back on the seat. "Go find help!"

"How?" Eric turns and looks off into the thick fog. He looks back around as blood continues dripping from his forehead and down the side of his face. "Where am I supp—"

"Go, damn it!" Leland suddenly slams his fist onto the horn, and Eric jumps backward, covering his ears with his hands. "I don't give a flying fuck! Just find someone to get me the hell out of here!"

Eric backs away, shaking. Blood continues dripping steadily from the gash across his forehead. He goes back around the van and finds a few bottles of water and some candy bars. He stuffs them in his pockets and heads off into the fog without another word.

Leland leans back, sucking air through his teeth as the pain continues to build. He closes his eyes and listens to the silence.

After a few minutes, he notices the quiet sound of something scraping and dragging slowly across the ground. Leaning over, he twists to try to peek out the window. There on the road, covered in blood, is a zombie. The same one that had caused him to wreck in the first place. She's using her arms to drag herself down the road. Her legs are broken and useless, and one of them bends in an unnatural direction. One of the shattered femurs is scraping across the asphalt, making a noise reminiscent of nails across a chalk-board. Her entrails drag along the ground behind her, leaving a sticky, red trail.

Drawing a long, shaky breath, Leland ducks back inside the vehicle, then reaches over and slowly rolls up the window. As he leans back in the seat, he sits silently, hoping the monster will be gone soon. The scraping continues outside his door until, at last, it goes silent. Leland lets out his breath.

He leans to the side to look out the window again, fully expecting to see one last glimpse of the zombie as she pulls herself off in the distance to disappear into the fog. There's no sign of her, though. The color drains from his face as he realizes the bloody trail doesn't continue straight. It curves and disappears somewhere in front of the destroyed minivan.

Suddenly, a hand appears over the front edge of the hood. The other hand grabs the tree, and the zombie begins pulling herself upward.

Leland's heart races as he sits there, weaponless and trapped. His eyes dart around him, looking for something to use to defend himself. There's nothing available up front—the wreck made sure of that. Just behind the passenger's seat, there's a whiskey bottle. He leans back and stretches out his right hand for it.

The zombie makes her way up onto the hood, and the metal pops loudly beneath her weight. She opens her mouth and roars.

Leland shouts and slams his left hand onto the horn. All his noise is drowned out by the sound of her wail.

She starts to punch the shattered windshield.

Leland keeps extending as far as he can, grunting as he struggles. He begins to sweat. The bottle is so close he can touch it but can't get a grip on it. The plastic and metal around his legs keep digging deeper into his flesh. Tears sting at his eyes.

The windshield bows in the middle and starts to loosen at the edges.

"You piece of shit!" He hurls insults off into the fog, where his son disappeared. He stretches. His sweaty fingertips slide across the clear glass. The bottle rolls away from his touch. "How dare you abandon me, you little brat?!"

All of a sudden, the center of the windshield gives way, raining glass down on Leland and covering him in dozens of tiny cuts. The zombie drags herself through the gap. Blood and guts fall down on Leland.

Throwing a hand down to his side, Leland grabs the lever there and makes his seat back fall backward. His hand finds the bottle, and at last, he grabs hold of it. Leland forces himself upright again as the zombie lunges. The alcohol, the concussion, the fear all hit him at once, sending his head spinning. He tries to swing at her but misses. She grabs his arm, and her teeth sink into his wrist as he jerks away, tearing off a chunk of his flesh.

He shrieks as he swings the bottle again, connecting with her cheek this time and knocking her sideways. Before she can recover, he hits her again and again, over and over, until he can no longer tell where she ends and the car begins.

As the adrenaline fades, his arm aches and burns in a way he's never felt before. He pulls his belt off and wraps it tightly around his arm to stem the bleeding. Then, he turns and glares into the wall of unending white fog where Eric went, and he screams.

Leland still holds a tiny glimmer of hope that he'll be saved. But deep down, he knows he's going to die here. Slowly. In agony.

And alone.

27

FINDERS

- Southern Missouri -

-- Day 29 --

Her tears have long since stopped and now, as Abigail sits on the muddy creek bank, her expression is vacant. For ages, she stares into the murky water, unseeing and fighting to keep any thoughts from her mind. The sun beats down on her, turning her face and neck a bright pink, but she's too numb to feel it. Abigail knows she shouldn't let her guard down like this, but inside, there's a darkness, threatening to swallow her whole. Even the loud growling of her stomach and the dry stickiness of her mouth doesn't break through the deep abyss of despair that's growing inside her. She doesn't have the strength to worry about physical comforts or safety.

Around her, birds chirp, squirrels dash up and down the trees, and puffy white clouds drift lazily across the sky. Nature—oblivious to the end of the world—continues on. Time slips by in a hazy blur. Abigail sits and stares off into the distance, softly rubbing the bandage on her arm, no longer able to keep her thoughts at bay.

I'm alone. For the first time in my life, I am completely alone. It's surreal. Last month, my family was happy and healthy and planning a big get-together for the Fourth of July. But now...

Jake only had a week after being bitten. Mom barely lasted a couple days. Now, everyone I've known and loved my whole life is just gone. Soon, I'll be gone too. Probably less than a week. I just need to get as far away from people as possible before it happens.

She stays there, unmoving for a long time as that thought—that need to run away—rattles around in her mind.

At last, Abigail stands up. She turns and walks slowly up the small hill, climbs into the car, and closes the door. She taps the lock button and stares out at the road in front of her. Up ahead, about a mile or so, are the deserted remains of one of the military roadblocks. Orange and white striped signs, abandoned cars, and decaying corpses all lie there, broken and abandoned.

She turns away. Leaning across to the other side of the car, she opens the glove box and pulls out a brittle, wrinkled map and as she begins to carefully unfold it, the door handle rattles. Unfazed, she flattens the map across the steering wheel before finally turning to look over her shoulder.

A zombie stands there, glaring through the window. If it weren't for the trail of dried blood down his chin and the black-streaked eyes, he would've been handsome. Abigail lets out a half-hearted chuckle at the sudden, inane thought before turning her focus back to the map.

Finding a simple county road that leads to a different highway on the map, she uses her finger to trace a route off to the north-west even though she doesn't have any particular destination. She doesn't know how far she'll make it anyway. Her only plan is to get somewhere with a lower population. Somewhere that she isn't likely to hurt anyone when she turns.

Abigail refolds the map and tosses it onto the passenger seat. The zombie roars and starts to pound the glass with his fists. Abigail twists around—still too numb to feel fear—and looks into his eyes. Turning the car on, she puts it in gear and starts to drive.

As the zombie's reflection in the rearview mirror starts to shrink, Abigail's apathy suddenly and unexpectedly turns to rage. She clenches her jaw, and her knuckles turn white against the steering wheel, then slams on the brakes and watches as the zombie keeps running toward her. Hot tears roll down her cheeks. She throws the car into reverse, twists to look over her shoulder, and stomps on the gas pedal. The tires squeal against the pavement. She flies backward, watching as the zombie gets closer and closer until there's a loud *wham!* Then there's a sickening *crunch* beneath the tires. When she finally stops, the zombie's body is lying in front of the car, his legs and torso crushed.

She steps out of the car, shaking and red-faced. She moves quickly around to the back—the bumper is caved in on one side and covered in blood—and she opens up the trunk. Grabbing the tire iron, she goes in front of the car and stops just outside the zombie's reach.

The zombie tries to roar, but its lungs can't quite hold enough air for that anymore. All that comes out is a weak, breathy moan.

Abigail stands there, transfixed by the dilated pupils set against that background of jagged black lines. Once upon a time, eyes like that had terrified her. But now, in this moment, they are fascinating.

She knows her own eyes will look that way soon.

Raising the tire iron overhead, Abigail yells as she brings it down with all her strength. Over and over again, she slams it into him, meting out revenge against this man for something that was never his fault. She keeps battering him until long past when he's unmoving, and his face is nothing but a bloody pile of gore.

Now, with an aching throat and barely able to raise her arms, she takes the bloodied tire iron back to the car. She tosses it in the trunk and closes it. The zombie's blood soaks into her shirt, dripping steadily off her hands and chin.

Abigail slides back into the driver's seat. Tilting the mirror, she looks up and wonders at the reflection that she hardly recognizes as her own.

- Southwestern Kansas -
-- Day 30 --

Abigail parks in front of the feed store. The peeling paint and cracked front window make it look as though it was abandoned long before the world ended, and it's no wonder. The place sits alone, in the middle of nowhere. She can't imagine it had much business even in its heyday. It doesn't matter, though. She only stopped here because of the growing heaviness of her eyelids. Double-checking that all the doors are locked, Abigail yawns, reclines the seat back as far as it will go, and closes her eyes.

A dream is creeping into the corners of her mind when her eyelids fly open. Someone is shouting in the distance. She sits up and turns to look out the window.

"Help!"

A young boy jogs slowly toward the car, looking half-dead with exhaustion. His feet drag with every step. His eyelids droop, and even from this distance, she can tell he's struggling to catch his breath.

Abigail watches. She has one hand on the door handle, ready to leap out and help him; the other rests on the gear shift, prepared to put the car in drive and speed away. A hot, shooting pain in Abigail's arm draws her attention and she looks down at the bandage on her forearm. Any minute, she might turn. She can't bear the idea of hurting a child, especially one who's begging her for help. But she wonders, *Is abandoning him any better?*

"Help me! Please!"

She sighs. Letting her hand slide off the gear shift, she opens the door and steps out.

The boy finally comes to a stop several feet away from Abigail. He doubles over and puts his hands on his knees, breathing heavily. "You have... to help. My dad is... trapped."

"What happened?"

He points over his shoulder in the direction he came. "He wrecked our van... Hit a tree and... it smashed up the front and trapped... his legs."

Abigail's eyebrows shoot up toward her hairline. "I can't promise anything, kid. That was... That was not good even back when hospitals were still a thing, and I'm definitely not a doctor. Can you show me where he is?"

The boy nods as he straightens up. "I think so."

Grabbing her bat and first aid kit, she takes off beside him.

"What's your name?"

"Abby."

"Thanks for helping me, Abby."

Under her breath, she mutters, "Don't thank me yet."

"What?" He looks up at her with innocent eyes.

"Uh... What's your name?"

"Eric."

Abigail nods and they continue on in silence.

The boy zigzags slowly between the trees, wearily dragging his feet and moving slower with every step. Before long, his knee buckles, and he lurches forward. Abigail reaches out and grabs hold of Eric's shirt, barely managing to break his fall. Holding him by the shoulders, she turns him around to face her.

"Okay, kid." Abigail pauses to look really look him over. He seems to be struggling to keep his eyes open. A deep, purple bruise covers one arm, and a scabbed-over gash mars his forehead. His clothes are caked in dirt; twigs and leaves are caught in his short hair. She squints at him. "How long have you been out here running?"

"A day and a half."

Abigail's jaw drops. "A *day and a half?* You... You were alone in the woods for a *day and a freaking half?* You stopped and slept during that, right?"

Eric shakes his head and sways on his feet as he does so. "I sat down a little bit, but I was afraid to stop and close my eyes for very long."

"Wow, I just..." Abigail stands and blinks at him, lost for words. "Okay, you can't keep going. Come on back to the car. It's time for you to rest."

"But..."

Abigail wraps an arm around the boy's shoulders and guides him back to the car. His protests quickly vanish into a wide yawn. Within a few minutes, she has him settled into the car with strict instructions that he is to stay there and sleep while she goes inside the feed store building to look for anything useful.

Truth be told, she really just wants to be alone to think.

She walks up the concrete steps. The jamb is busted, and the door swings open with just a touch, its hinges squeaking loudly as it moves. She takes half a step inside and reaches one hand out in search of a light switch. She finds it, but nothing happens. Leaning forward, she peeks inside. The sun shines brightly through the door and a couple windows at the end of the building. That'll have to be good enough.

Lifting the bat up to her shoulder, Abigail steps inside. In a matter of minutes, she's walked through the entire building. She's confident that she's alone, so she lowers the bat and begins to look around as her mind races.

Packages of canned dog food line one of the shelves. She looks at the nearest label—chopped, ground liver—and for the first time in days, her stomach rumbles loudly. She picks up several cases of various flavors and hurries them out to the car's trunk.

Eric snores softly in the car's back seat.

Returning to the building, Abigail looks around for anything to drink. First, she notices a small refrigerator next to the cash register. She gathers up all the sodas and teas and sets them by the door. Then, seeing the water cooler and the unopened, five-gallon jug at its side. It takes her a few trips, but she finally manages to get all the drinks into the car as well.

At last, she climbs back into the car. She's only half-ready to talk to the kid. Fortunately for her, he's sprawled across the back seat, thoroughly passed out. Abigail lays back in the driver's seat, resolved to speak to him as soon as he wakes up. In the meantime, she decides she'll close her eyes for just a minute.

- Southwestern Kansas -
-- Day 31 --

Abigail opens her eyes a crack as the sun shines brightly through the windshield and lights up her face. She's disoriented. She doesn't realize immediately that "just a minute" turned into sleeping through the entire night. But eventually, she realizes why the sun is suddenly on the opposite side of the sky.

Holding her hand up to block the light, she tilts the seat upright and slowly angles her face toward the rearview mirror to check her eyes. No black specks.

Yet.

Yawning, Abigail twists around in the seat to look in the back. Eric is still lying on his stomach, with the side of his face smushed against the seat, and he's snoring softly. His legs rest at an awkward angle against the door. One of his arms hangs limply onto the floorboard while the other must be tucked underneath his belly.

The growling in Abigail's stomach cuts through the quiet atmosphere inside the car.

Quietly turning around, Abigail opens the door and steps out, walking around to the trunk. She opens it and stops to look. Hesitantly selecting a can, she pulls it from its case and looks at it. At the bottom, it says, "Turkey and chicken in brown gravy." She moves her hand to see the top half of the label. A panting golden retriever looks back at her from above the bolded words "Canine's Choice."

Abigail's lip curls in disgust. But as her stomach rumbles again, she sighs, lifts the tab, and pulls the top from the can. Slowly, she lifts the open container up to her face and tips a tiny bit into her waiting mouth. The flavor is so much better than she expected—surprisingly good, in fact—she nearly moans in satisfaction. Chewing quickly and taking another bite, she wonders if the exquisite flavor is due to her overly-empty stomach or if dog food has always tasted this fantastic.

Leaving the trunk lid open as she continues to eat, she returns to the front of the car and slides into her seat. She notices that Eric is sitting up, looking at her. She quickly swallows the food in her mouth. The two of them look at each other in silence for a moment before Abigail finally blurts out, "Hungry?"

"Yeah."

Getting back out, she retrieves a couple water bottles and a can of dog food for him. She offers them to him as she gets back inside. Eric makes the same face she did when he notices the can's label. He hesitates for a moment, but finally, reluctantly, he takes a bite.

The two sit in uncomfortable silence as they finish their meal and avoid each other's gaze. As Eric polishes off the last few bites, he sets the empty can down and looks at Abigail. "So, are we gonna go find my dad now?"

"Well..." Abigail pauses. She picks up their empty cans and stares at them, momentarily distracted by the thought that there's no more garbage service. She still hates to litter, but wonders to herself what other choice she has now. Giving her head a shake, she tosses their empty cans out the window, then turns to face the boy again. "Do you know which road you were on when you wrecked? Or which town you were in?"

Eric shakes his head.

"That's what I was afraid of." Abigail sighs heavily. "So, if we don't know which road he's near, we can't drive there. Best we could do is try to retrace your steps."

"Okay..."

Abigail sighs again. She loathes being the one to break bad news to this kid, but who else is there? "So, assuming you ran in a perfectly straight line and we could go straight to him, it'd take us at least a day and a half to get to him. But, unfortunately, I doubt you went in a straight line. So we'd have to take that long, and there's no telling if we'd even find him after all that walking. You with me so far?"

"I think so."

"At this point, your dad's been trapped for at least two days now, almost three. Probably bleeding during that time. By the time we found him—well, *if* we found him—it would've been something like five days since the wreck. Even if we found him and he somehow managed to survive that long, bleeding and without supplies..."

Eric's eyebrows crinkle up as he looks at her. "What?"

"I'm sorry, kid. I... I don't know how to explain this gently, but..." She inhales shakily and then exhales slowly. "I doubt he'd survive that long. And even if he did, I'm not sure I could get him out. And then, if I somehow managed to get him out, I wouldn't be able to do much—if anything—for the bleeding or the infection that's likely to happen after. I'm really sorry."

Eric swallows hard. "So what does—"

"I can't help you save your dad, kid."

He looks at her, blinking slowly as he processes her words. And then, he surprises her. She'd expected tears and fighting. Instead, even as the sadness shines in his eyes, she can see the tension go out of his shoulders, and he leans back in the seat without a word.

Tilting her head to the side, she studies the boy intently. A million thoughts run through Abigail's mind. She starts with what she hopes is the simplest one: "How'd you get that gash on your forehead?"

"Huh?" Eric touches his fingertips to the long scab and winces. "Oh. I hit my head when we wrecked."

"And what about that big bruise on your arm? Was that from the wreck too?"

"No." Eric looks away. His jaw is firmly set and he refuses to elaborate.

Abigail nods. She unwraps the bandage from her arm and holds the bite out for him to see. "I'm heading west, see how far I can get. I don't know if it's a good idea for you to come with me, kid."

His eyes go wide as the color drains from his face. "Please don't leave me like Evie!"

The two stare at one another. Abigail doesn't understand who Evie is but watches silently as Eric's eyes fill with tears. "Fine. You can stay with me for now, if you want. But there's a condition."

"What?"

She looks at him and waits until he meets her stare. "As soon as my eyes start turning black, you have to leave me."

He chews his lip.

"Look, kid. I get it, but if you can't agree to that, then I can't take you with me at all. I don't want to hurt anyone, and I'm afraid I will if you stick with me too long."

At last, Eric nods and blinks away his tears.

And with that, she starts up the car and puts it in drive.

The sun is still high in the sky, but the tank is running low with no gas stations in sight. On top of that, Abigail is exhausted. Eric is passed out in the back seat once again. So, when she spots the driveway jutting off the side of the narrow dirt road, she doesn't hesitate to turn in.

Rolling slowly up the driveway toward the barn, she looks

across the unmown grass. A few cows wander through the yard, grazing near a broken gate. Chickens wander freely.

As she comes to a stop in front of the barn doors, she glances back at the pile of black, ashen remains of a house and wonders what happened there.

28

SICK

- Northern Utah -

-- Day 30 --

Brad brushes Evie's long hair back behind her shoulders and gently rubs a hand across her back as she doubles over again. Nothing is left in her stomach, but her insides don't seem convinced. When the nausea finally ebbs, Evie drops onto the ground next to Brad, shivering. Sweat drips from her forehead. Momentarily returning to the pickup, Brad retrieves a small blanket, walks over, and wraps it around Evie's shoulders.

After promising he'll be back soon, Brad stands up and heads over to where Melvin and Joan are sitting.

"Seems like she's got a pretty good fever going right now." Brad carefully keeps his voice low as he talks to the other adults. "And I know she's dehydrated."

"Hmm." Melvin shakes his head gently, frowning. "Poor kid."

"Do you think she's contagious?"

Brad sighs heavily. He looks over at Evie as she sits there, facing away from the group with her knees clutched against her chest. Turning back to Joan, Brad shrugs. "I have no idea. Hopefully not, but... I just don't know."

"She's probably going to turn soon. Next thing you know, she's going to be biting us as we sleep."

"Joan," Brad rolls his eyes. "She wasn't bitten."

Joan folds her arms across her chest, looking over at the girl. She purses her lips but doesn't say anything more.

The wrinkles along Melvin's forehead deepen as he looks over at her. "Well, whether it's contagious or not, we've got to do something for her."

Brad nods. "I agree."

"Like what exactly?" Joan's eyes dart from one man to the other, and she raises her eyebrows at them expectantly. When they don't answer, she goes on. "We can't go to a doctor or a hospital. We don't have any nausea meds. We don't have any crackers or ginger ale. We don't even have any peppermints. So what can we do besides sit here and wait it out?"

Melvin leans back against a tree trunk, shaking his head slowly from side to side. "Son, I hate to admit it, but I think she's right. As awful as it is, there really isn't—"

"No!" Brad hisses the word at his father. Then he takes a deep breath and tries to continue more calmly. "I cannot just sit idly by while she's this sick. She can't keep anything down, and her temperature keeps rising. That was dangerous enough even in the before times."

"Oh, *well,* in that case, let's just load her in the pickup and take a nice little drive down to the nearest walk-in clinic then!"

"You don't have to be snarky about it." Brad glares at Joan. "But yeah, basically."

The trio stands in silence for a moment, staring at one another, before Joan finally lets out a deadpan, "What?"

"There was that shopping center a few miles back. I'm not sure what all they had, but there's bound to be a grocery store or pharmacy or something there that has basic medications. We'll head there and—"

"Brad, that's way too risky!"

Brad closes his eyes and inhales, then exhales slowly. When he looks at her again, he goes on, "Okay, *I* will go there and get her some meds."

"No." All eyes turn toward Melvin. "We're not splitting up. And besides, we agreed we weren't stopping inside any towns or cities if we could help it. Towns mean people, and where there was people, now there's zombies."

"Alright, look. I am going to look for meds with or without you. Because—" Brad catches Joan's eye as she tries interrupting him with another argument. With one eyebrow raised, he stares at her until she clamps her mouth shut. "*Because,* even if that kid didn't need it right now and even if she's not contagious, one of us three is going to have a fever at some point. Or a bad cough. Or a severely upset stomach. I'm honestly surprised we haven't gotten sick before now with the random crap we've been eating and the questionable water sources we've had this past week. So, I *am* going. Now you two need to decide if you're going with me or staying here until I get back. I'm leaving in five minutes."

With that, Brad turns on his heel and walks over to Evie and sits down on the ground beside her. Evie's eyes are closed, and she looks like she's finally getting some rest, but as soon as Brad is settled next to her, she leans over and buries herself against his shoulder. Wrapping his arm around her, he gently strokes her hair.

At the sound of footsteps, Brad turns. Melvin and Joan come up beside him.

"We're all going with you. Like I said, I really don't think we should be splitting up. Us three will just wait in the truck while you go searching. I don't think you should be going in alone..." Melvin pauses as he shoots a disappointed glance over at Joan. She turns her face away as he continues. "But I'm not too great at running, and Evie sure isn't fit to run right now either. And Joan... Well, she already told you her stance."

"Okay."

Brad leans down and softly tells Evie that they're going to go find her some medicine. She mumbles some incoherent reply. Scooping the girl into his arms, Brad stands up, carries her to the truck, and slides her into the seat. He climbs in beside her. The others get in as well, and they start to drive.

A few minutes later, Melvin is backing into a parking spot near the front of a large convenience store at the end of the long strip of buildings. He puts it into park but leaves the motor running as he looks out across the lot. Several dozen abandoned cars remain there, a monument to their lost owners.

"I still don't think this is a good idea." Melvin turns to Brad. "But if you're still planning on doing it, get a move on so we can get out of here quick."

"Stay here, Evie. I'm going to go look for that medicine, okay?"

Evie's head moves up and down the tiniest fraction of an inch.

Brad gets out and grabs his sledgehammer from the truck bed and turns toward the convenience store, but something catches his eye to his left. A small hardware store sits there. He heads in that direction first.

He approaches the glass door, pulls it open, and enters the dark interior. A bell overhead announces his entrance. Quickly reaching up, he silences it and stops to listen, but all is quiet. Turning to the side, he finds the light switch and flips it up and down a few times, but the room remains dark. The only light is the small sliver of sunshine leaking through the front door and the eerie red glow from an exit sign at the back of the room.

After standing still a few minutes and waiting on his eyes to adjust to the dim interior, he grabs a basket and hurries down the first row of shelves. It doesn't have what he's looking for, but on a whim, he grabs some rolls of duct tape and quickly moves on to the next aisle.

Finding a box of disposable respirator masks, he pulls one from the package, slips it onto his face, and drops the rest in his basket. Again, he hurries on.

When he locates the safety goggles, he comes to a halt. Three hang on the shelf. He puts one on and sets the others inside his basket. He's suspected for a while now that getting the infected blood in your eyes or mouth is a terrible idea, but he hadn't had an opportunity to do much about it. But now that he's found the goggles, there aren't enough for everyone. He stands there, tapping his foot, trying to think of an alternative.

At last, he has an idea and hustles down a few more aisles. Then, in the far back corner, he spots the welding masks. He grabs one, tosses it in the basket, and heads back out into the sunshine.

Brad sets the basket in the back of the pickup. Joan is turned around in the seat, looking confused. She mouths something to him that might have been, "What the hell are you doing?"

He mouths back, "Almost done."

With one last glance out across the lot, Brad heads toward the grocery store entrance. The doors slide open at his approach. He lifts the sledgehammer to rest on his shoulder, takes a deep breath, and steps inside. He stops momentarily as he walks in and is greeted by the bright lights and upbeat muzak still playing over the store speakers. The cheery atmosphere feels utterly surreal and entirely wrong, given the current state of the world. Something about it sets his teeth on edge and makes him wish he were back in the unlit hardware store.

Choking back his fear, he grabs some reusable shopping bags from beside the nearest register and hurries off toward the pharmacy area. Before long, he's filled the first bag to the brim with a variety of medications he thinks might be useful sometime. Pain relievers, fever reducers, nausea meds, and so on go into the bag. Toothpaste and other toiletries fill the next bag. He loops the bag handles over his left arm and holds the sledgehammer in his right hand.

Brad turns to head toward the grocery section. He's only taken a few steps when he freezes in his tracks. Why is it so quiet now? His head whips to the side, searching his surroundings. His heart pounds in the deepening silence. The muzak suddenly starts again with a new song, and Brad jumps. He laughs and continues on his way, but that nagging fear has him moving even more quickly than before.

Moving past the checkout counter, the air smells sickly sweet. Gnats fill the room, swarming in black clouds over the slowly decomposing remains of the cheap flower bouquets by the cash register. The hair on the back of his neck begins to rise, and he swears he can feel eyes looking at him. He breaks into a jog.

The bags slap against his side and the pill bottles rattle noisily as he heads into another aisle. He skids to a halt. Oatmeal and granola bars are shoved into the next bag, along with some nuts and trail mix. These two bags of food go over his right arm. Awkwardly maneuvering the sledgehammer around the groceries, he cradles it to his chest and turns to leave.

Brad starts back the way he came, and something stops him in his tracks. His chest feels tight; he begins to sweat through the sides of his shirt. He's not sure why, but his feet refuse to carry him that way again.

Slowly, he backs up a few paces, then suddenly spins around and bursts into a sprint. Footsteps pound behind him. A zombie's roar tears through the building, echoing off the tile floors and block walls.

He tries to move faster. The bags slam into him with every step, and the weight of everything in his arms slows him down. His heart pounds. His breath comes in ragged gasps. He can't swing the sledgehammer without dropping everything, but he refuses to risk losing what he came here for.

The zombie is gaining on him.

Brad jams a hand into the first bag and yanks out a blue bottle.

He rips the plastic tamper seal off with his teeth, then quickly unscrews the cap.

Daring to take one glance back, he sees the zombie. He can't be more than ten feet away. Brad faces the front again, ignores the burning in his chest, and forces himself to move faster.

At the end of the next row, Brad grabs onto the shelf and turns around the corner into that aisle. The bags swing out to his side, tossing out some of his supplies. He doesn't have time to deal with it, though. He chucks the opened bottle of liquid behind himself, then picks up speed again.

A second later, the zombie turns and hits the patch of spilled liquid. The zombie's feet fly out from underneath him, and he crashes loudly into the metal shelves, sending mounds of plastic bowls and plates clattering to the floor. The shelves rock precariously.

Brad makes it to the exit just as the zombie rights himself. The zombie shoves the wobbling shelf, and it topples over, finally slamming against the floor. He roars and takes off sprinting, his liquid-medicine-coated shoes squeaking loudly against the hard floor with every step.

Brad rushes out the door and flings himself into the truck bed, shouting at his father to drive. Melvin throws the truck into gear and speeds off across the lot and out to the road.

The zombie bursts through the doors. He stops on the sidewalk. He roars his frustration at them.

Ignoring the monster's wail, Brad forces air into his tired lungs and looks down at the bags on his arms. The nausea meds and fever reducers sit there at the top. He smiles as he leans back, victorious.

29

RASCAL

- Southwestern Kansas -

-- Day 34 --

The car is parked inside the dark barn. Eric is nowhere to be seen. Abigail is tucked into the shadowy corner of the backseat, trying not to worry about the kid she knows will have to leave her soon. The thought crosses her mind that maybe he's already gone. But that thought doesn't bring the relief she thought it would.

Aside from the protectiveness she feels toward the kid, she feels almost numb. Hopeless.

She sits in darkness, waiting for the change she knows is coming.

Abigail jumps at the unexpected sound of knocking beside her, and she turns to see Eric's silhouette standing just outside the car door. She sighs as she opens the door just a crack. "Look, kid, I'm sorry, but I don't know when I'm gonna turn. I just think it's best if I'm alone right now."

"I know. I just..." He pauses and starts to back away.

Sighing again, Abigail swings the door the rest of the way open. "What is it?"

"I thought Rascal might cheer you up."

"What?"

Something lands in her lap abruptly, and Eric wordlessly turns and dashes away. Abigail reaches up and switches on the dome light to see a gray cat staring up at her. Chuckling slightly, she sets a hand on his back. Immediately, he starts purring, kneads her legs with his paws, then curls up to sleep.

"Well, hi, Rascal."

Abigail watches as he opens his eyes. He lets out a soft meow, and she scoops him up to cradle him in her arms. Over and over, Rascal bumps his forehead against her chin. Clutching the purring cat to her chest, she lies down in the seat. As her tears slowly begin to fall, so do the walls she'd been building around up her heart.

Abigail's eyelids flutter open. It's later in the day, but it's brighter inside the barn now as the setting sun peeks in through the open loft doors. The gray tomcat is still lying tucked close to her chest, snoring softly.

She pushes herself upright. Rascal opens his eyes, meows a couple times in annoyance, stretches, then curls up again on the seat; he's soon back to snoring. As Abigail sits there, rubbing the sleep from her eyes, she hears the front door of the car open, and Eric climbs into the passenger seat. He turns around in the seat to face her, and she looks over at him.

"You feeling any better?" Eric chews his lip as he watches her, anxiously waiting for her response.

"Yeah. Thank you... What was your name again?"

"Eric."

"Thank you, Eric."

He grins, reaching down into the backseat to scratch Rascal behind the ears.

"First of all, how'd you come up with his name?"

Giggling, Eric says, "I dunno. He just looks like a Rascal."

"I can see that." Abigail laughs. "So, how'd you know that Rascal was what I needed?"

Eric's smile fades. He shrugs. "That always made Evie feel better. When she was sad or scared, I'd bring her a teddy bear. She'd cry and hug it, and then she'd be happy again. You looked sad, so I thought you might want something soft to hug too."

A lump forms in Abigail's throat. She swallows hard and sniffles before finally finding her voice. "That was very kind of you, Eric."

The pair sit in silence for a time. Eventually, Abigail tilts her head as she looks at him. "Who is Evie? You've mentioned that name before."

His lip begins to tremble. He quickly blinks back his tears and then turns his face away from her. "My twin sister."

"Oh. Did she..." Abigail's heart aches at the boy's sadness, and her words trail away as she struggles for a tactful way to ask her question. "Do you want to tell me what happened to her?"

There's a long pause. At last, Eric speaks in a choked voice. "We were camping and got split up. One of those... Those monsters chased us, and... And my dad left her there! And... And she..."

Eric's voice gives out as he bursts into sobs. Abigail quickly climbs out of the car and goes up to his seat. She gently scoots him over and sits down beside him, stroking his back and letting him cry until he can't cry anymore. When he finally goes quiet and looks up at her, his eyes are red and puffy, and Abigail's shoulder is thoroughly soaked.

Looking down and picking at a loose thread at the bottom of his shirt, Eric changes the subject. "What were you sad about?"

"Well," Abigail sighs. "I've lost my entire family since this all started. But on top of that, I was bit a few days ago. So I'll become one of those zombies any day now."

"How do you know that you'll become one?"

"I... Well..." Abigail stammers as the innocent question forces her to think through what she truly knows about the situation. "I mean..."

"Does everybody become a zombie if they get bit?"

"I... I thought so, but..." Abigail pauses as she leans over to look at her eyes in the rearview mirror. Still, no signs of black. "You know, that's a really good question, Eric. I don't know."

"Well, I hope you don't become one." Eric yawns widely and snuggles up against Abigail's side again. "I like you, Abby. You feel safe."

30

ACCUSATIONS

- Northern Utah -
-- Day 33 --

Brad suddenly opens his eyes in the dim, pre-dawn light. Lying there in the bed of the pickup, he props himself up on his elbows to look toward the corner of the truck bed near his feet. His father —although sitting upright against the corner with his head resting against the glass—is still sound asleep and snoring softly. Turning his head to the right, he sees Joan lying there, stretched out alongside him. For a moment, he's taken back to a time before all this started, back when the world was still right. He grins at her sleeping form. But the new realities slowly creep back in. His smile fades as he remembers that it had been her turn to keep watch. Fondness turns to frustration.

Brad reaches out, just about to shake Joan awake and ask her how she could be so careless. But he stops. He jerks his head toward the front of the truck as he realizes something he'd missed a moment ago: the passenger side door is ajar.

Standing up, Brad jumps out of the pickup bed and hurries around the side. As the truck bounces from his sudden movement, Melvin and Joan are both startled awake.

"Evie?" Brad yanks the door the rest of the way open.

"What's going on?" Melvin rubs his eyes with his knuckles.

Brad slams the door shut. "She's not in there."

Joan sighs, lays back, and pulls the blanket up over her shoulder. "She can't be that far away."

Storming back to the pickup bed, Brad grabs Joan's blanket and yanks it off her. "Why weren't you keeping watch? It was your turn! If you were getting too tired, you should've woke me!"

Rolling over and pushing herself up, Joan glares at him. "I would've woken up if anything came close!"

"Would you? You didn't wake up when she opened the door and waltzed away!"

Melvin sits in the corner, looking at the pair as they glower at one another. Leaning forward, he picks up his shovel and clears his throat, disrupting the staring contest.

"Gah!" Brad growls his frustration. He picks up his sledgehammer from the corner of the truck bed as he looks off into the trees. "Come on! We've got to go find her."

"I still don't have any kind of weapon." Joan climbs out of the truck. She plants her hands on her hips as she looks at Brad. "What exactly do you expect me to do if we come across a zombie?"

"Well, I guess you better follow us and just *keep watch* then, huh?" Brad turns around and stomps off toward the trees, quickly disappearing into the forest before the others can catch up.

Melvin steps out of the pickup bed with his shovel in hand. He extends it out before himself, silently offering it to Joan. She rolls her eyes and storms off after Brad. Melvin sighs and goes after her.

Joan stops near the trees. The sun is beginning to light up their little campsite, but the forest is still cloaked in shadow. Melvin walks up beside her and quietly looks off into the foliage where his son had just vanished. They can't see Brad. From somewhere in the distance, Brad's voice—muffled by the dense leaves—calls out Evie's name.

Raising the shovel up to rest on his shoulder, Melvin mutters under his breath, "So much for not splitting up." He shakes his head. Taking a deep breath, he steps into the forest and motions for Joan to follow.

Joan grabs a fallen tree branch, slides her mask and goggles into place, then follows close behind.

"Evie!"

Melvin pauses to listen. He can faintly hear Brad calling the name as well, but there's no response from the little girl. He moves forward a few more feet and stops again.

"Do you hear that?"

Joan ducks down and turns her head to the side. There's a faint rustling, like something is digging through the undergrowth. "Yeah. I think it's coming from over that way."

Turning toward the noise, Melvin moves past a pair of trees, then stops another time. Several feet in front of him, a man is crouched down, reaching for something underneath a fallen tree.

"Hey. You need help?"

The man doesn't respond. He keeps reaching for the thing, grunting softly as he tries to grab it.

"Hey, mister!" Melvin and Joan take a step closer.

Clapping a hand on Melvin's shoulder, Joan hisses, "I don't think this is a good idea."

"Yeah, may—" Melvin gasps. Just behind the man, there lies something that looks very much like a little girl's sneaker. Finding a small rock, Melvin picks it up and flings it at the man.

The stone clips the man's knee. His head jerks toward Melvin. The black eyes fix on Melvin, and the zombie roars.

Melvin rushes forward, shovel held high, and he whacks the zombie across the face. With a loud *thunk*, the zombie's cheekbone caves in. He stumbles sideways and falls.

Melvin teeters from the shock of the impact. His lungs are struggling for air. He tries to straighten up and lift the shovel again, but there's an uncomfortable pressure in his chest, and his vision swims. Knees buckling, he slumps over against a nearby tree.

The zombie leaps to his feet with another roar and charges forward. Melvin clenches his teeth. Suddenly, there's a shriek behind him. Joan dashes forward with her branch held overhead. She brings it down hard on the top of the zombie's head, and the thick branch snaps in two. The zombie's legs give out from underneath him. He collapses to the ground.

Chest heaving, Joan stares at the zombie as she slowly backs toward Melvin. She takes the shovel from his hands, then she moves forward again. The zombie starts to push himself up onto his hands and knees. Rushing at the zombie, Joan brings the pointed end of the shovel down into the base of his skull. He collapses and blood sprays out in a tall arc, showering Joan from the top of her head all the way down to the tips of her toes. But the zombie doesn't move again.

Brad pops out from behind a cluster of trees, huffing and puffing from his rush to find the source of all the commotion. He watches as the blood geyser slows to a small trickle. Joan grabs a handful of leaves and uses them to swipe the blood from her goggles. As she tries to clean off the worst of the mess and catch her breath, she gestures toward Melvin.

Brad hadn't noticed Melvin before now. He hurries over to help his father to his feet.

"I had some pain in my chest. But it's fading now." Melvin straightens up but keeps his hand on the tree trunk to steady himself. "I'll be okay."

"Are you sure? You —"

There's a rustling noise behind the trio. Everyone turns. Brad raises his sledgehammer. Joan pulls the shovel out from the corpse's neck, sending a smaller burst of blood pouring out.

The rustling continues. Brad inches closer to the sound near the fallen tree. He tightens his grip on the sledgehammer.

Suddenly, a little girl scoots out into. Brad drops the sledgehammer and rushes up to her, dropping to his knees and wrapping her in a tight hug.

"Why did you run off?"

Evie swallows hard. Her eyes are red, and the tears flow freely down her face. "I... I had to pee. That one snuck up on me, and I hid under there."

"Why didn't you wake me up and tell me where you were going? I was so scared when you were gone."

"I'm sorry." She stiffens up as she looks between the faces of the adults and then back to Brad. "Please don't be mad at me!"

"I'm not mad at you. I was just scared. Tell me next time, okay? It's not safe to go out there alone, especially at night."

"I w-won't get in trouble if I wake you up?"

"Of course not." Brad hugs her again, then stands up. "Now, let's get back to the truck."

"Wait."

Brad looks down at her, puzzled. "What for?"

"I still have to pee."

- Northern Utah -

-- Day 34 --

"Even if she wasn't before, she sure as hell is now!" Joan glares at the girl, no longer caring if the child hears.

"Damn it, Joan!" Brad stands up, blocking her view of Evie. He walks close, grabs Joan by the shoulders and waits until she meets his gaze. "She has not been bitten! She's already told you a dozen times. What is it going to take to get you to knock it off with these constant accusations?"

Joan growls at him, "What's it going to take to get *you* to believe..." Suddenly, she takes a deep breath and straightens up, all traces of anger vanishing from her face.

"Wh-what's... Uh..." Brad leans back, furrowing his brow at her sudden calmness. He turns to look at his father. Melvin has one arm around Evie's shoulders as he stands there, looking just as perplexed as Brad. Melvin shrugs, and Brad turns back to face Joan again. "What's happening right now?"

Ignoring the question, Joan steps around him. Brad turns, following her with his eyes as she walks up in front of Evie.

"Let's go for a walk, okay? Just us girls."

Evie looks up at Melvin, then over to Brad before returning her gaze to meet Joan's. "Why?"

"Well, you and me really haven't had a chance to get to know one another. And it'll give you a chance to show me that you haven't been bit."

"Hold on, now." Brad steps up beside Joan. He grabs her by the arm and turns her to face him. "Do you mean *metaphorically* she can show you? As in, you're going to *talk* and get this stupid obsession out of your head? Or are you proposing having her undress and you do some kind of physical body inspection?"

"Oh, come on." Joan rolls her eyes. "It's no worse than getting a checkup at the doctor. Just a few seconds to look for bites, and then it'll be over, and we can all move on."

"But you're not a doctor! And this is for you, not her!"

"What's the harm? If she doesn't have—"

"Have you completely lost your mind, Joan? 'What's the harm?' Are you kidding—"

"I'll do it."

All eyes turn toward the girl.

"Evie," Brad walks over and kneels down in front of her. "Are you sure? Are you really comfortable with this?"

"It's fine." Evie chuckles nervously. She continues, barely above a whisper, "It's better than her being so mad at me forever."

Brad stands up and turns to Joan. "You swear you'll drop it after this? No more accusations?"

With her index finger, Joan traces an "X" across her chest.

"Fine. If you're going to do it, hurry up and get it over with."

"Come on, girl." Joan picks up Melvin's shovel and takes a step toward the trees. She slides her mask and goggles into place, then stands there, waiting for Evie to join her.

"I don't think we should split up. Just do it here and be done with it."

"Ha! You don't want *me* to inspect her, but you think it's somehow gonna be better if two grown men are watching too?"

"That's not what I meant, and you damn well know it!"

"Fifteen minutes. We're just going to walk around for a bit and talk, she'll show me she doesn't have any bites, and then we'll come right back." Joan turns to Evie again. "Okay, girl. You coming or not?"

Evie nods, situates her goggles over her eyes, and walks up beside Joan. Together, the two of them disappear beyond the trees.

Brad looks down at his watch for the millionth time. It's barely been five minutes. He crosses his arms, uncrosses them, walks over to the truck, sits down, then abruptly stands up again.

"How long should this take? It should only take, like, what? Thirty seconds? Something's wrong. Something's definitely wrong. Don't you agree?"

Melvin barely manages half a word before Brad continues his rambling.

"I know Joan said fifteen minutes, but why in the world would it take that long? She's just looking for bites. There's no reason it should take so long. Something's wrong. Isn't it?"

"Son—"

"I need to go look for them. What if they've gotten lost? Or attacked? Or what if—"

"Brad!" Melvin grabs Brad by the shoulders and gives him a shake. "Take a breath!"

As he grinds his teeth together, Brad's eyes meet his father's. Finally, Brad takes a deep inhale. As he exhales, the muscles in his jaw relax ever-so-slightly.

"It's not gonna do any good to get yourself worked up into a lather. I need you to keep your wits about you. Alright?"

After another long inhale and exhale, Brad nods.

"Okay then. Before you get any more worked up, why don't you try hollerin' for 'em? They probably aren't too far off. Maybe they're just talking, like Joan said."

Brad nods again, then turns toward the wall of trees. "Evie! Joan! Everything okay?"

The men stand in silence, waiting for a reply. Brad shoots a glance at his father. Melvin's calm appearance falters. He steps closer to the line of trees and calls out, "Joan! You two alright?"

"Eevieee!" Brad cups his hands around his mouth and shouts as loud as he can. "Where are you?"

A few birds take flight from the commotion on the ground below them, but otherwise, there's no response from the forest.

Brad marches over to the pickup and grabs his sledgehammer, then turns back around and hurries toward the trees. "I'm going to go find them."

"Right behind you."

It's slow going at first as the weeds and thorny bushes snag at their clothes and try to trip their feet. Soon though, the two men make their way into a narrow clearing next to a fast-moving stream. They stop and look around but can't see any sign of the others.

"Eeeevieee!" Brad slowly spins around as he shouts.

"Girls! Where—"

Brad lays a hand on Melvin's shoulder, and the older man goes silent. "Did you hear that?"

Before Melvin can respond, Brad suddenly takes off, sprinting along the edge of the stream. Rocks slip beneath his feet on the muddy ground, but he barely slows his pace as he regains his footing and keeps going. Trees and overgrown bushes block his view and wall him in by the water.

Melvin follows, trying to keep up. But before long, his chest is aching, and he has to slow down and catch his breath.

The narrow band of water at Brad's side is moving faster and faster, gurgling as it speeds over rocks and debris. There's a shrill scream up ahead. Brad's heart leaps into his throat. He plows on until, at last, he skids to a halt at the edge of a sheer drop-off. Water pours over the edge. Brad leans forward to look at the ground far below. As the dizziness starts to take hold, he staggers backward.

"Brad!"

He spins toward the high-pitched voice. Evie and Joan are standing about fifty feet away from him, near the ledge of the cliff. They're both facing him, and Joan's arm is wrapped tightly around Evie's throat. Tears stream down the girl's face; the woman's eyes are wide, and she bristles with energy.

"Help! She—"

Joan clamps a hand over Evie's mouth. For a split second, Joan's eyes dart to the sledgehammer in Brad's hands. She steps sideways, closer to the drop-off, dragging a struggling Evie along with her. "She's gonna turn. We have to get rid of her before she attacks us!"

"I hear you." Brad drops the sledgehammer at his side and raises his hands in surrender. He slowly moves forward as he speaks. "Let's you and me go talk about this, okay? Just let her go and—"

"No! She'll get away."

"Okay, okay." Brad avoids Evie's eyes, afraid he'll anger Joan even more if he turns his attention toward the scared, little girl. He licks his lips as he takes another step toward them. "I'll tie her up, and Dad can keep an eye on her while we talk. I just want to know what your plan is. Okay? Can we talk before you do anything rash?"

"You wouldn't listen before now! Why would—" Joan's words disappear into a shriek as Evie's teeth sink into the woman's palm. Reflexively, she jerks her hands away.

Evie darts off toward Brad. Joan looks up and shouts as she charges after her. Brad's eyes widen, and he bolts forward, spinning around Evie to get between her and the crazed woman.

Brad stops and plants his feet just before Joan crashes into him. The impact halts her in her tracks. She steps back and rushes again, trying to swerve around his side. Brad swings his arm wide. His forearm slams into Joan's chest and sends her stumbling backward. His eyes widen as he realizes what's about to happen, and he reaches out, grasping for her hand. Her fingers slip through his as she tips back and disappears over the cliff edge, screaming.

As her voice suddenly turns to silence, Brad turns around. His face is frozen in shock. His eyes seem focused a million miles away.

Melvin is standing next to the water's edge, hugging a sobbing Evie. He holds the girl close and looks over at his son, unsure who needs to hear this more. "It's gonna be alright. You done good."

- Northern Utah -

-- Day 35 --

Melvin picks up the last of their gear and sets it in the truck bed. Then taking a step forward, he looks into the cab through the open driver's side window. Evie sits in the center of the front seat with her knees clutched tightly against her chest, staring at the floor-board. A few streaks of dried blood still coat her chin. Brad sits beside her, silent and unmoving, as he stares vacantly out the passenger window.

"Anybody hungry? There's a can of chicken and dumplings and a jar of diced peaches in the back."

Neither of the truck's occupants acknowledges Melvin or his words. He sighs. He wishes more than anything that he could do something to help them.

Pulling a shirt from one of the suitcases in the back, Melvin grabs one of their water bottles, pours some water over the shirt, and wrings it out. He slowly slides onto the seat next to Evie. Gently cupping her chin, he tries to turn her face toward himself. She resists at first but eventually gives in. He gently wipes the blood off her face. She still doesn't speak or look at him. When at last she's reasonably cleaned up, he lets go of her face. She puts her chin back on her knees and wordlessly resumes staring at the floor.

Melvin sighs again. Unfolding the bloodied, soggy shirt, he sees that it's one of Joan's. One, in fact, that Brad had bought for her last Christmas. He remembers happier times.

The silly jokes she used to tell and the way she'd make Brad snort with laughter...

Brad's eyes lighting up when he'd hear her voice on the phone...

The way she'd look up at Brad, barely able to contain her grin when he was around...

The time that Brad was out of state on a trip with a couple of buddies and Melvin had started feeling chest pains one afternoon. The hospital had kept him for observation. Joan showed up with a checkerboard and kept Melvin entertained and distracted until Brad could make it back around dawn the next day...

Now misty-eyed and blinking rapidly, Melvin steps out of the pickup and uses a bit more of the water to clean up the shirt as best he can. He wrings it out, folds it up, and sets it gently into the storage box in the pickup bed.

He climbs back into the driver's seat, starts the engine, and puts it in drive.

"Where are we going?"

Melvin looks down at the little girl. "Somewhere we can learn how to live again."

"Where's that?"

"I don't know, Sweetheart." Melvin hugs Evie with his right arm, gently moves her feet to the floorboard, and fastens the seat-belt across her lap. Facing forward again, he starts to drive. "We've just got to keep going until we find it."

31

KEEPERS

- Western South Dakota -

-- Day 36 --

Just after dawn yesterday morning, Abigail had searched the barn and found a couple pairs of safety goggles and a few dusty-but-not-too-moth-eaten bandanas. Since the car was low on gas, she and Eric transferred their supplies to the abandoned pickup. Fortunately for them, its tank was full, and its key was still in the ignition. They'd climbed inside—Eric cradling Rascal and refusing to let go, of course. It took Abigail a few tries before she remembered how to drive a standard, but before long, they'd set out on the road again.

After barely an hour of traveling, the sky had turned an ominous shade of greenish-gray and Abigail had nervously parked the truck beneath an overpass to wait out the storm. It had been a stress-filled couple of hours as the winds shook the pickup and hail pounded down on each side of their shelter. When the weather's assault finally ended, they decided to stay put for the night in case another storm rolled through.

Now, as the truck coasts slowly down the abandoned highway, the sun shines brightly. Broken tree branches litter the road and the ditches. Abigail drives cautiously, avoiding the carnage caused by the storm. Eric dangles his hand out the open window, catching the warm morning breeze.

"Stop!"

At the sudden exclamation, Rascal meows loudly, and Abigail jumps. She glances over at Eric. The boy is staring at her with wide, panicked eyes. She turns back toward the road as she continues driving. "Why? What's wrong?"

"Just stop, Abby!" Unfastening his seatbelt, Eric practically flings himself at Abigail, then latches onto her arm. "Please, you have to stop the truck!"

Rascal meows again and drops into the floorboard, quickly disappearing beneath the seat.

Baffled by his apparent distress, Abigail brings the truck to a stop and turns to look at the boy. "What is it?"

"Sh!" He crawls back over to the passenger side of the pickup and turns so his ear is near the open window. He waits, listening.

As her bewilderment grows, Abigail silently watches him.

"There!" Eric spins away from the window to stare at Abigail. "Did you hear that?"

"Yeah, Bud, there's a zombie. But wh—"

"No! Not that!" He huffs with frustration. "Someone screamed. We have to help them!"

"Are you..."

Abigail's words trail away as she notices the shrill sound cutting through the air, and her heart skips a beat as she realizes the high-pitched note sounds like it's from a young child. She looks at Eric again, hesitant to leave him here, alone, while she tries to go find the voice. But taking him with her seems equally risky. She chews her thumbnail as she weighs her few options.

Guilt gnaws at her as she considers simply ignoring the screams and driving away.

As if reading her thoughts, tears start to form in Eric's eyes. His voice cracks as he pleads with her, "Please, Abby. We can't leave them like Evie."

"Okay." Abigail grabs her bat as she opens her door. She gestures for Eric to follow. "Let's go. But stay close to me and keep an eye out."

Together, the pair hurry away from the road. As they run, Abigail pulls the goggles over her eyes and lifts the bandana from her neck to position it to cover her nose and mouth. She orders Eric to do the same.

As they make their way around a wide cluster of trees, the pair comes to a clearing and stops. Across from them is a woman. With only a broken tree branch, she's fending off a zombie when he roars and lunges at her again.

Telling Eric to stay hidden, Abigail then charges toward the zombie with the bat held high. She swings. He twists to the side, effectively dodging the blow. Abigail's momentum carries her forward and around, causing her to lose her balance and crash hard into the ground.

Abigail cries out in pain as she hits her bandaged injury against a rock and that burning agony reignites in her arm. Tears sting in her eyes. She struggles to keep attention focused on the zombie.

The other woman swings her branch at the zombie. It connects, but the wood gives way this time, shattering into long splinters. Her eyes go wide. She tries to turn and run, but it's too late.

The zombie lunges at her. He grabs her by the shoulders and sinks his teeth deep into her neck. She screams.

Abigail finally manages to refill her lungs, and she rights herself. She runs toward the monster.

As he lets go of the woman, her legs give out. The zombie spins toward Abigail. He roars.

The metal bat catches him in the throat and silences him. He stumbles sideways. Abigail swings the bat around and hits him again before he has time to recover. It finds its target at the base of his skull. Blood sprays out, covering Abigail's goggles in a fine mist. His body goes limp, and he collapses into the dirt.

Abigail turns away and walks up to the woman; she's lying on her back and gurgling, choking on the blood that's quickly filling her mouth and throat.

"Mom?" All of a sudden, a little girl darts out from the bushes. She throws her arms across the woman's chest. Tears flow down the girl's cheeks. "Mommy?"

The woman's eyes dart to the little girl. Obviously growing weak already, the woman grabs the little girl's hand and squeezes. The woman's eyes, though, find Abigail. She tries to speak but only manages to cough wetly.

Abigail nods in understanding. "I'll take care of her. I promise."

Even through her pain and fear, the woman seems to relax slightly at the reassurance. She looks at the little girl again and silently mouths the words, "I love you." Then, she exhales one last time, her eyes roll back, and it's over.

"Mommy?" The little girl shakes the woman as if trying to wake her from a nap. "Mommy!"

Abigail walks up and crouches beside the mother and daughter. Noticing a shiny bit of metal beside the woman's hand, Abigail looks down. Around the woman's wrist is a delicate, gold band holding a small strip of metal. It's engraved in cursive: *Kristen*. Abigail gently unclasps the bracelet and tucks it into her pocket.

She'll give the bracelet to the little girl someday. But not now. For now, the girl is lost to grief.

- Western South Dakota -

-- Day 37 --

"Sweetheart?"

The girl doesn't react to Abigail's voice. Last night, the poor thing had clung to her mother's corpse and sobbed inconsolably until sleep had overtaken her. Abigail hesitates to wake her now, but they can't stay here forever. And after staying up all night to keep watch, Abigail isn't sure how much longer she can remain on high alert like this. She walks up, lays a hand on the girl's shoulder, and gives her a gentle shake.

The girl begins to stir. She sits up. Her hair is matted and covers half her face; dried blood and tears stain her clothes and skin. She slowly opens her eyes and groggily looks around. Until her gaze lands on the body beside her, and her lip trembles.

"Sweetheart?" Abigail quickly moves close and kneels next to the little girl.

With tears clinging to her eyelashes, the girl's focus turns toward Abigail. She doesn't speak, though.

"Sweetheart, I'm so sorry for what happened. I wish I could do something to make you feel better."

The girl stares, unresponsive.

"It's alright to be sad. My name is Abby, and I'll be here if you ever want to talk about any of this, okay? What's your name?" Abigail pauses, but she still doesn't get a response from the girl. "It's not safe to stay here. We need to leave."

All of a sudden, the girl turns and throws her arms around her mother's neck. She begins bawling again.

"Sweethea—"

The girl goes silent at the sound of the snapping twig echoing through the still air. In unison, all three heads jerk to the right.

Abigail shivers. She grabs her bat and stands up as she pushes Eric behind her. "Eric, you get her to the truck. I'll be right there."

Eric nods. He walks over, grabs the girl's wrist, and tries to pull her along with him. She resists. The two children begin to bicker. As the leaves in the distance start to rustle with movement, the kids' eyes widen, and they stop their fighting. The girl leaps up, and Eric is finally able to pull her toward the waiting pickup.

Keeping her eye on the bushes, Abigail backs away, following after the kids. The leaves shift just on the other side of the clearing. Her palms begin to sweat, and she tightens her grip on the bat.

Roaring, a zombie bursts through the shrubbery and charges at her. She gulps. Planting her feet, she raises the bat over her shoulder and waits.

As the zombie gets within reach, she swings the bat. It connects with the side of his head. He falls to the side. Barely a second later, he pushes himself back to his feet.

Abigail gapes at him. The left side of his head is completely caved in and spurting blood from an empty eye socket. Entirely unfazed, he roars and charges at her again.

She lets out a yelp but quickly regrips the bat. She swings again, connecting with the side of the monster's neck this time. His legs buckle underneath him.

Slowly, Abigail starts to back away. His black eyes—still simmering with bloodlust—follow her as she moves, but his arms and legs no longer work. For a brief moment, Abigail almost feels sorry for him, lying there, paralyzed and trapped in his own body. But before long, she turns around and darts away.

As Abigail climbs into the driver's seat of the truck, Eric throws himself at her. He wraps his arms around her neck and cries softly.

"I thought y-you weren't c-coming back."

Abigail rubs light circles on his back as she returns the embrace.

The girl sits tucked against the passenger door, hugging a purring Rascal. Tears trickle down her cheeks as she quietly watches Abigail and Eric through her dark, tangled mess of hair.

Shifting Eric to her other side, Abigail looks at the little girl. "What's your name, Sweetie?"

"Macy."

"Hi, Macy. How old are you?"

The little girl sniffles and swipes the back of her hand beneath her dripping nose. She doesn't speak any more, but holds up six fingers for Abigail to see.

"Come here, Macy. You're safe now."

Macy scoots closer. Her face crumples, and the tears begin to fall in earnest.

Abigail wraps an arm around each of the children and slowly rocks them back and forth until the sun disappears from the sky.

32

TRAPPED

- Southern Montana -

-- Day 40 --

Abigail pulls into the parking lot of the small rest stop as the noon sun beats down through the windshield of the pickup. Eric sits next to the passenger door. Macy sits in the center, fidgeting rest-lessly as she squeezes her legs tightly together.

"Okay, wait here."

"But..." Macy whines out the word.

"I have to make sure it's safe. I'll be back in just a second." Grab-bing her bat, Abigail gets out of the truck and hurries toward the building. She's barely gone a dozen steps when she hears the truck door open behind her. She turns around just in time to see Macy dart past her. "No! Macy, wait!"

"I'll get her!" Eric sets Rascal in the seat, hops out of the passenger side door, and runs after Macy.

Abigail groans and takes off after the two kids, cursing under her breath. She barely manages to catch up to them before they go inside the building—and even then, it's primarily due to the fact that Eric is distracting Macy as she struggles to push open the heavy door.

"You gotta wait, Macy!"

"I can't!"

"Macy," Abigail wraps an arm around Macy's waist and pulls her backward, away from the door. "Stay here for just a second. I have to make sure it's safe first."

"Hurry!" The word gets stretched out as Macy hops back and forth from one foot to the other.

Abigail nods and ducks inside. The lights are no longer working, but a skylight in the center of the room chases away the worst of the shadows. Before long, Abigail returns, pulling the door open and ushering the kids inside.

Wasting no time, Macy pushes past Abigail and disappears into the nearest stall. Eric walks to another halfway down the room.

Abigail hesitates. There's no lock on the restroom door, and she hates leaving them all completely vulnerable, even for a few minutes. At last, she shoves the trash can up against the door and hurries into her own stall. It's not much, but it'll at least give her some warning if anyone tries to follow them in. Quickly taking care of business, Abigail comes back out and washes her hands.

"Hey, guys? Wait for me in here. I'll be right back."

"Wait!" There's a flush, and then Eric's stall door slams open. Still busy fastening his pants, he runs up to Abigail with wide eyes. "You're not leaving us, are you?"

For what feels like the millionth time since she met the boy, Abigail lays a hand on his shoulder and says, "Of course not."

Eric looks up at her, unconvinced.

"We're a team now, Bud. As long my eyes aren't turning black, you're stuck with me." Abigail plants a kiss on his forehead and squeezes his shoulder. "Now go wash your hands and wait on Macy."

"Okay." Eric grins as he turns to go toward the sink.

Going outside, Abigail grabs an empty box from the back of the truck and returns to the building. There's a well-stocked vending machine a few feet away from the bathroom doors, and she hurries over to it. The goggles are already in place, but Abigail pulls the bandana up to cover her mouth. Then she steps up and swings the bat into the glass on the front of the machine. The glass shatters. She quickly knocks the last few jagged pieces out of the frame before reaching inside to start taking the food. The box is soon filled, and she walks quickly back to the truck with it.

Abigail dumps the food into the truck bed and turns to go back and gather another load. A tall, round-bellied figure disappears into the bathroom, and Abigail's heart stops. The box clatters to the ground, and she sprints back to the building.

The creature roars, the sound amplified by the rigid walls.

Both kids scream.

Abigail can hear a thin stall door slamming somewhere inside as she bursts through the entrance. The thick, metal door slams against the block wall.

"Abby!"

"Help us!"

The kids are nowhere in sight. The zombie is lying facedown on the floor, his head and arms stretching underneath the far stall door. He's pushing with his feet, trying to fit himself through the large gap. He makes it another inch further before his large waistline catches on the bottom edge of the door and brings him to a stop.

Eric yelps.

Macy starts sobbing loudly.

Abigail lets out some kind of war cry and charges forward. She gets to the far end of the room and swings a foot hard into the zombie's side. He roars. She slams the bat into his back. He twists, trying to grab at her, but catches his arm on the stall support post. Trying to push himself upright, he slams his neck into the stall door and falls back to the floor. He pounds his fists against the floor, shakes the divider walls, roars again, then goes still.

"Uh..." Abigail steps back and stares with one eyebrow raised high. "I think he's stuck."

Cautiously, Abigail moves forward and pokes the zombie with the baseball bat. He jerks his elbow back into the support post again. His roar bounces off the walls. But he still doesn't get out.

"Kill it!"

"Macy, I know this is really scary, but I think it's stuck. I can't get to its head to kill it from here. Try to be brave for me while we figure out what to do, okay?" Abigail pauses to stare at the zombie. "Hey, Eric? Can it reach you two?"

"No. Macy is standing on the toilet, and I'm squished against the back wall."

"Good. Can you two crawl under the side and get into the next stall?" As she asks the question, Abigail pushes open the door of the adjacent stall. The zombie's hand whips across the floor toward her and slams into the stall support post. "Never mind."

Abigail looks at the flimsy stalls, wondering if she can use the bat to break them apart without hurting the kids. Or she might be able to find a screwdriver and take one of the panels off, but that would require leaving the kids alone long enough to go look for tools.

"What if we go over the top? I can lift Macy up, and you grab her arms and pull."

"What about you?"

"I think I can stand on the pipe with the flushy deal and pull myself most of the way."

"I don't know..." Abigail bites her lip. "This seems risky."

"Do you got a better idea?"

Abigail sighs loudly. "You're right. Give me a second."

Drawing a deep breath, Abigail grabs ahold of the walls of the nearby empty stall and takes a wide step into the space. The zombie's hand swipes at her, his fingers brushing against the edge of her shoe, but it can't grab on. She awkwardly brings her other foot inside, dodging the swiping hand, and steps up onto the toilet seat.

"Alright, Macy. Eric is going to help you up, and I need you to grab hold of me. Okay?"

Macy lets out a soft whimper.

Abigail takes that as all the confirmation she's likely to get. She reaches her hands over the top of the divider, praying that this goes better than she's imagining. "Ready when you are. Just *be careful*!"

There are some shuffling sounds in the far stall as Eric gets into position, and Abigail can see the tips of his shoes underneath the divider.

Eric crouches down as much as he can in the small space between the toilet and the divider. "Okay, Macy. You gotta climb on my shoulders. Yeah. Give me your hands."

Some more shuffling as Eric grunts and then straightens up. Suddenly Macy's head and shoulders appear above the divider wall. Abigail leans forward as far as her precarious footing on the toilet seat will allow, grabs Macy underneath her arms, and pulls. "Good job, Eric. I got her."

The frightened little girl cries out as her shins scrape across the top of the divider, but soon enough, she's safely on the other side, and she wraps her arms tightly around Abigail's neck.

"Alright, Macy, Sweetie. You did good." Abigail carefully steps down. The attacking hand swings out again, threatening to trip her. Macy shrieks, and Abigail winces at the shrill sound by her ear, but she steps wide out of the stall and into the middle of the room. "Now, I need you to let me go so I can help Eric. Okay?"

Macy nods but doesn't loosen her grip. Abigail has to pry the little hands loose. She sets the six-year-old down, then hurries back into the stall before the little, trembling fingers can latch on again.

"Okay, great work, Eric. Macy is safe. Start climbing when you're ready."

More shuffling. A few seconds later, Eric's head appears over the top. He grabs the divider board and twists, swinging his leg up to hook his foot over the top.

Abigail grabs one wrist and his ankle to keep him from slipping back down, but he's too heavy for her to pull over.

Just then, the zombie roars, and Macy screams. The loud echoes are enough to drown out the softer sounds of cracking and creaking that come from the thin divider panel.

Eric takes a deep breath and pushes off with his other foot so that all his weight is on the divider.

Abigail shifts one hand away from Eric's foot to grab hold of his waistband. She pulls. Her eyes widen at the loud *crack* from somewhere off to her left. She tries to stop, to tell Eric to get down, and they'll think of something else. But it's too late.

The divider buckles, and Eric falls backward. Abigail falls, too, barely managing to grab hold of the stall door to break her fall.

The zombie roars.

Abigail gasps as both kids scream. She bolts out of her stall to see the zombie pulling itself forward beneath the now-lopsided door. She lunges forward, rips the door open, and before the zombie can twist around, she brings the bat down hard into the back of his head. The bat makes contact, but bounces harmlessly off the thick layer of flesh around the back of his neck. The zombie slides another inch closer to Eric. Abigail swings again, harder. And again and again, until at last, the lifeless body collapses to the floor.

Adrenaline and terror still filling her veins, Abigail hurries to the back corner, scoops Eric into her arms, then turns and carries him outside.

Macy latches on to the hem of Abigail's shirt, and she follows.

Once outside in the bright sunshine, Abigail sets Eric on the ground. She pulls both kids in close and wraps her arms around them. After the two of them finally calm down and dry their tears, Abigail ushers them all back into the truck. As she starts the ignition, she wonders how much longer they can all keep running like this.

- Western Wyoming -
-- Day 42 --

Abigail drives the pickup beside the lone cabin and stops in a patch of gravel, sets the parking brake, and leans forward to look through the windshield. With a twist of her hand, the engine shuts off. She leaves the keys in the ignition, just in case.

"Stay here."

Eric puts a hand on Abigail's arm. She turns toward him and lightly pats his shoulder. Then she looks back and forth to both of the kids. "Honk if you see anything bigger than a squirrel pop out of the bushes, okay? And keep the doors locked until you see me coming back. I'm gonna go check it out."

Both Macy and Eric nod. Macy leans into Eric, half-hidden behind his shoulder, and softly says, "Be careful."

"I will, Sweetie."

Abigail grabs the baseball bat and climbs out. Softly closing the door of the pickup, she pulls her goggles and bandana into place. Abigail stands there patiently, listening for movement. After several seconds pass quietly by with nothing more than the chirping of the birds and gentle water brushing against a shore, she lifts the bat up to her shoulder and starts to creep forward.

Scanning her surroundings as she moves slowly ahead, Abigail goes up to the front of the cabin and presses her back against the wall. She moves sideways until she reaches the corner, then leans forward to peek around the edge. Giving one more quick glance to the waiting pickup, Abigail turns and disappears around the side of the building.

Macy's teeth bite into her lower lip, and her fingernails dig into the flesh of Eric's arm. Wincing, Eric looks down at her grip, pries her fingers loose, then turns to look out the driver's window again. His eyes go wide. Macy lets out a whimper. There's movement on the far side of the building, near the trees. Eric quickly pushes Macy off the seat and into the floorboard, pressing a finger to his lips. Tears start to fall from Macy's eyes, but she obediently clamps both hands over her mouth and stays quiet. Eric slides across the seat and ducks down low, barely keeping his eyes above the bottom edge of the glass as he keeps watch.

From between two large pine trees, a man steps out into the clearing. His face is covered by a welder's mask, and a shovel is clutched in his hands. Eric slams his palm against the horn.

The man jumps. He turns toward the vehicle and starts walking that way, even as the noise continues.

Abigail comes running out from behind the near side of the cabin and stops between the man and the pickup. Eric lets the noise die and puts one hand on the door lock, the other on the handle, ready to open it for Abigail if she needs to get in. She stands sideways in front of the door, bat lifted and prepared to swing.

"Don't come any closer!"

The man stops. He lowers the shovel to the ground at his feet and lifts the mask off his face. "I'm sorry, ma'am. Didn't mean to scare you. I was only checking to see what we were hearing over here. Can't be too careful these days."

Abigail nods. She relaxes slightly, lowering the bat a few inches and pulling the bandana back down to her neck.

More movement behind the trees draws the attention of both the man and Abigail, and they turn in that direction just as a young girl emerges. All of a sudden, the pickup door flies open and slams into Abigail's back, sending her stumbling forward and causing the bat to fall from her hands. She stares wide-eyed as Eric sprints past her.

"Evie!"

The girl's neutral expression switches to one of open-mouthed disbelief as Eric crashes into her and he wraps. He throws his arms around her. The girl pulls back a bit, blinking at him. She begins to smile even as the tears start streaming down her face, and finally, she throws her arms around him and squeezes.

"What's going on?"

Abigail looks down as Macy grabs her hand. "I, uh... I think we found Eric's sister."

The man turns to Abigail, and his expression mirrors the one Abigail had just a moment ago, with one eyebrow raised high and his mouth half-open. "He's Eric?"

Everyone turns to look at the twins as they continue their embrace.

"Yeah." Abigail chuckles. "Small world."

The man turns to Abigail and extends his hand. "I'm Melvin. That there's Evie, of course. My son, Brad, is back at our cabin. It's just over there a ways."

"Abby." Abigail dutifully shakes Melvin's hand, then gestures toward the girl hiding behind her. "This is Macy."

"And who's that?"

Abigail looks at him, puzzled. Just then, she feels something rubbing against her ankles, and she glances down at the gray cat. "Oh, that's Rascal."

Melvin looks from the cat to the pickup, then back to Abigail again. Something about that feline and that truck seems familiar to him, but he shrugs off the thought. "Well, I don't know how long you're planning on staying, but it's sure nice to have some new company. Y'all wanna come over and visit?"

Abigail hesitates, but then she cautiously lowers the bat to her side. She glances at Evie. The girl seems to have been well taken care of, so Abigail decides it's worth the risk to trust these strangers. She nods. "Lead the way."

Melvin turns and heads back toward the trees. Along the way, he gets Evie's attention, telling her to come with him. Evie and Eric refuse to let go of one another, but after a quick glance at

Abigail, the twins follow Melvin. Abigail and Macy bring up the rear.

A few minutes later, they all step into another clearing with a cabin in the middle, nearly identical to the one Abigail had parked at.

Brad is sitting on a tree stump near a small fire. Introductions are made, and Brad is polite, but his smile doesn't meet his eyes. Until he finds out that Evie has found her brother. He beams at her, and the girl breaks away from her long-lost brother just long enough to receive a bear hug from Brad. As soon as Evie walks away, the sadness in Brad's eyes returns.

Just as the adults all sit down around the fire and Macy starts to climb onto Abigail's lap, Eric and Evie come running over.

Eric bounds up in front of Abigail. "Can we go in the house and play? Evie said there are some board games in there."

"Yeah." Abigail grins. "Just don't wander off outside, okay?"

"Okay! Come on, Macy!"

"Can I?"

Abigail nods.

Macy jumps up, smiling as the three run off toward the building. As they open the front door, Abigail hears one of the twins excitedly announce to the younger girl, "We always wanted another brother or sister!" Abigail can't help but smile at the sweet words.

"Is Macy yours?"

Abigail looks over at Melvin. "Biologically? No. I've just had a crash course on being 'mom' since the world ended."

"Looks like you've been doing alright so far."

"Poor sweetheart cries herself to sleep every night, missing her mom. I don't know what the hell I'm doing."

"Well, '*knowing what you're doing*' wasn't ever a requirement to being a parent. I've been a dad for a long time, and I'm still making it up as I go. And I had the advantage of getting my kid to adulthood before zombies came into the picture. Trust me, you're doing good by those kids."

Blushing, Abigail turns and pokes at the fire with a thin stick. A small cluster of sparks fly up and drift away on the breeze.

"So, how'd you find Eric?"

For the next couple of hours, Abigail and Melvin tell each other about their lives since the apocalypse happened. Brad sits there but doesn't contribute much, except when Melvin asks him a direct question. At last, Brad gets up and silently disappears into the cabin.

"Don't take it personal. He's having an awful hard time right now, especially since Joan died."

"Who was that?"

"His girlfriend. She'd been a real nice girl right up until the zombies took over. I think it all just got to her, though. She kinda went off her rocker, and... And she..." Melvin glances toward the house, then lowers his voice and slides closer to Abigail. "She tried to kill Evie."

Abigail gasps.

"He killed Joan to save Evie. Now the guilt is just eating him up inside. I've been telling him it's not his fault, but it just doesn't seem to sink in."

"Yeah, I can imagine."

The pair sits in silence for a long time. At last, Melvin looks up at the setting sun. "Gonna be dark soon. Y'all want to stay here for the night? You can get that other cabin set up tomorrow."

"Well..."

"I doubt you're gonna get them kids pulled apart tonight, and I can't imagine you'd be willing to let them stay with a couple of strangers. And, no offense intended, but Brad isn't gonna be letting Evie run off with someone he just met."

Abigail chuckles. "True. Yeah, I suppose we can stay for tonight."

33

END OF THE END

- Western Wyoming -

-- Day 43 --

Pink and orange rays of light reflect off the calm water as the sun makes its way up above the horizon. A gentle breeze stirs the leaves in the treetops. Brad sits on a wooden bench next to the rocky shoreline of the lake with his sledgehammer lying on the ground near his feet. At the sound of approaching footsteps, he tenses up and turns to look back over his shoulder.

"Sorry." Abigail raises her free hand in a gesture of surrender. The other one holds the bat loosely at her side. "Wasn't trying to sneak up. I woke up when I heard someone open the door this morning. I just wanted to come out and make sure you were okay."

Brad nods. He silently turns toward the water again.

"It's beautiful out here this morning. Mind if I sit with you for a bit?"

Without a word, Brad slides over to make room on the seat.

The birds chirp in the trees, and the wind gently flutters

Abigail's hair. For a long time, Brad and Abigail sit there, quiet and unmoving, watching the sunrise.

"I had plans."

Abigail jumps slightly at the sudden comment. Brushing a stray lock of hair behind her ear, she turns to look at Brad.

"I had decided to go back to school. Not sure what I was gonna major in yet, but," Brad shrugs as he continues staring out across the water, "I was going back. I'd decided I was going to get an education and find a career. Get myself out of that podunk little town, you know?"

He goes quiet. Abigail waits patiently for him to continue.

"I made that decision… I don't know, a couple weeks before all this went down. I even started searching for schools, sent off a couple applications." A sad smile appears on Brad's face. "For once in my life, I found some real ambition. I don't mean… Well, I always worked, always pulled my own weight and all that. But I just did what I was supposed to do. Never put much thought into it, just did what I had to, and that was that. And then, when I'd finally decided to *try*, to do something that was important to *me*… And then the world…"

Brad's words trail away, and he sighs. He runs his fingers through his short hair and then lowers his hands to his lap once more. "Now, I'll never even know if I was accepted. I'll never know what I might've gone on to do. Where I might've ended up."

Again, Brad goes silent. But he sits rigid, tilting forward as if he's about to leap up at any moment, so Abigail leans back and waits for him to find the words.

"Now, it's all, everything, just… Just gone. My plans, my home, my friends and family… And now there's this kid that I never planned for… Even the woman I thought I'd marry is gone!" Brad buries his head in his palms. When he speaks up again, his voice cracks, "It's my fault she's gone!"

"No, Brad. You didn't have a choice. You—"

"What the hell do you know about it?!" Brad turns and glares at her. "You don't have any idea what it's—"

"You think I didn't lose everything too?!" Abigail slams a hand against the bench. "At least you still have your dad!"

The anger in Brad's face abruptly vanishes, and his eyes go wide. "Oh, God. I'm… I didn't mean… I—"

"I know." Abigail exhales loudly as she leans back. "It's alright. I'll admit, I've had my fair share of breakdowns since this all happened. Lots of cursing and crying and yelling. There just usually wasn't anybody around to witness it whenever I did it."

Brad turns to face the water again, unwilling to meet Abigail's eyes. He leans back, folding his arms across his chest.

"Your dad told me about what happened with Joan. And I do know that feeling of guilt."

Brad looks at Abigail from the corner of his eye. He opens his mouth as if to interject, but Abigail continues without giving him a chance.

"When this all started, my brother, Jake, came to my house. He decided he didn't want me to be alone during all this. I was grateful he was coming there. I didn't want to be alone either, so I happily accepted. You want to guess when he got bit? The minute —the very *minute*—he stepped out of his car in my driveway. If he hadn't come to protect me, he might still be alive right now. Maybe I should've demanded he stay home, but no. I had to be selfish and accept his help." Abigail sniffles. Clearing her throat, she goes on. "He swore to me that he didn't regret it for a second. But you know what? His fate is not even close to the last one I feel guilty about. I'll save those for another day if you ever want to hear about them. But Jake turning into… Well, that nearly broke me."

This time, it's Abigail's turn to pause as she searches for the right words. She turns toward Brad and leans forward, staring at him until he finally meets her gaze. "But I didn't let it. I think Jake would've been mad at me if I had let it destroy me. And to tell you the truth, sometimes that thought is the only thing keeping me going. That I wouldn't want to disappoint Jake."

Abigail looks at Brad, waiting, letting her words sink in. Finally, she continues, "I know what you went through with Joan isn't exactly the same. But she made her choice. She let fear win because she couldn't handle this new reality. And you were forced to make a horrific, impossible decision. You had to choose between someone you loved but no longer knew and an innocent person you had just met. I can't even imagine how hard that was, but you saved that little girl. And that little girl already looks at you like you hung the moon."

"I know!" Suddenly standing up, Brad goes to the water's edge, grabs a rock, and hurls it across the lake. After the rock splashes heavily into the water, he turns back to face Abigail. "You think I don't see how she's adopted me? I already feel like she's practically my own kid, but... But what if... What if something happens to me? What will happen to her then?"

"You think I don't know that feeling too? I somehow ended up with twice as many as you!"

Brad's lips curl up at the edges. "Touché."

"Look, tomorrow was never promised. Even before all this, any one of us could've died at any minute. A car crash, an aneurysm, a run-in with the wrong person. Did that stop you from living back then?"

Tilting his head to the side, Brad raises his eyebrows slightly as he mulls over the question. But he doesn't speak. Walking back over, he sits back down on the bench.

"And I..." Abigail lets her words trail off. She looks at Brad for a moment, weighing her options. Fear of his reaction makes her hesitant, but she already feels as if Brad is the most trustworthy person she's ever met. At last, Abigail pushes up her sleeve.

Brad's jaw drops, and he reflexively slides away across the bench. As his eyes fix on the still-healing wound on Abigail's forearm. A moment later, he leans closer to stare at her eyes, searching for any sign of black. When he doesn't see any, he sits back and lets her continue.

"Everyone I know turned in a week or less. I got this more than two weeks ago. I may not make it much longer. But, based on what I've seen, I'm honestly beginning to wonder if I'm immune. Or if I maybe just got lucky this once, and maybe it'll be the next bite that does me in. Either way, what choice do I have but to keep going as long as I can and hope for the best?"

Just as Brad opens his mouth to respond, a roar sounds from somewhere in the distance. Both turn and look in that direction.

"These past... What?" She pauses, staring vacantly as she tries to count back through the days. "Two months? I don't know, but it feels like I've lived an entire lifetime since this all started. I've nearly given up more times than I care to admit. Probably would have caved entirely if I hadn't felt like I was letting down the memories of everyone who had ever loved me."

Another roar. This time, a little bit closer, a little bit louder. Abigail keeps talking. "Now I need to be there for those kids. I need to make Jake and my parents and my uncle proud. I need to *try*. So, you know what? I'm done giving up. I'm done running. Here is just as safe as anywhere else, and I'm making this place my home."

Abigail stands up, slips her bandana and safety goggles into place, and takes her bat in hand. Leaning down, she grabs the sledgehammer. As she rights herself, she offers it to Brad. "Are you with me?"

Brad stands up. Drawing a deep breath, he straightens his shoulders and takes the weapon from her. "Yeah. I am."

NOTE ABOUT THE FOLLOWING TEXT:

Well. You may have noticed that there is a *second* chapter 33. That's not a mistake. Er, well... It's done intentionally, anyway. I suppose you might argue that it's not—*ahem*—"correct" to do that... But it's my book and I wanna, and who's gonna stop me? [*Insert maniacal laugh here.*]

So, here we go.

This second chapter 33 (labeled as 33A) is an alternate ending and it picks up right at the end of chapter 32. I really liked this alternate ending and felt like it worked with the overall story. But, it also seemed short and abrupt. Honestly, it felt like kind of a cop out. So, I decided to go with the ending that you (presumably) just read.

But you know what? I hated to just scrap this ending. So I decided to include it as well. If you liked the main ending, feel free to stop reading here and pretend like this next one doesn't exist. If you're curious, or you would've liked for this to end a different way, you're welcome to read on. No matter which you option you choose, thank you for taking the time to read my story!

33A. END OF THE END
(ALTERNATE ENDING)

- Western Wyoming -
-- Day 43 --

Abigail wakes up, blinking out at the unfamiliar surroundings. It takes her a moment, but she slowly remembers where she is. Her head aches terribly. She stifles a groan as she rolls over on the brown leather couch and her blanket slides down onto the floor. The wall clock ticks softly. Abigail stares as the second hand jumps forward and back, forward and back, over and over without making progress. Something about watching that clock with its almost-dead battery feels ominous. Shivering suddenly, she pushes herself upright.

Abigail stands up and squeezes her eyes shut as a wave of vertigo washes over her and has her swaying on her feet. When the dizziness finally passes, she reopens her eyes and walks over to the window. She leans her forehead against the cool surface of the glass and looks outside toward the trees, watching the silhouettes of their branches shift slowly in the pre-dawn breeze.

Straightening up, Abigail heads into the bathroom, closes the door, and slides her hand along the wall until her fingers find the light switch. She squeezes her eyes shut, sucking air through her teeth as the room is suddenly filled with the bright glow. She leans on the edge of the sink draws a deep breath. When Abigail finally gathers her nerve and slowly opens her eyes, she sees exactly what she'd expected: hazel irises, oversized pupils, and an abundance of thick, zig-zagging black lines. She trembles as she stands there staring at the sight.

There was nothing yesterday, but now...

At last stepping away from the vanity, Abigail squares her shoulders and resigns herself to her fate. She'll leave. She listened to her uncle and didn't give up while there was still hope. And in that, she saved two children. Now, she can hold her head high as she goes somewhere quiet to wait for the end.

Abigail opens the bathroom door and stops. Standing in front of her is Evie, blinking tiredly as the bathroom light washes over her.

"Hi, Abby." Evie starts to squeeze past, into the bathroom, but then she freezes as she notices those dark-lined eyes. She gasps and steps backwards until she's pressed against the opposite wall.

Abigail opens her mouth to speak, but movement off to her right draws her attention. She looks over just in time to see Macy appear around the corner. The little girl's eyes widen. Abigail reaches out, ready to comfort the child, to tell her goodbye before she leaves. But as she does, Abigail's vision goes dark and her thoughts seem to vanish entirely.

As Abigail disappears inside her own mind, the last thing she knows is the shrill sound of a little girl's scream.

PLEASE LEAVE A REVIEW

Thank you so much for taking the time to read my book! You'll never know how much it means to me.

If you have a few minutes to spare, I would really appreciate if you'd leave a review for this book on Amazon, Goodreads, or any other site where it's listed. More reviews increase the chances of my book finding its way to new readers.

ACKNOWLEDGMENTS

To the readers: Thank you for taking the time to read my book! Whether you love it *(yay!)*, hate it *(can't win 'em all, I suppose)*, or something in between *(I'll take it)*, thank you so much for reading this book!

To the cover artist, Perky Visuals: Thank you for making a picture that's truly worth a thousand words!

To my husband: Thank you for your words of encouragement! And thanks for all your help with my research (A.K.A., all those late nights of eating popcorn and watching zombie movies with me)!

To my fellow Runaway Daydreamers: Thank you for helping me find the right words when they just didn't want to be found. And thanks for helping me make my way through this whole, crazy process! Keep on daydreaming!

ABOUT THE AUTHOR

C. Britt lives in the midwestern United States with her husband, cat, and two dogs. She enjoys spending time sewing, photographing nature, playing video games, and (of course) dreaming up fictional worlds to write about.

Follow C. Britt:

https://www.linktr.ee/cbritt

https://www.cbrdpublishing.com/c-britt

amazon.com/author/cbritt
goodreads.com/cbritt
bookbub.com/authors/c-britt
facebook.com/CBrittAuthor
threads.net/@cbrittauthor
tiktok.com/@authorc.britt
instagram.com/cbrittauthor

Printed in Great Britain
by Amazon